It's About TIME

ISBN: 979-8-9884967-7-9

First Printing 2025
10 9 8 7 6 5 4 3 2 1

CONTENTS

To the greatest gifts in my life.

To my daughters, whose bravery and strength continue to inspire me. Your courage to rise through every challenge and pursue your path with grace fills my heart with pride.

To my husband, whose unwavering love has been my anchor and light.

To the brave women who shared their stories in these pages, thank you for your vulnerability and truth.

And to the many women who have shaped my journey with their wisdom, friendship and guidance, this book carries a piece of each of you.

With deep gratitude,
Kelley G. Lamm

WHEN LOVE HAPPENED

There are moments in life when time pauses, when the world grows quiet, the chaos fades and something shifts deep within your soul. These moments may come wrapped in heartbreak or bursting with joy. Sometimes, they arrive softly on an otherwise ordinary day, but their impact is undeniable. They mark a turning point. A spark. A beginning.

This book is full of those sparks.

For me, *It's About Time* was born from a life I never thought possible, a life built not on survival, but on safety. On love. On a partnership so steady and true, it anchored me in ways I didn't know I needed. After years of appearing strong while silently breaking… of holding others up while losing sight of myself… of standing in crowded rooms feeling alone… I reached a breaking point. Abuse, sickness and loss had fractured me mentally, emotionally, physically. Smiles masked sorrow. I was constantly giving, constantly chasing, constantly rebuilding.

And then, *love happened.*

Not the undying love of a parent or the unconditional love for my children though those are sacred and unmatched, but a different kind of love. A love that didn't demand or take. A love that didn't leave me wondering if I was enough. This love lit a fire inside me, not one that burned, but one that warmed me from within. A steady, healing flame.

It reflected back a version of me I had long forgotten, joyful, passionate, bubbly, strong and deeply alive. This love didn't save me; it reminded me I was already worthy. Already whole. Already everything I needed to be.

And it came when I least expected it.

I had been single for 11 years after a marriage that dissolved, protecting my peace and doubting love's return. Then one night, on our second date, he looked at me and said, *"If I fall in love with you, know that no one will love you the way I do."* In that moment, I knew *he was the one.* That was the moment everything changed. That was *when love happened.*

This anthology is a tribute to moments like that when everything shifts, and life pivots into something deeper, more honest, more beautiful.

Thirty-Five women. Thirty-Five stories. Each one bravely sharing the moment that changed the trajectory of their life. Stories of heartbreak, healing, rediscovery, resilience and reinvention. Stories that will make you laugh, cry, reflect, and above all, feel seen.

These pages are filled with truth. With strength. With grace. And with hope.

May their stories wrap around your heart like a soft blanket. May they spark something inside you. May they remind you that you are never alone, and that your moment your pivotal, beautiful, soul-awakening moment is waiting too.

Because it's about strength.

It's about healing.

It's about truth.

It's about love.

It's about time.

With all my heart,
Kelley G. Lamm

"You have to stop crying, and you have to go kick some ass."
Lady Gaga

"I couldn't find roles that I felt were complex or dynamic,
so I decided to create them."
Reese Witherspoon

Angela Skurtu

RESET: A SEX THERAPIST'S SOBRIETY JOURNEY AND INTIMATE AWAKENING

I walked into my daughter's bedroom and laid down next to her, cuddling her to help her wake up. I could not remember what happened the night before, because I had blacked out drunk. I felt nervous and worried about what I had done. *How could I have driven with her in the car like that? Why did I do things like that? Where had we gone? What did we do?* I remembered having the idea of going to the YMCA to swim, but I didn't remember much of what happened after that.

She woke up and laid next to me. She was around 6 or 7 years old at this time. "Mommy, last night was a disaster." she said to me. My heart sank.

"What happened, baby?" I asked her.

"We got kicked out of the YMCA," she told me. I was frozen as she told me some other details. I don't actually remember much after that about what she said because I sunk into a pit of self-loathing. *How could I have done this? When did I lose control? What kind of mother am I?* I did my best to apologize and tell her I wouldn't let that happen again. And I hugged her.

The rest of that week was filled with little hints of that night. While I couldn't remember what happened, the consequences of what had happened continued to show up. The next day, I saw a trail of things I had left here and there. I had left clothes on the floor that I had forgotten to put in the laundry basket. I had left things in the car. There were crumbs in the car from eating a cupcake. Then there were things missing. *Where was my special necklace?* My daughter had made me a little clay necklace with her thumbprint for Mother's Day when she was in kindergarten. I had worn it that night. It was missing. I never found it.

I wish I could say *that it* was the night I stopped drinking for good. It was one of the lowest points of my life. But it wasn't. I did my usual.

I stopped drinking for about a month or two, determined that I would end things, but then slowly, I found myself making the typical excuses. *If I can just keep it to a couple drinks, then I can still drink. If I can just stay home and not drive, then I won't hurt anybody.*

That night I did make the decision to never drink in front of my daughter again. *Had I ruined her life forever? Would she be one of those kids who's super anxious because she was raised by an alcoholic mother? Not on my watch! I'll avoid ever drinking in front of her again, and that will fix it! I can be a responsible drinker and a good mom! I can do it, right?* These were the deals I made with myself over and over again. I would make a huge mistake—really hurt someone I loved or even hurt myself physically. I would commit to stop drinking for a month, six months, a year. I always had high hopes, but inevitably I would stop for a few months, then make an excuse to take that first drink, telling myself, *I can control it this time.* I would drink "responsibly" for a few weeks, even several months. Then inevitably, I would have one night that turned bad and caused huge consequences.

Alcohol has been at the forefront of my life since I turned 21. I wasn't a young drinker. I grew up in a very religious family, and I have always been a rule follower. So, when other teens and young adults drank and smoked pot, I avoided it. I always used to say, "I don't need those things. I am high on life!" Then, my 21st birthday came, and my sister brought home my first bottle of wine. She told me, "You have to drink on your birthday! It's a big deal." So, I drank, and I liked it. *A lot.*

She showed me how to drink. She would hold her nose and guzzle a glass of wine. I didn't know anything different. When I got buzzed, the feeling was amazing. I used to say alcohol in my body felt like cocaine. Not that I had ever tried cocaine, but I remembered this hilarious skit on SNL where Andy Sandberg sang, "I don't know why, but today feels like it's going to be a great day!" That's how I felt when I drank alcohol—like my body could do anything and forget everything.

That started my quest to become a regular drinker. It got better and worse over the years. Back in my twenties, everyone was drinking to excess so you honestly could get away with it without many people noticing it. We were all binge-drinking lushes back then, partying and going out for nights on the town. But there were definitely some bad stories around that time that I remember.

One night, I was going out on my own. I lived in Hawaii during my college years, and it was difficult to break into friend groups. I was lonely. Most of the locals stuck with their friend groups they had made in high school. Don't get me wrong. They were kind people, but they didn't let you in. They knew most haoles (the island term for someone who is not a native Hawaiian, especially white people) would not be on the island long. So, they didn't invest in friendships outside their local circles. That left me with military people and sometimes students. Really, living in Hawaii was the loneliest time of my life.

I took to the bottle and went out looking for a husband. I took the car and a bottle of wine and went out for the evening. I was also broke, so I didn't pay for drinks at the clubs. I would pre-game it in my car in the Ala Moana parking lot until I felt drunk enough to go out alone. It was a pretty dangerous move when I look back at it. But I was young, and I wanted to feel alive.

I went to the club to meet potential suitors. Funny how I never seemed to meet a "good guy" when I was completely smashed and drunk. You mean, good guys aren't attracted to that behavior? I don't remember everything about the night, but there was a guy and his friend who noticed me and let me hang out with them.

"Oh, I know your type," the guy said. I didn't know what that meant, but I smiled through my drunken stupor. We danced, and I asked for another drink. He seemed miffed and said, "This better be worth it." I still don't think I quite understood what he meant, but I was grateful for the drink. We danced and kissed. I was all over him. Then at one point, he showed me his hand with a ring on it and said, "I'm married." I was terrified and ran away. I literally ran out of the room to the bathroom. My face was hot, ashamed. Mortified. *How could I have kissed a married man? What was wrong with me?* I left the evening unsure how to forgive myself but still blaming myself for choices I made under the influence. That's the tough part about alcohol. You do things you really wouldn't do sober, but you still have to take responsibility for the actions you take when the light of day hits. I felt horrible for a long time after that, but I still never blamed the drinking.

Fast forward to years later. I married my now ex-husband when I was young. I was unhappily married, and my drinking had become worse. I remember my ex telling me I needed to change my drinking—that it had become a problem. I would listen to him on the surface and try to make changes, but then I would not fully believe him. Underneath my drinking, there was a problem. I felt I could blame my drinking on him. I was unhappy and I drank to deal with our marriage.

He used to beg me to stop and say my drinking was destroying our marriage. I secretly believed he was destroying our marriage. I drank to deal with that and to deal with him. But, since I didn't have any plans to leave him, I did have to at least try to make changes. I would manage it here and there and come up with plans for shifting my drinking. I would set goals for myself, limit my drinking to one night a week. Over time, I would avoid drinking around him. I would stay up late drinking to sober up before the morning. There was no way I would let him blame drinking again.

When he asked me to quit, I was dead set that I would never quit alcohol. I didn't care what he said or wanted. Drinking was my friend, and it was all I had to rely on. Little did I know I had come to rely on alcohol for so many things. I relied on alcohol to sleep, to quiet the voices in my head, to manage social anxiety and to have fun when I was bored. *How in the world could I live a life without alcohol?*

I divorced him in December 2018, so I couldn't blame my ex anymore for my drinking. Then in 2020, I was in a new relationship with my now husband, Shane (we married in October 2024). The pandemic hit and day drinking was all the rage. I was drinking pretty heavy, and things were becoming a bigger issue in my life. I had learned to use alcohol to cope with everything. The hard thing is I could still run a business, pay my bills and even parent to some degree. I was drinking every night to cope with life, but so was everyone else at that time, it seemed. I didn't feel like anything I was doing was wrong by society's standards, but it was definitely impacting my relationship with Shane and my daughter.

I started recognizing that I needed to change this behavior. I could see the writing on the wall. My boyfriend was going to leave me if I didn't change my drinking habits. This time, I actually had a good one. I couldn't blame my behavior on him. I couldn't say that we had a bad relationship. Quite the contrary, he was amazing. He was kind, gentle, patient and great in bed, which is important to me. I'm a sex therapist, after all!

The only problem was me and my addiction. I had to make a change but I didn't know how. All this time, I had been trying to manage it and pretend like I had control over my alcohol. But I really didn't have control. I would "manage" it for a time and then screw up again. I would black out. I would say hurtful things. I'd start a fight over nothing. I would treat Shane or my daughter like crap. Alcohol does that.

I started the process of trying to quit. I truly want anyone reading this to really understand how challenging it was and is to quit alcohol. I started trying to quit in 2020. I drank my final drink of alcohol on May 19, 2023. I know this because I wrote it in my calendar. I am now sober for two years. But it took me three years of consistently trying to quit. Starting. Stopping. Managing. Going back. Even before 2020, I knew alcohol was a problem. I was never serious about quitting before my divorce.

That's what we need to look at when we talk about quitting alcohol. The process it takes before you take your last drink. From 2020 to 2023, I had to figure out all the things that alcohol was solving in my life. In those three years, alcohol slowly hurt everyone in my life in ways for which I still must learn to forgive myself.

My first big low started with my best friend, Amber. Somewhere in 2021, I was getting a breast reduction. I successfully quit for a time but then had severe pain after my breast reduction surgery. I turned back to the bottle to manage my pain. One night, Amber and I were watching TV, and I passed out and she couldn't wake me up. She was terrified. She went upstairs to ask Shane to check on me. He saw that I was breathing and made sure I was propped up, so I wouldn't die or choke on my own vomit, should I need to vomit. Then he sent her on her way. I wished that it was my last night. But it wasn't. I quit for a few months, then got right back on the alcohol horse.

Then sometime in 2022 the YMCA incident occurred with my daughter from earlier in this story. I wish that was the end of things. But it wasn't either. Each time I tried to quit, alcohol dragged me back. I wish I could say kicking and screaming, but I can't. I went back because I loved alcohol. The rush, the high I felt, the warm blanket I felt in my skin when the alcohol kicked in. I actually believed at some point that I was more of my true self when I was drinking. They were all lies I told myself. In the end, none of it was real.

The last straw was when I was at a conference. My boyfriend was watching my kid, and I ended up flirting with someone. Nothing happened, but I realized I crossed a huge line in my relationship. My boyfriend could tell something was wrong as soon as I got home. He asked me point blank, "Did you cheat on me?"

I sighed deeply and answered honestly, "I didn't, but I blacked out drunk. I honestly wouldn't know if I did. I don't think I did. But I know I crossed some serious lines and that's not OK." He was incredibly hurt and rightly so. *How could I have done that? Who am I, and why did I think that was OK?* That conference took place on May 17 through May 19 2023 and that is how I know when I took my last drink. I wrote down the first day sober as May 20, 2023.

It was that low that started my real journey toward recovery, and it truly was my last drink. I have learned a lot about myself in recovery. To truly quit alcohol, I had to replace all the things that alcohol was managing in my life. First, I had to find hobbies. I started gardening. I needed to find things that were fun that didn't include drinking. I learned to go dancing and roller skating. I learned to hang out with friends who weren't drinkers. I was lucky in this department. My boyfriend and now husband never really drank. My family didn't really drink anymore. All my friends already avoided drinking. That was a huge help. I saw people in my life who had positive lives without drinking.

I also had to learn to seek help for my needs outside of drinking. I had to learn to use yoga instead of alcohol to quiet my brain. I realized that alcohol in some ways was how I rebelled in this world. I needed to find more healthy ways to rebel that didn't include drinking, like dangerous hikes and jumping off cliffs into waters below.

One of the hardest things I learned about myself sober was that my daughter was one of my biggest triggers. She has ADHD with hyperactivity. Every time I struggled with her as a parent, I was turning to alcohol to cope. As a mother, you are supposed to love your kid unconditionally. Yet, whenever things happened with her that I didn't know how to address, I was drinking to cope. I had to start researching ADHD to learn how to parent her differently. I had to learn to set boundaries and really listen to my own needs as a mother. I needed to take breaks from her and have my own life that she sometimes wasn't a part of. That was a challenging lesson to overcome.

Now that I am two years sober, I am so incredibly grateful for my life. I am way happier and doing a much better job in a lot of ways. I am a better mom, a better businessperson, a better wife and a better friend. I still have a long way to go. As I get stronger and better, I find new ways that alcohol caused harm in my life. That's something they don't tell you in sobriety. As you get stronger, the people around you that were hurt want to share how you hurt them. I have to practice a lot of self-compassion as people share these stories. I also have to practice gratitude that I am now in a healthy enough place to listen.

I was drinking for four of the six years I have been with my now-husband. There is a lot of unlearning that we continue to do. He tells me regularly that he is not always sure which versions of me from that time were real and which versions of me were the alcohol. I honestly can't tell him which ones were or weren't me either. I forgot a lot of what I said and did. I apologize to him and thank him for working with me through that time, and I continue to ask that we talk through things going forward. I am so incredibly grateful that alcohol is in my past. And I can't wait until my time sober in my relationship has been longer than my time drinking.

ABOUT ANGELA SKURTU

Angela Skurtu, M.Ed., LMFT-S, ACST-S. Angela is a keynote speaker and author of the books *"From F*ck No to F*ck Yes Sex!"* (2025), *"Helping Couples Overcome Infidelity: A Therapist's Manual"* (2018), and *"Pre-Marital Counseling: A Guide for Clinicians"* (2016). She is a Licensed Marriage Therapist and Supervisor (AAMFT) and a Certified Sex Therapist and Supervisor (AASECT). You can find Angela's information at OpenBedroomDoors.com.

Angela on a personal level: I help couples who are best friends take their relationship from the *"friend zone"* to the *"sexy zone"* by normalizing conversations about sex. I love this work. Every day, I am privileged to walk with couples in their time of need and help sexually empower them. For many of the couples I work with, sex is mired in shame. Instead of feeling comfortable in their body, sex is scary, lonely and creates anxiety. My work with couples is all about helping them find their own creative sexual style and become their authentic sexual selves. My passion is to help individuals find their sexual voice and their personal sexual identity. I'm Angela Skurtu and *I open bedroom doors!*

Scan the QR code to watch a full interview with Angela

Anne Marie Boedges

DOWN TO THE STUDS

Some moments divide our lives into before and after. This is one of those moments.

I'm from a big Irish Catholic, small-town family. My brother, Dave Varel, and I always had a dream to have our own design and build company together. I design and he builds. Then we wanted to have our own home renovation TV show. It would have been a version of "This Old House," but with a more modern twist. We've always had this desire to create and share things we are passionate about with the world.

My brother was a fine craftsman, a carpenter and a tree farmer. He felt like he could do this full circle; what we take from the earth to create, we put back in. He'd walk a site and identify trees like old friends—knowing which would make the strongest beams or the finest trim, and which should be left to shade the land for another hundred years. His reverence for nature wasn't just professional, it was spiritual. And he loved to teach everyone about all the trees and acorns and nature along the way, and especially what trees were no good, such as the Bradford pear.

I'm Anne Marie Boedges. In 2013, at 32 years old—nervous but determined—I opened Anne Marie Design Studio. Within four months, my brother came right alongside me so we both could make our dreams happen. I went to school for interior design at Maryville University, and had already been designing kitchens, baths and homes since 2005. I always wanted to have my own company and had a strong desire to do things the right way. My wonderful husband, Jon Boedges, was my biggest fan and inspiration at this time, not only acknowledging my desire to start my own company but helping me to realize the dream was actually achievable. He has continued to support my business in my accounting and IT departments and has done more than his share of taking care of the children. I have been truly blessed with his support.

My brother, David, and I had made so many fun collaborations and stunning transformations. In six years, we grew three times our original size in clientele, sales and office staff and expanded our showroom. As time flew, we kept growing in skills and pushing the envelope.

Then in March of 2020 the COVID-19 pandemic hit. Like everyone else, we were scared and uncertain, trying to find footing in a world that no longer made sense. But by April, we had a plan in place. Luckily, we had the best clients, and everyone who was stuck inside their homes, sheltering in place or working from home decided they didn't like anything about their homes, and our phones rang off the hook.

We started demolition on a large-scale project on March 8, 2020, the week before everything shut down March 15, 2020. The client's six-person family was on spring break in Florida. They chose to stay there, so we were able to work in their home for the next four months. As so many things were still out of our control, we felt blessed. We were able to keep most of our staff working designing, selling and installing projects. Steve Beinart and Dave, our fabulous senior craftsmen duo, were able to be on job sites every day, and despite everything, they still were able to make impactful headway on many projects.

But during August 2020, COVID-19 hit hard our hometown area of Clinton County, Ill., where my brother lived. In a 30-day period, we lost multiple aunts and uncles to the deadly disease that was scouring through nursing homes where they had no vaccines, medications or cures. My brother also got COVID, along with his wife and two children, during that month. We talked daily, learning about all the symptoms and coming up with plans for extended work dates off. Dave had every single symptom and was doing everything the CDC said he should do. He never went into the hospital, he just stayed ill at home. I remember being scared and I would get anxious headaches from overthinking about what was happening.

I'd sit up late into the night scrolling articles, searching for hope, remedies or reassurance, desperate for control over something that felt uncontrollably dark. With the kids homeschooling and not seeing many friends or family for long periods of time, we had our own personal home stresses of COVID.

But it was during this time that we got the absolute worst phone call I will ever receive. I hate reliving it. On Sept. 6 we were visiting my sister in Kansas, like we normally would do every Labor Day weekend. We all took COVID tests and ensured we were healthy enough to see them. My brother woke up very early that day, thinking he was having a panic attack. But he didn't realize he was having a heart attack. His wife was right by his side calling 911. He didn't survive the ride in the ambulance. We never got to hug him, tell him goodbye, or tell him how much we love him. My world shattered into a million sharp pieces.

I'm the youngest of six kids, and David was number four. He was the life of the party. Everyone wanted to be where David was. Everyone was his friend. He was a drummer in a band growing up. He took me to my first concert and taught me about the music of Rush and Pink Floyd. He taught me how to drive—even if it was at the age of 12. He showed me how to find my own confidence when my best friend went to a different high school. And when I went through the breakup that I thought I wouldn't survive, he was there. He taught me how to build a coffee table and how to use a router and table saw. He taught me the difference between pecan and hickory, maple and sycamore and showed me how quarter sawn wood was cut. He showed me how to make a veneer of exotic wood. He taught me how to build a house. He also taught me to be a more patient wife—though I'm still working on this—and helped me to parent when he was so close with us while raising our kids.

Our family is so close. This was the biggest loss I've ever experienced. I've gone through grief, but this devoured me.

The days after David's death were a blur of pain, logistics and heart-break. But even in that darkness, something stirred a need to keep going, for him, for our family, for myself. I don't know how, as a sister, aunt and sister-in-law, I got past it, but the sun kept rising and setting, and I found myself in a caregiver position. We took the kids and my sister-in-law in almost every weekend that first year. I went to their house almost daily for a few months, even though we lived 60 miles apart. I also decided to train for a marathon during that year. I started in April, and the race was to be in November. I couldn't finish, but I got close with 18.6 miles. And I kept running. That was my therapy.

As for my company, I knew my brother would be so disappointed in me if I let things fall apart. My gracious, hardworking team stepped up in ways I didn't even see. Outside contractors stepped up, and through the grace of God, were able to help complete projects we already had in the works. Their devotion wasn't just to the business. It was to Dave, to me and to the mission we all believed in. That kind of loyalty is rare, and I will never forget it. With everyone's priceless dedication, we were able to keep scheduling new projects. I learned what real patience was and how to actually ask for help. Learning how to lean on my team was crucial during this uncertain time in my life and career.

And I especially looked to my other lead carpenter, Steve Beinart, for support. Steve was not only left alone amid a client's whole-house renovation, but he had just lost his best friend. Dave and Steve had been good friends and co-workers for almost 26 years at this point. Steve became a rock for me during this heart-wrenching time. He had personally been through deep loss in his own life, and his kind heart and willingness to listen and guide me was (looking back) so helpful in my growth.

Steve was really a mentor for all of us, including Dave's wife and children. He taught us many critical things about what to do and not do after losing a loved one, such as: don't buy or sell anything big for one year, don't drink and keep moving forward.

Anne Marie Design Studio, as a company stayed strong and kept growing as I learned to take action sooner than later in my life on matters that are important to me. While I have always put family first, the notion that we do not know God's plans really stands out so much more now. So, I make it a point not to miss my kids' games whenever possible. I take them to fun places that are special to us (like the skate park, bike rides, Sky Zone, the movies and on runs), and I spend more one-on-one time with the kids just listening and acknowledging things they are passionate about.

And I take action on big dreams I have instead of just manifesting them now. I shared big dreams with my brother to teach and share everything we could about design and best building practices. And this massive loss pushed me to make these a reality.

I began to say yes, not out of obligation, but from a place of courage born from heartbreak. Instead of saying no to opportunities to expand my media, I began saying yes—yes to creating a YouTube channel when I didn't know how, yes to sharing design tips live on local TV each week, yes to co-hosting a radio show, yes to coaching and teaching, yes to running, and yes to leading, loving and living. My newest endeavor is teaching kitchen and bath design at my alma mater, Maryville University. Saying yes was and still is fulfilling. Now when everyone around me says to start saying "no" more often, I wonder what opportunities and what relationships could I be missing out on? Saying yes brings growth and new life to so many situations. I hear all too often that I do "all the things." I am so proud that I am able to, and thankful that I have family, friends and a team of people in so many walks of my life who support me and possibly admire me just a little bit. I'm learning to receive that admiration, not deflect it. Because it's not about being superhuman. It's about surviving the unthinkable and choosing to keep building anyway.

Grief taught me that time is never guaranteed. But it also taught me how much I could grow in its wake. My 15-year-old son is now dreaming and creating on his own platforms and finding that being a risk-taker and being willing to jump when others hesitate is the way to implement growth on his own. The willingness to be innovative and to show grit and determination on his own path with a clothing line is proof of that.

My young daughter can see how impactful David was in my life and how my involvement in so many things is a true testament to why God has put us all here—to do great things.

So, if there's one thing I hope you take from my story, it's this: Stop waiting for the perfect moment. Say yes. Say it boldly. Say it often. Say it for the people you've lost, and for the life still ahead of you.

ABOUT ANNE MARIE BOEDGES

Anne Marie Boedges, president and principal designer of Anne Marie Design Studio, LLC has been helping clients fall in love with their homes all over the St. Louis area since 2001. She obtained her bachelor's degree in interior design from Maryville University in St. Louis, Mo., currently teaches a Kitchen and Bath Design Course at Maryville University, co-hosts The Inside Out Show on The Big 550, KTRS, and shares her Tuesdays Design Tips on Studio STL on Fox 2. Anne Marie has won numerous prestigious awards through the years, including Kitchen of the Year with St. Louis Homes and Lifestyles magazine, St. Louis A-List Awards for Kitchen and Bath Remodeling, and 40 Under 40 with ProRemodeler. Specializing in Kitchen and Bath Design + Build, Anne Marie's positive and down to earth approach helps clients feel anything is achievable. Designing from her Studio in Wildwood, Mo., her unique attention to detail distinguishes her work amongst the rest.

Scan the QR code to watch a full interview with Anne

Audra Harrold

THE $1.50 TURNING POINT

I can identify many pivotal moments in my life, and trust me, there are many. Some moments were obvious. They were punch-me-in-the-face kind of obvious. Other moments came across like a soft tap on my shoulder or something shifting in the shadows. How could I choose just one? I took some time rewinding the reel of my life and reflecting over moments that stood out and after doing so, I can confidently pinpoint my most defining pivotal moment to date.

It occurred recently. On my birthday. June 5, 2025. At Costco.

Before fully feeling the gravity of this moment, I need to take you back through the noise, the beautiful chaos and some barely-held-together days. Because without the storm, this would just be another date in time passing by. Across the decades of my life, I have experienced a fair share of plot twists: cross-country moves, career reinventions, a divorce, starting a business and the roller coaster that goes along with it and then ultimately flying off the tracks into a fiery crash, a terrifying cancer diagnosis, the chaos of raising two boys as a single mom, financial ruin and the slow, steady dance of starting over again and again.

About 16 years ago, my family moved from eastern North Carolina to St. Louis, Mo. My boys were young, ages 3 and 5, and the promise of a fresh start in a new city was welcome and exciting. I was looking forward to a life of sporting events, orchestra concerts, making new friends, raising my boys and embracing my new city with everything it had to offer. I also rode and competed horses, my own horse having been shipped from NC as well. Things were good. Not just good; they were really good. But within two years, my marriage was over, my horse was severely injured and ended up retired at a friend's farm, I was unemployed with a large resume gap, and I found myself staring down into a new city and a future that no longer looked like the one I had envisioned. Some might say this could be my most pivotal moment, but it's not.

I kept going because mothers do. Women do. I had to rebuild a life for my boys and for me. This time around it came in the form of becoming an entrepreneur. While I was riding horses, I became frustrated that my riding clothes didn't fit right. Or rather they didn't fit like they used to when my body was 22. My post-baby body was stubbornly pushing back and refusing to cooperate with how my clothes fit. I found myself tugging and shifting instead of focusing on my ride on an 1,100-pound animal with a mind of its own. So, I decided to do something about it. I started my own equestrian clothing brand. SassyBull. A pink bull. An oxymoron. A woman with kahunas – like me. All of the tugging and shifting bloomed into something, and SassyBull Equestrian apparel was born. And just like that I stepped over the threshold into the magical and colorful world of fashion. Some might say this could be my most pivotal moment, but it's not.

SassyBull was my love and my passion. I did not come from a fashion background, but I was hungry to learn. Very hungry. I surrounded myself with people who were experts. I sat by their sides, I asked their advice, I flooded their inboxes with questions craving knowledge of everything fashion from sourcing fabrics, creating tech packs and working with manufacturing. I went to trade shows, I created a youth council, I showed up at horse events. What was missing? A solid plan with a razor-sharp budget. It was a true entrepreneurial story: I simply ran out of money. I over-inventoried and made about every mistake a new entrepreneur can make. I trusted the wrong people and made poor decisions. After a few years, I finally called it quits. It was over. Some might say this could be my most pivotal moment, but it's not.

But it gave me my first taste of what I truly love: fashion.

After I pulled up my big girl panties and wiped my tears with leftover T-shirts, I shifted into a different role in the fashion industry. I worked in a small batch manufacturing facility working with local designers and while I was there, I realized what was missing. It was community. Sure, we can have fashion shows and parties, and trunk shows with famous designers but that doesn't help the fashion professional who is struggling to get to the next level or find their next client and to truly make a living. There needed to be community. That is how I found myself at the intersection of fashion and purpose by co-founding STL Fashion Alliance as a nonprofit built to guide and champion the next generation of fashion professionals. To guide them to *not* make the mistakes I did, is what I was thinking. To truly provide support and resources and all the other things I would have loved to have at my fingertips had it been available. I finally felt like I wasn't chasing meaning behind what I was doing; I was standing in the middle of it.

STL Fashion Alliance is the real deal. It is an organization that truly supports local. From professionals to students at both the high school and college level the Alliance is exactly what it says. An Alliance. A bond between people who support each other. I have boot-strapped the organization from inception. It is something I believe strongly in and have poured my heart, soul and money into. STLFA is seasoned and ready to level up and grow. I am incredibly proud of the work I have done and will continue to do to support fashion and also serve as a bright flashing warning light to others to help detour around disaster. Some might say starting STL Fashion Alliance could be my most pivotal moment, but it's not.

While I was busy building something for others and trying to rewrite the course of my life, life had a plan of its own. It's like I had packed my bags for smooth sailing and life declared, "wait a minute" and changed the forecast and put a hole in my boat. It's almost like I couldn't have things be too good for very long. This time life threw a nasty one at me.

Cancer.

Diagnosed during a routine screening, no warning signs, no fanfare. Just the disorienting slap of a new chapter beginning without permission. I spent Christmas in the hospital that year, a section of my gut removed. Add in the bonus sidecar surgery (as I called it), which included a full hysterectomy due to the uterine fibroids that my doctor said were "impressive" and in the way. Trust me I was super surprised but definitely *not* impressed.

Recovery came in stages: physical first, then mental and emotional. As any cancer survivor will tell you, life will always be "before the C" and "after." Life and how I see it are different. A second lease on life, yes, but with an asterisk. Many might define a cancer diagnosis and getting to the other side to be the most pivotal moment, but it's not mine.

So that brings us back to Costco. I'm sitting at a plastic table in the Costco food court on my 52nd birthday with a $1.50 hotdog and drink in front of me. I am sitting across from my youngest son who just graduated from high school and will be off to college in a few short weeks to London. As we talked over our hotdogs and discussed our shopping list, what I saw was a beautiful adult emerging right before my eyes, and then it hit me. My boys are launching fully into their lives. I did a great job shaping kind, curious and bold young men. I nurtured and parented them, and then I gave them the encouragement, support and the wings to leave the nest and fully fly.

And in that moment. That pivotal moment. I realized it is not just their time to fly, I realized it was my time, too. I needed to find my wings again that have been folded up against my body for decades. It is my time to fly again.

The second half of my life will be louder. Braver. Stronger. Focused on building but also on breathing and taking in every moment. I want to pour more energy into me and what I love. I want to help young creatives through STLFA to help them see what's possible and to nurture vision into vocation. I want to create space where talent thrives and not merely survives. I want to inspire and empower.

I want to be fully, unapologetically *here* for the next chapter. For the fashion and the failures (how about a few less failures please?). I'm here for the quiet walks and the wild leaps. For the unknowns and the once-in-a-lifetimes. I want to stand in the fullness of my own story and say, "This is my awesome and amazing life." And anytime I forget how lucky I am, or get derailed by self-doubt, or find myself drowning with no life preserver, all I have do is get in my car and drive to Costco. Order a $1.50 hotdog meal, sit down, unfurl my wings and remember who I am, what a beautiful life I lead and what a powerful light I bring to the world. This realization…this was my most pivotal moment.

And if you ever need some life encouragement, or someone to help you rediscover your wings, give me a call and I'll meet you at Costco.

ABOUT AUDRA HARROLD

Audra Harrold is co-founder and executive director of the STL Fashion Alliance, where she leads efforts to support and elevate the St. Louis fashion industry through connection, education and grants. A seasoned professional with a strong foundation in design, manufacturing and nonprofit leadership, Audra brings a well-rounded and deeply informed perspective to her work. She also works in partnerships and education with Stars Design Group, which is a global design and production house specializing in custom apparel with manufacturing partners around the world.

Audra's fashion career began with launching her own equestrian sport brand, an experience that gave her a hands-on understanding of what it takes to bring a concept to market from ideation and design through production and sales. She also has worked closely with a small-batch manufacturing factory in New York and St. Louis, gaining full-circle knowledge of product development and apparel production processes.

Deeply committed to education, Audra is passionate about helping students understand the diverse career pathways in fashion. She serves on the Missouri Department of Elementary and Secondary Education's Family and Consumer Sciences and Human Services Education IRC Committee at the state level, shaping curriculum and competencies for fashion-related programs. She also contributes her expertise as an advisory board member on the Fashion Business and Design Advisory Council at Lindenwood University. She extends her expertise outside the US and most recently traveled with University of Georgia fashion students and faculty throughout Peru studying textiles and sustainability.

Audra's previous nonprofit roles with the American Cancer Society and as program director at the Saint Louis Fashion Fund further underscore her strengths in program development, community engagement and strategic leadership. Her extensive experience, industry connections and commitment to building an inclusive and thriving fashion ecosystem position her as a respected leader and advocate for fashion in St. Louis and beyond.

Random facts about Audra: She has two rescue dogs, Lollipop (boxer) and Roxann (bulldog), is not a fan of olives or mushrooms and loves to escape the real world with a good fiction book.

Favorite quotes:
"Sometimes you have to rethink the things you thought you thought through."
Winnie the Pooh

"In order to be irreplaceable, one must always be different."
Coco Chanel

Scan the QR code to watch a full interview with Audra

Caryn Dugan

A PLANT ON EVERY PLATE:
A JOURNEY FROM FEAR TO FLOURISHING

As a teenager, I was known to friends as the "human garbage disposal." I happily cleaned every plate, especially if it involved melted Velveeta or fried bologna. Food was joy. Food was comfort. Food was community. But health? That wasn't something I thought much about—until it became impossible not to.

In 2008, cancer took my dad far too soon. His absence left a hole in my life, one that would grow even larger just 10 weeks later when I was diagnosed with cancer myself. Grief, fear and disbelief were my constant companions. Everything I thought I understood about food, health and control was shattered.

But amid that darkness, I found an unexpected source of light.

I turned to medical journals, books, articles, interviews—anything I could get my hands on. I was desperate to understand how my body had failed me—or more accurately, how I might have failed it. Over and over again, I kept landing on one central truth: what we eat profoundly shapes how we live, how we heal and how we thrive.

So, I made a choice. A radical one, especially for someone who once counted nacho cheese as a food group.

I traded processed comfort for whole, vibrant foods. I gave my body a second chance. And as my own health returned, something inside me clicked. This wasn't just about *me* anymore. This was about *we*—all of us walking around in bodies that want to heal, if only we'd stop getting in their way.

That shift led me to Washington, D.C., in 2011, where I trained with the Physicians Committee for Responsible Medicine and became certified to teach plant-based cooking and nutrition. I came home to St.

Louis determined to spread the word. I didn't have a business plan or a strategy—I had conviction. And that was enough to get started.

At first, I taught people in grocery store community kitchens, then I was hired by the Community Support Center to educate cancer patients and their families about the connection between food and health. Soon I was anywhere someone would let me roll in with a blender and a smile. The impact was immediate and profound. People wanted to know what I knew. They wanted to feel better. They wanted a way in. So I gave them one.

That mission—*a plant on every plate*—became my guiding light. One person at a time, one meal at a time.

In 2011, I launched STLVegGirl, the city's first fully plant-based culinary education entity. It started with in-home classes and meal prep, then evolved into collaborations with restaurants, corporate wellness programs and eventually regional media appearances. I started popping up regularly on local affiliates NBC, CBS and FOX morning shows, sharing simple plant-based recipes that were as healing as they were delicious. Earning that bachelor's degree in broadcast journalism from Washington University in St. Louis served me well here.

It was time to spread the message a little more and bring some heavy hitters in the plant-based world to STL, so in 2018 we put on the Plant-Based Nutrition Summit at Washington University, which sold out and drew attendees from 16 states and two countries!

But something was still missing: a home.

On August 13, 2019—the 11th anniversary of my dad's passing—I opened the doors to the Center for Plant-Based Living in downtown Kirkwood. It was the first center of its kind in the country, dedicated solely to plant-based culinary and nutrition education. And it was so much more than a business. It was a tribute.

In that space, we held cooking classes, workshops and speaker events. We piloted the first-ever Forks Over Knives Community Program. And we launched St. Louis' inaugural Plant-Based Restaurant Week. Each event, each class, each person we reached confirmed what I already knew: people are hungry for change—they just need someone to show them how.

When the pandemic hit, we, like everyone else, adapted. I expanded our virtual programming and soon realized that the reach and flexibility of online access offered something the physical space couldn't. In 2024, I made the bittersweet decision to close the Kirkwood location and go fully digital. The mission didn't end—it grew.

Today, the Center for Plant-Based Living continues as a robust virtual membership along with a vast array of free resources. For just a dollar a day, members have access to a growing library of 150-plus plant-based recipes, on-demand cooking classes, monthly live support calls and a welcoming community of people on similar journeys. It's food and support, always at your fingertips.

Through the Center, I now work with corporate wellness teams to bring plant-based education to their employees, giving companies the tools to support the health of their people from the inside out. It's preventative care, served on a plate. The Center also has partnered with the Hospital for Special Surgery (HSS) in New York, utilizing CPBL's membership to enhance outcomes in their patient care. HSS is the world's leading orthopedic hospital, 15 years in a row.

And that's not all.

A few years ago, I partnered with Dr. Jim Loomis to launch *The Doc and Chef*, a video series where he tackles the science of nutrition and I demonstrate what that science looks like in your kitchen. We keep it approachable, engaging and evidence-based, each episode backed by a blog post full of citations, resources and practical tips.

We've taken *Doc and Chef* on the road—presenting everywhere from cruise ships to the US Air Force to the Romanian Lifestyle Medicine conference in Moldova! It's a joy to watch audiences light up when they realize that food can be powerful, joyful, and yes, *fun*.

But for all the certifications, accomplishments and airtime, my favorite moment is still the same: when someone tells me they finally feel better. That they didn't know it could be this way. That they didn't think it was possible for them.

And I get it. I really do.

Because I didn't grow up with quinoa in my pantry or kale in my smoothies. I grew up with boxed dinners, grief and a lot of questions. I wasn't born into this life—I fought my way into it. And every time I help someone else do the same, it feels like a small victory for the girl I used to be.

This work isn't just about plants or prevention. It's about power. About reclaiming agency over our health. About saying, *I deserve to feel good in my body*—and then doing something about it.

So yes I still love food. But these days, it's the kind that energizes, protects and connects. Food that respects the miracle of the human body. Food that heals.

It's taken years of learning, unlearning, experimenting and listening. But every step has been worth it. Because now, when someone asks me, *How do I begin?* I give a smile and say:

"Start with a plant on every plate."

And maybe that's what this moment is about. It's about time.

It's about time we stopped settling for chronic disease as the norm.

It's about time we gave ourselves permission to feel vibrant again.

It's about time we stopped fearing food and started celebrating it.

It's about time we saw our bodies not as projects to fix, but as miracles to nourish.

ABOUT CARYN DUGAN

Rooted deep in the St. Louis food and wellness scene, Caryn Dugan is STLVegGirl, a plant-based nutrition and culinary and lifestyle educator with a simple mission, "A Plant on Every Plate™."

Caryn adopted a plant-based diet in response to tragedy; in 2008, cancer took her father at an early age and 10 weeks later, tried to take her. In response to her diagnosis, she searched for an answer and found one in the growing body of literature supporting a whole food, plant-based diet to bolster our natural immune system. Adopting a plant-based diet herself and beating cancer, she sought to share her knowledge to help others.

In 2011, Caryn studied in Washington, DC, under the direction of Neal Barnard, M.D., at the Physicians Committee for Responsible Medicine's (PCRM) Food for Life program, becoming a certified instructor. Bringing this knowledge home, she teaches immune boosting, plant-based cooking classes at the Cancer Support Center of St. Louis for the benefit of others who have, like her, met cancer at the door.

Caryn went on to form STLVegGirl, LLC, St. Louis' first fully plant-based entity providing cooking instruction, personal cheffing, meal delivery and collaborative restaurant events. She regularly appears in cooking and nutrition segments on St. Louis affiliates of NBC, CBS and Fox morning shows.

Caryn has continued to earn her spurs as a graduate of:
• Rouxbe Cooking School Plant-Based Professional Program
• Plant-based Nutrition Certificate through Cornell University

- Wellcoaches as a Certified Health and Wellness Coach
- Wellness Forum's Plant-Based Certified Personal Chef Program
- Complete Health Improvement Program (CHIP) as a Lifestyle Medicine Institute Certified Program Facilitator

She also teamed up with Forks Over Knives to create the first-ever *Forks Over Knives Community Program,* which piloted in St. Louis and sold out every time. Most recent speaking engagements include presenting culinary instruction in Naples, Fla., to a group of 100 attendees at Total Health Immersions, Health Retreat where immersionists reportedly marked weight and inches lost, a decrease in insulin and blood pressure medication administration, and chronic illness reversal all within the span of seven days.

International exposure includes Naked Food Magazine featuring Caryn in its Spring 2017 anniversary edition where she received three pages.

Caryn executed St. Louis' first Plant-based Nutrition Summit at Washington University in July of 2018, where this one-day event featured world-renowned experts such as Michael Greger, M.D., and Caldwell Esselstyn, Jr., M.D. The event sold out and represented in attendance were 16 states and two countries.

A notable accomplishment is the opening of our nation's first plant-based nutrition and culinary education center, the Center for Plant-based Living in the historic Kirkwood downtown neighborhood of suburban St. Louis. The center offers plant-based cooking classes, programs, speaker's series, philanthropic efforts, etc. The COVID-19 pandemic has encouraged her business to shift, and she now also has a strong virtual presence where she can share the Center on a global level. They now also offer a membership for just $1 per day where members have access to a full library of past classes and recipes, access to ongoing virtual classes and monthly support calls.

2022 also made way for St. Louis' first Plant-based Restaurant Week, led by Caryn and the Center for Plant-based Living.

The Center also partnered with the Hospital for Special Surgery (HSS) utilizing CPBL's membership to enhance outcomes in their patient care. HSS is the world's leading orthopedic hospital, 15 years in a row.

Caryn and Jim Loomis, M.D., medical director of the Center, have teamed up to create a trailblazing YouTube series called *The Doc and Chef*. Each episode is topic-driven: Dr. Loomis breaks down the science, and Caryn brings it to life with a simple cooking demo that shows what the science looks like on your plate. Every episode is supported by a companion blog post, complete with scientific citations for the claims made.

In addition to the YouTube series, the duo travels extensively to present *Doc and Chef Live* at conferences, health immersions and retreats. They've had the honor of presenting to the US Air Force, headlined wellness programming on commercial cruise ships, and are set to speak in Moldova at the first-ever Romanian Lifestyle Medicine Conference—hosted jointly by the Moldovan and Romanian Societies of Lifestyle Medicine.

To learn about the trailblazing Center for Plant-based Living, please visit CPBL-STL.com

Scan the QR code to watch
a full interview with Caryn

Dr. Cassandra Walker Suggs, Ed.D, EJD

THE DECISION

It was the late 1960s, the country was still reeling from the assassinations of both John F. Kennedy and Malcolm X just a few years earlier. Death seemed to be on the minds of many Americans, and that did not bring comfort. It was supposed to be a time of freedom with the passing of the Civil Rights Bill and the integration of schools, yet it still felt heavy at times in the day to day lives of many.

One woman in particular who lived in the bustling city of Chicago, Ill., was feeling the pressure of the world engulfing her. She and her husband were expecting their second child, one they had been waiting years to conceive. It should have been a joyous time, but it was shrouded in gloom.

"I am certain mam that you or your child or both will die if you have this operation while pregnant." Was the stern remark from the doctor to the young woman in distress. She rung her hands tightly as her wedding ring moved round and round on her narrow fingers. The doctor's voice sounded almost muted as she stared at the floor contemplating all that was being said.

"I want a second opinion." Is what she quietly found strength to say. Offended, the doctor marched out of the room and moments later his nurse came in with another doctor's name and phone number scribbled on a piece of paper. The young woman gathered her personal items and headed to her car.

On the way home she thought about what she and her husband had been through the last four months. Finding out they were pregnant again, celebrating with friends and family and even going over potential girl and boy names, filled their days. Then one day a routine appointment revealed that the occasional pain in her side turned out to be ligaments that were forming and wrapping around her colon, a deadly situation if not corrected with surgery. Lost in her thoughts, before she knew it, she was home and did not even remember driving there.

She and her husband talked most of the night about what the first doctor warned her 'you and your baby or both will die if you have surgery while pregnant." The only option she was told was to abort the baby and then proceed with the complicated surgery. No decision in her life had ever come to such a price as this one.

Later that week, she and her husband found themselves sitting in front of the second doctor. He looked over her X-rays with a serious yet informed expression. He made a few hmms and umms and then looked up at them with a concerned look on his face. This is a difficult situation because of where the baby is in your womb and the location of the ligaments wrapping around your colon. Your doctor was correct about the potential outcome.

To which the young mother replied, "I will not abort my baby in the hope that I can survive, you will have to do the surgery with me pregnant. My child deserves a chance to live!"

The young lady sighed and looked at her hands, brown and slender, long fingers that were now shaking, so much so that her husband gently reached out and held them. Then the doctor said, "I believe I can do the surgery and you and the baby can both survive."

She exhaled loudly and started to softly sob. Her husband held her tight. "That is all we wanted to hear, doctor, that I could keep my baby and there was a chance we can both live."

They prepped her for surgery that day. Before she was carted off to the operating room, she and her husband prayed "Dear Lord, you gave us this child and we believe you have a purpose for this child's life. Please bring that purpose to fruition and guide the doctor's hands so that we both can come out of the surgery alive, in Jesus' name, Amen."

That winter was a cold one. One of the coldest Chicago had in years. The traffic was bumper to bumper on this cold February day. It was also Abraham Lincoln's birthday, a holiday in Illinois so many were off work. It seemed like a lifetime ago that this young man had to make the decision with his wife to have a serious surgery or not. He kept thinking about how difficult that was just a few months ago and he kept thinking about the outcome of the surgery. He snapped out of his daydream as the cries of a baby were heard down the hall signaling to the father that his new baby daughter was born. He ran to the room to find his young wife and their baby girl safe and sound. Noticeably on the side of the wife was a scar from her colon surgery several months before, also noticeably was her beautiful smile as she held her new baby girl full of promise and of LIFE! They both made it through that difficult surgery and the mom's and dad's prayers were answered.

The prayer that God had a purpose for their child was also answered as I type this story today; I am that baby who the doctor said would not survive! My mother Odessa Floyd Walker is the courageous mother who did not give up on me and most importantly did not give up on God!

Now many years have passed and I am married with four grown sons and five grandchildren. As of 2025, both of my parents are alive and are celebrating their 70th wedding anniversary. Life has some tough times but everything works out for the good for those who love God and are called according to His purpose. Romans 8:28. My life's verse. You have a purpose for your life as well!

ABOUT DR. CASSANDRA WALKER SUGGS, ED.D, EJD

Cassandra Walker Suggs, Ed.D., EJD, is an Emmy-nominated television talk show host, award-winning author and nationally recognized newspaper columnist whose career bridges education, media and advocacy. A dynamic leader with a heart for equity and empowerment, she currently serves as the incoming assistant superintendent for the Affton School District, following her impactful work as director of educational equity and access for the Rockwood School District.

Cassandra is a two-time Emmy nominee for her work in television and the author of two national award-winning books for adolescents. She was also honored as a National Award-Winning Columnist for *The St. Louis American* and named Teacher of the Year in 2018.

She holds a doctorate's degree in heritage leadership, social justice, sustainability and participatory culture from the University of Missouri–St. Louis, an Education Specialist degree (Ed.S.) from the University of Missouri–Columbia and an Executive Juris Doctorate from Purdue University Global Law School, where she graduated with the highest GPA in the Class of 2024. She also earned a Certificate in Administrative Leadership from Harvard University.

Beyond her professional achievements, she is a proud wife and mother of four adult sons, and remains deeply committed to mentoring, storytelling and building inclusive spaces where all people are seen, heard and valued.

Scan the QR code to watch
a full interview with Cassandra

Chelsea Haynes

SKY SCRAPER SEASON

When you get down, look up!

Look up to the heavens and see all that you were created for and purposed to be in this world.

Sometimes when we look up, we will see nothing but clear skies, open air and the beauty of nature's ceiling. If you grew up in a large, metropolitan city like me, often the skies are full of skyscrapers towering over you. These buildings may seem magnanimous, powerful and overbearing, but they most certainly are always beautifully breathtaking, showcasing both life and light—all qualities that we as humans should try to achieve.

What if we, too, are designed to function like those skyscrapers? What if we are purposed to be big, bold, beautiful buildings with an iconic impact on the world, just like those towering dwellings?

Think about it.

Historically, skyscrapers were constructed to maximize land use and to accommodate growing urban populations in limited spaces. They were designed to show off natural light and to display gorgeous design elements.

Doesn't that describe us as human beings? Our mission and our purpose in this life is to infect and impact peoples' lives within the limited space God has called us to. And each of us has been uniquely designed, crafted and constructed by Him to properly infect the "buildings" we have all been assigned to. No matter how big or small we feel, we can all have a powerful impact every bit as bold as some of the world's largest buildings.

Throughout my journey of becoming, I learned that each of us has a skyscraper season—a deep season of personal growth that allows us to shoot up like a skyscraper and to refine our purpose and calling in life. In those seasons of life, I have grown into myself as a woman, a leader, a television host, a better daughter and sister, and hopefully one day, a wife and mother. In some of my darkest days, when I have felt lost, confused and struggled to open my mouth and pray, seek clarity and encourage myself, God told me I was in my skyscraper season—a season of deep, foundational work, so the world can see my name, my structure, my purpose, my design, my foundation, my strength, my culture significance and my influence on the community.

More importantly, anytime I am reminded of my personal skyscraper season, it is even more beautiful to encourage others and share with them that they also have them. Based on my own story, here are six attributes to remember how to root yourself when it comes to recognizing your Skycraper Season:

Skyscrapers have names and purpose.

The Empire State Building.
The Burj Khalifa.
The Shanghai Tower.

All of these iconic buildings have a name that people across the globe instantly recognize, and you, too, have a name—a name that is packed with meaning and purpose. Our names are the gateway to our identity, family, culture and history. So what's in a name?

For me, my name is Chelsea Olivia Haynes. Rooted in Olde English, a Chelsea is a port, or a landing place that allows people to come in and out, a true reflection of my bright, bubbly and encouraging spirit. My name embodies how I am a fixture in the community, allowing people to take what they need on dark days, providing a solid infrastructure and stable platform, ensuring the transfer of goods and services between passengers and the vessels and destinations in which they travel.

My middle name, Olivia, is a derivative of olive. Olives symbolize peace, renewal and friendship. In addition to this, biblically, the olive tree represents the Holy Spirit and God's blessings, lifelong faith and the ongoing journey of devotion to the Lord. They say the name embodies the true strength needed to thrive in adversity and the capacity for renewal, growth, strength and resilience.

Just as I know my name and my purpose here on this Earth, I challenge you to seek out the meaning behind your name. Whether it was a name your earthly parents intentionally chose or the name that was inspired by God, your name holds weight and its impact can often give you insight into exactly what you should be doing here on Earth.

This is a powerful peek into not only your identity but into your purpose and the spheres of influence you will affect. As you walk into your Skyscraper Season, you will endure a tough building phase, and once your building is complete, so many will reap from the longevity of your skyscraper, erected for the entire world to see.

Skyscrapers have a design and a solid foundation.

Renowned architects, such as Frank Lloyd Wright and Antoni Gaudí, left a legacy through the creativity and innovation of their designs. Their acclaimed works, such as the Guggenheim Museum and La Sagrada Familia, respectively, have inspired others for generations and imparted the depth of their imagination in cities all across the globe. And you, too, have a beautiful design that will impact the world.

Take a moment to consider how you're designed.

Are you artsy and creative, or do you prefer rules and routine? Are you a high-energy individual, or do you tend to take things with a more mellow, even-keeled approach? Do you focus on the details or the bigger picture, the final product or the planning stages? Are you an early bird or a night owl? Are you an athlete, or do you prefer to sit in the stands? Every single one of us has a unique design to influence and impact the world God created for us.

As a television host, my big, bright, high-energy personality might not be the best fit for grieving families who visit the funeral home to plan their loved one's homegoing celebration, but it's encouraging and inspiring to so many people I come in contact with in front of the screen and off-air.

At this very moment, I challenge you to take a moment to really consider your own design. How are you wired? What makes you tick? Are you truly walking in your purpose?

Seriously, stop reading!

Take a moment to think about it.

Now that you've processed how you function, consider the foundation. The buildings mentioned above and the architects who created them knew their incredible designs meant nothing if the structure was unstable and not durable.

Your foundation is the strongest part of who you are. It's how you set the tone and the standard for your life. It's how everything flows in and out of who you are, your principles, your morals and the way you treat others. When we draw parallels to ourselves as a building structure, the foundation serves as a way to avoid defects, stay grounded and prevent overloading.

As humans, it is imperative to build a strong foundation. When the foundation is strong, people will wonder, why the person is so great, so beautiful or so ___________________. Yep, go ahead and fill in the blank with all of your best qualities.

What makes me grounded is my faith in Christ, my passion for performing and the arts, pure kindness, joy, peace and treating people as they deserve to be treated. My foundation is rooted in a healthy relationship with self-confidence in who I am, my hair, my skin, my voice and any other quirks that make me unique. When you have a solid foundation, you can continue to grow and build your life on a solid rock, rather than sinking sand, on something sturdy rather than a shaky surface.

Imagine the things you want people to remember about you and, my friends, don't just talk about it. Be about it. It is through this foundation, the deep groundwork, that your skyscraper can withstand gravity and other forces that will try to wear you down. However, going back to that foundation, never changing from the root of who you are, is the perfect recipe for finalizing the build and evolving with time, but never truly letting go of your name, your purpose and your design.

Skyscrapers have an impact and influence on the community.

Historically, skyscrapers were created to reduce housing costs and level inequality, but also to serve as architectural landmarks to continue to define a city's unique identity and skyline. Consider the St. Louis Arch. It is an icon of the beloved Gateway City. But more importantly, it is a way for both citizens and tourists to provide spaces for social interaction and cultural events.

If we keep up with our analogy of us as humans being skyscrapers, we too, were named, purposed, designed and founded to have impact and influence on our direct spheres of influence.

The impact that we are destined for includes our purpose and design and contributes to a beautiful ecosystem of success. Whether it's business or the arts, we all have unique and innovative roots, ideas and designs that not only impact ourselves and our families, but our places of employment, our communities, our cities, our regions, our countries and our world.

No matter how big or small, your impact leaves a mark. You are a cog in a much bigger wheel.

You have the power to decide which campaigns to support, in which local stores to shop and how children in our community learn both inside and outside of the classroom.

I have been blessed to impact many communities including my hometown of Houston, Texas, and more specifically, the suburb I grew up in, Missouri City, Texas. Ironically, I have since lived in two 'Missouri cities'—Columbia, Mo., and St. Louis, Mo. Both cities have played an integral role in my growth and development as not only a professional, but as a person. I have also lived abroad in Barcelona, Spain, and in Knoxville, Tenn., and have island roots to the city where my father was born, Bridgetown, Barbados.

I mention all of these places because each one has been a part of me, but more importantly, I can see different ways I have impacted all of these places, no matter how big or how small.

As you embark on the journey of being a skyscraper, you have to acknowledge your influence and impact, not from a place of ego, but as a way to shine and sparkle with humility by the weight of who you were created to be.

All in all, I leave you with this:

You don't have to be rich or famous to influence and to impact the world; you just simply need to be you. Boldly embrace your name, your purpose, your design, your foundation, your impact and your influence.

At 28 years old, I have accomplished a lot. But this is only the beginning. The best part about skyscrapers is that they often don't thrive alone. They are part of a community, each of them standing boldly and proudly next to another, serving different peoples, cultures and communities from all across the world.

Are you ready to soar? You better buckle up, buttercup! It's your Skyscraper Season!

ABOUT CHELSEA HAYNES

Engaging. Effervescent. Encouraging.

A wise man once said, "there are two great moments in a person's life; the day you were born and the moment you discover your purpose." To know your purpose is to understand why you pursue life passionately. Raised in a suburb of Houston, Texas, as a young girl Chelsea enjoyed theater arts. At any early age, Chelsea knew her place was in front of people using her voice to inspire and to instruct others. Chelsea discerned it was necessary to cultivate her gifting to become a lifestyle and entertainment journalist, and she enrolled at the University of Missouri to study broadcast journalism and Spanish.

Fluent in Spanish, Chelsea has a passion for food, fernweh, sharing her faith with others and being in fellowship with a variety of people from different cultures.

Chelsea solo-hosted, the hour-long, magazine-style program Studio STL on FOX 2 in St. Louis, from 2021- 2025 and served as the in-arena host for the NHL's St. Louis Blues from 2022- 2024. Prior to her gig in The Lou, Chelsea was a storyteller and fill-in host on Living East Tennessee in Knoxville, Tenn. Before launching her TV career, Chelsea lived in Columbia, Mo., as she studied broadcast journalism and Spanish and spent six months abroad in Barcelona, Spain.

A blossoming blogger, Chelsea explores spiritual truths and encourages her peers to deepen their faith through daily devotionals as they pursue the peace of God in the midst of an unpredictable world. An eternal optimist, Chelsea enjoys reading magazines and keeping up with entertainment news, watching television, traveling, practicing her Spanish and shopping for the perfect pair of shoes.

In her spare time, she's a Luxe Travel Specialist booking trips for clients all over the globe with Altitude Travel: TheAltitudeTeam.com.

Scan the QR code to watch
a full interview with Chelsea

Dr. Christy Jenkins, N.D.

THE TIME TO HEAL
FROM KNOWLEDGE TO CALLING

There comes a moment in every life when time stands still—not because the world stops moving, but because you do. For me, that moment came in a hospital room, holding my mother's hand, watching her fight a battle that her body was no longer prepared to win.

I've been a board-certified naturopathic doctor since 2004. For years, I offered consultations, treatments and protocols designed to help people live better, feel stronger and heal naturally. I believed in the power of holistic medicine—deeply. But even with all of that knowledge, I couldn't save the woman who gave me life. And that reality reshaped everything I thought I knew.

Her passing wasn't just a personal loss. It was my pivot. It forced me to confront a haunting question: Was there more I could have done?

That question stayed with me—through sleepless nights, through prayers and through the quiet moments of grief that no title or certification can shield you from. But it also led me somewhere sacred—back to the drawing board, not just as a doctor, but as a daughter determined to make meaning out of her mother's life.

Two years ago, that meaning took form in the launch of my own line of supplements centered around one of the most overlooked yet critical organs in the body, the liver.

Most people don't realize how vital liver health is to their overall well-being. They don't know that fatigue, weight gain, skin issues, poor sleep and even mood disorders can often be traced back to liver dysfunction. And worse, many are told by doctors, "Your labs look fine," while their symptoms scream otherwise.

In my practice, I saw this pattern far too often. And I knew it was time to do something about it.

I developed a complete Fatty Liver Cleanse system rooted in naturopathic principles but built with practical application. It included:

- A homeopathic liver remedy designed to gently stimulate detox pathways
- A superfood powder to replenish essential nutrients and reduce inflammation
- A pharmaceutical-grade chamomile extract to calm the nervous system and support the gut-liver-brain connection

These products weren't just items on a shelf. They were the embodiment of a mission: to reach people before it's too late, to give them real options—not just prescriptions—and to help them heal before they break.

And the truth I want every reader to know is that we are not overmedicated because we're broken. We're overmedicated because we're uninformed. Our bodies are intelligent. They respond to support. They respond to nature. And most of all, they respond to intentional care.

This chapter is not just about my journey. It's about yours. Whether you're new to holistic health or have tried everything and still feel stuck, I want to invite you into a new possibility: that healing is not only possible, it's within reach. It's about time we believed that again.

The Turning Point: From Practitioner To Innovator

For years, I did what every responsible practitioner does. I stuck to what I was trained in: nutritional guidance, botanical medicine, homeopathic remedies and personalized detox plans. And I helped many people improve the quality of their lives.

But something kept pressing in my spirit that there was more. I was called to build something.

It wasn't about reinventing medicine. It was about reclaiming it, stripping away the dependency on overprescribed pharmaceuticals and showing people how to engage with their health from the inside out.

After losing both of my parents, especially my mother, I couldn't shake the feeling that we live in a system that reacts to illness instead of preventing it. My mom wasn't uneducated. She did what her doctors told her to do. She took the prescriptions. She followed the advice. But what she needed wasn't more pills. She needed restoration—nutritionally, emotionally and physiologically.

That realization became the foundation of my supplement line: not just selling products, but delivering solutions. My mission became helping people detoxify their lives—starting with the liver and radiating outward.

I began incorporating these new formulations into my existing practice, and the results were undeniable. People who had struggled for years began seeing shifts in their energy, sleep, digestion and even emotional regulation. Clients were more engaged, more hopeful and more willing to take ownership of their wellness.

Chamomile Wasn't Just for Sleep

Chamomile became one of my most powerful tools. But not in the way most people think. Yes, it helps with sleep. But more importantly, it soothes inflammation, supports digestion and balances the gut-brain-liver axis. It calms the nervous system in a way that pharmaceuticals often can't—without side effects, dependency or dulling the senses.

I created a specialized Chamomile Elixir that was designed to do more than relax you at night. It was made to restore your baseline, the foundation, the part of you that holds all the stress, toxins and unresolved tension.

This elixir became my number one seller. Not just because of its flavor, but because of its function. People would message me saying, "I didn't know how much my body needed this." They weren't just sleeping better—they were living better. That's when I knew I was on the right path. I wasn't here to just "consult." I was here to create solutions rooted in faith, science and a deep calling to help people heal.

A Different Kind Of Health Message

If you're reading this and you've never heard of naturopathic medicine, don't worry. You're not alone. So many people have only experienced the health care system through prescriptions, co-pays and 10-minute appointments.

Naturopathic medicine is not mystical or fringe. It's rooted in biology, physiology and science. But it takes a whole-body, whole-life approach. We ask "why" instead of masking the "what." We look for the root cause. We do not just suppress symptoms. That's what makes holistic healing so powerful. It's not about avoiding conventional medicine. It's about using every natural tool available before we jump to drugs or surgeries.

In my view, true health is when your body is supported enough to do what it was designed to do: to heal.

It's About Time We Stop Settling

I named my contribution to this book "The Time to Heal" because I believe this is a divine moment for many people. A moment where we stop accepting chronic symptoms as "normal," where we stop accepting that illness is inevitable, and where we finally start listening to the messages our bodies are sending.

If you're exhausted, foggy, inflamed, anxious or just not yourself, that is not something you should normalize. It's something you should investigate. And holistic care offers the roadmap to do exactly that without more side effects, more prescriptions or more confusion.

The turning point in my own life was not when I received my degree. It was when I realized my calling required more. It required me to build, to educate, to serve and to lead others into healing they didn't know was possible.

I don't claim to have all the answers. But I do know how to ask the right questions. And I believe you deserve a health care approach that sees the whole you—body, mind and spirit.

My Mother's Legacy, My Life's Work

It breaks my heart that my mom didn't get to see what I've created. I often wonder how she would feel, knowing that her struggle gave birth to something that's now changing lives. I carry her memory with me in every formula, every consultation and every success story from a client who feels like they finally found hope.

Her passing was the moment time stood still for me. But it was also the moment I woke up. I stopped waiting for systems to change. I became the change. I stopped expecting people to "get it" and started building tools that help them feel it for themselves.

Every product I've created, every class I've taught and every protocol I've built has been shaped by the belief that we were meant to thrive—that life doesn't have to be lived under the weight of pills and problems.

A Personal Invitation To The Reader

If this is the first time you're hearing about holistic health, I want to welcome you. You don't have to know all the terms. You don't have to be perfect. You just have to be open—open to learning, open to healing and open to asking if there's a better way. Because there is.

You may be reading this chapter feeling like you've tried everything, like no one really understands what you're going through, like you're tired of not being heard. I've sat across from that feeling more times than I can count. And I want you to know there's another way forward. You don't have to walk it alone.

Final Words: It's About Time

The time to wait is over. The time to ignore symptoms is over. The time to believe healing is for someone else is over. It's about time for you to choose you. And when you do, I'll be here ready to walk with you, guide you and empower you toward the kind of health that doesn't come from a pill, but from within. Because optimal health is more than the lack of illness. It's the presence of peace, clarity and the freedom to live fully.

You deserve that. And it's about time.

Dr. Christy Jenkins, N.D.
Founder, Drs Blend Cleanse
Board-Certified Naturopathic Doctor

ABOUT DR. CHRISTY JENKINS

Dr. Christy Jenkins is a board-certified naturopathic doctor, wellness innovator and the founder of Naturo Health Solutions. With more than 30 years of clinical experience, she is widely respected for her expertise in liver health, functional detoxification and holistic wellness. Dr. Jenkins is especially known for helping clients uncover the root causes of illness—often after conventional medicine has failed to provide answers.

She leads a multidimensional wellness center in partnership with her daughter, where they combine advanced natural therapies with faith-based healing to support long-term vitality and longevity. Her work is grounded in the belief that optimal health is more than the absence of illness—it's the presence of peace, purpose and cellular restoration.

Dr. Jenkins is the formulator behind a growing line of therapeutic products including her signature fatty liver cleanse, her groundbreaking Chamomile Elixir and a collection of functional foods that merge flavor and healing, including wellness teas, lattes and now, a buzzworthy line of chamomile-infused desserts.

Her latest innovation, the St. Louis Red Velvet Chamomile Cookie, is a tribute to her roots and a bold new expression of food-as-medicine—infused with anti-inflammatory benefits and crafted to support the nervous system and digestive health.

Dr. Christy Jenkins is not only a healer, but a pioneer who is devoted to creating a legacy of well care, not sick care, and restoring hope for those who feel overlooked by traditional systems.

Scan the QR code to watch a full interview with Christy

PERFECTLY IMPERFECT
A MARRIAGE STRENGTHENED BY GRACE

Fighting For Each Other

How do we choose a lifetime with one person in a world that constantly tells us to walk away? How do we uphold a covenant of marriage, promising to stay through the joy and the pain? How many times must we forgive, let go, offer second chances and fight for not against each other?

My story is not one of giving in to divorce or settling into a cold, disconnected partnership. It is a story of suiting up for battle, not against my spouse, but alongside him. It is about choosing to grow in love, to stand firm when it would be easier to run and to fight for the sacred bond of marriage. It is about protecting what matters most: our love, our faith and our family.

Childhood: Learning How to Hide

To understand my story, you need to know where I came from. I grew up in a home filled with conflict. Dinner was either silent and tense or loud and volatile. My father was often absent, either physically at the local tavern or emotionally disconnected at home. When he was home, the air was thick with resentment.

By first grade, I had already mastered silence. It was just more peaceful. I was so quiet, my teacher thought I had learning challenges. But the truth was harder to see. I was simply trying to survive in a home filled with ongoing tension, conflict and unspoken pain. There were hidden secrets in my parents' marriage that none of us fully understood at the time, though we felt their weight in every room. After 20 years, my parents' marriage ended in divorce.

A turning point for me came around the time I was 10 years old. A neighbor, Joann, had invited my mom, my brothers and me to church. There, I discovered a new kind of love—a safe, unconditional love found in Jesus. He became my refuge, my comfort and the father my heart longed for. Unfortunately, we only stayed in the church for a brief period of time. My father never attended.

As time passed, I grew into a young woman who feared confrontation, avoided vulnerability and did not know how to verbalize my deepest feelings. I now see that when I entered into marriage, I was missing essential tools such as openness, honest communication and the courage to share my truths.

Over time, by God's grace, I rebuilt my relationship with my mom and dad. What once felt broken was slowly restored, and now we have honest conversations about the past. We cry and laugh together, and I have seen redemption in places I never thought possible.

A New Kind of Family

In 1981, a year after high school, I met Brian, a funny, outspoken and persistent young man who would eventually become my husband. His upbringing was the opposite of mine. His family was close-knit, faith-filled and affectionate. I jokingly refer to his parents as June and Ward Cleaver. They were everything mine were not. They laughed together, vacationed together, played games together and went to church three times a week where his grandfather was the pastor.

By the time I was 21, I told Brian I wanted a ring on my finger. He proposed in 1984. I committed to five years of marriage, not because I did not love him, but because deep down, I did not believe marriages were meant to last a lifetime. Looking back, I wonder why did he want to marry a woman with trust issues and such low expectations of marriage? The answer: he loved me. And I loved him, in the only way I knew how.

The Vows We Say Without Understanding

In 1985, at the age of 23, I stood in front of family, friends and God and made promises I did not fully understand. "To love, honor and cherish, till death do us part."

Like many young brides, I entered marriage with more emotion than preparation. I knew what I did not want, mostly based on what I had seen growing up, but I had little idea how to build something lasting. The part "till death do us part" felt like a line from a romantic movie, unrealistic and overwhelming.

The truth is the majority of us say our vows not yet able to grasp that love is not just a feeling but a discipline, a decision made daily in the trenches of real life.

The Love Letter That Saved Us

In the year 2000, after 15 years of marriage, I hit a wall. I felt more alone than ever. I felt unseen, unheard and emotionally adrift. Brian was traveling constantly, his job growing heavier and more demanding with each passing year. I had slowly grown accustomed to his quiet absence, both away and at home. I found myself avoiding conflict. The more I stayed silent, the more bitter I grew. Emotionally drained and disconnected, I began preparing my heart to leave.

Then, one day I shattered his world with the devastating confession that I wanted to end our marriage, a word he never dreamed would touch us: divorce.

After months of separation and silence from me, pleads from him, something so unexpected happened that it stopped me in my tracks. One day, without warning, Brian wrote me a "love note"—his first ever. My hand trembled as I opened it.

He poured out his heart. He said he was sorry for not being there in the ways I needed. He told me he still loved me, deeply, fiercely. He wanted us to stay together, and he was willing to make changes. He was fighting for us. For me. At the end, he wrote a line that pierced through the walls I had built around my heart: "I am casting you a line. Please grab it, and I will pull you in."

That line, so simple, so vulnerable, broke me open. I remember staring at the words, tears blurring the ink. It was more than a metaphor. It was a lifeline. A plea. A promise.

That line, the literal and metaphorical one, saved our marriage.

Learning How to Communicate

We committed to rebuilding our marriage and saw a counselor who quickly diagnosed our dynamic. To me, she said: "You have a voice. Use it." To Brian: "Do not defend. Do not talk. Just listen."

I was a competent leader at work, yet I struggled to tell my own husband how I felt. The years of silence would always end in explosions of frustration. I resented how I bottled everything inside, and he regretted how he reacted when I tried to share my feelings. But slowly, I forced myself to speak honestly. And Brian committed to truly listening, allowing his defenses to come down. We stumbled. We repeated patterns. We continued to work on us.

My heart continued to soften. My faith and hope strengthened. We finally started putting our marriage first. We were honest with each other. We apologized more. We forgave faster. We still stumbled and repeated patterns, but we remembered why we chose each other. There is a saying: "Speak the truth in love." But I like to take it further: speak the truth with grace, with love and with hope for the future. Grace is unearned. It is what keeps us coming back to the table, repeatedly, even after we have messed up.

Three Marriages, One Man

The Evolution of a Love That Lasts

Marriage is not a single moment, but a living journey, one that changes, stretches and deepens over time. It is easy to look at couples who have been together for decades and imagine smooth sailing, but behind every lasting union are seasons of struggle, surrender and strength. This is the story of my 40-year marriage, not one seamless narrative, but three distinct versions of love shared with the same extraordinary man. Each season has refined us, and each time, we chose to stay not because it was easy, but because it was worth it.

Together, we have raised two incredible children, welcomed two beloved bonus children, and are now blessed with four precious grandchildren who fill our lives with joy, laughter and meaning. From the outside, it might look like a fairy tale, but the truth is, our journey has taken many unexpected turns.

I often say, half joking, fully honest that I have been "divorced" three times from the same man. Not legally, of course. But emotionally, spiritually and relationally, we have gone through three distinct versions of our marriage. Each season required us to reintroduce ourselves, to learn about each other all over again, and to recommit to a love that has grown deeper, more weathered and more rooted with time.

Through it all, one thing has remained steady: Brian. His unwavering integrity, faith, strength and steadfast love have been the constant thread holding us together. This is our story, three seasons, one man and a love that endured.

Season One: The Early Years

The first version of our marriage began when we were young, wide-eyed and wildly unprepared. We were building careers, raising babies, chasing dreams and learning what it meant to become "us." Sleep was a luxury, money was tight and time together felt like a race against the calendar.

There were diaper changes, school drop-offs, youth sports, late-night work projects, work trips, lake weekends to catch our breath and big aspirations that demanded everything we had. We loved each other deeply, but we were often too exhausted or distracted to say it out loud. The busyness masked the cracks, communication breakdowns, emotional distance and the slow fade that can happen when two people stop truly seeing each other.

Fifteen years in, I hit a wall. I felt lonely in the very life we had built together. I was tired, emotionally disconnected and quietly preparing my heart to leave. I did not know how to express the ache I was feeling or if it would even matter if I did. I felt invisible. And I was ready to walk away.

But Brian never stopped showing up.

Even when I withdrew, when I did not have the words for what I needed, when I had one foot out the door, he remained—not with pressure or panic, but with steady grace and presence. I was slipping away, and instead of letting go, he wrote me the love letter.

We didn't fix everything overnight. But we were committed to each other and in the daily choice to keep showing up. The cracks started to disappear, and over time, they filled with grace. And somehow, that season of heartbreak became the soil for a stronger, more honest love.

Season Two: The Empty Nest

The children grew up, and suddenly the house was quiet. It was just us again, only we were not the same people we had been at the beginning. For a while, the silence felt foreign. We had poured ourselves into parenting and our careers for so long, we had to relearn who we were as a couple.

But we began to rediscover each other. We found joy in slow Saturday mornings, unhurried and uninterrupted dinners, dancing, playing games and late-night talks that had nothing to do with carpool schedules. Our conversations turned toward travel dreams, spiritual growth and how we wanted to spend this new chapter together.

We dated again, on purpose. We laughed more easily, prayed more earnestly and fell in love, not with who we used to be, but with who we were becoming. Brian was intentional, thoughtful and fully present. He pursued me, not just out of habit, but out of love. And I found myself falling in love with my husband all over again.

Season Three: Retirement and Grandparenting

Now, we are in our third season, a time of slower rhythms, deeper roots and unexpected challenges. Retirement, for all its beauty, required a major adjustment. We had to redefine our days, our sense of purpose, and even our identities apart from the careers that shaped us for decades.

Together, we asked the big questions: How do we spend our time and money? Where do we want to live? How do we maintain our individuality while nurturing us?

What I am most grateful for in this season is how we have learned to have conversations, not conflicts. We have become partners in the truest sense, spiritually and emotionally. We are a team, and we know how to win together.

These days, love looks like presence. It's in the way he walks beside me through our neighborhood, in the way he flips pancakes for the grandkids, in the way he listens when I share a thought that has no point or makes no sense, but that I just needed to say it. It is in the quiet moments, the coffee on the porch, the shared memories, the simple joy of being here together.

Each of these three seasons has required us to begin again, to have new roles, new challenges and new versions of ourselves. But each time, we have chosen each other all over again.

I have learned that love matures when it is tested, that grace is essential, that small things matter more than grand gestures, that laughter and prayer are glue in tough times, and that a marriage rooted in faith, friendship and forgiveness can weather any storm.

Most of all, I have learned that the man I married at 23—the one who has loved me through every version of myself—is still the one I want beside me every morning.

Learning to Love with Grace

I mention grace a lot. It took me years to understand what love truly meant—beyond the butterflies, the romance and the shared memories. Love, real love, must be rooted in truth and watered with grace. Without both, love becomes either too harsh or too fragile. It is looking at your partner not through rose-colored glasses, but with eyes wide open and deciding to love them anyway. Grace means giving, even when it is not earned. It means choosing to listen when you would rather shut down. It means extending your hand when your pride wants to pull away. Grace is not a weakness; it's strength wrapped in humility. It offers a soft place to land when the world has been harsh.

I also had to learn to offer grace to myself. For years, I was my own worst critic, berating myself for not doing enough, rehashing past failures, not being enough. We are meant to glance at the past, learn from it, but not live in it. The real journey is ahead of us. That is where hope lives. That is where transformation happens. I have learned to dream forward, both in life and in marriage.

The Road to Hana

Marriage, to me, is a lot like the legendary Road to Hana in Maui. If you have ever driven it, you know it is not for the faint of heart. It is a winding, narrow highway with more than 600 curves and around 60 one-lane bridges. There are waterfalls around nearly every corner, panoramic ocean views, lush rainforests and moments where the path feels too risky to keep going. But if you stay the course, you are rewarded with the kind of beauty you could never experience on a straight, predictable road.

The journey of marriage is thrilling and breathtaking, but also terrifying and unpredictable. There are moments of wonder, like holding your newborn child or celebrating an anniversary you were not sure you would reach. But there are also sharp turns, like the death of a parent or a career setback. There are moments when you lose your way, when it feels easier to turn around than push forward.

But if you stay committed, if both people keep showing up, keep choosing each other those challenges become sacred. They become part of the story. You do not just love your spouse for the easy parts. You love them because of everything you have been through together, the arguments, the forgiveness, the resilience. Every struggle, every reconciliation, is a mile marker on your shared map. Now, I am not suggesting staying in an abusive relationship. There are real, painful reasons why some marriages cannot or should not continue. But if there is still love, if there is still respect and the desire to rebuild, then I believe it is worth fighting for.

When we drove the Road to Hana, there were times we had to slow down, pull over, even back up to let someone else pass. Marriage is the same. You will have to yield. You will need patience. If you are driving with someone who is committed as much as you are, then even the detours can become part of the adventure. And when you finally arrive, when you look back at everything you overcame, you will realize it was not just about the destination, it was about the journey.

Our Love Story

Now, in retirement, our home is filled with the echoes of grandkids' laughter and second chances. One of my greatest joys in life is reflecting on the journey my husband and I have shared and being able to say, without hesitation, that I am married to my best friend and soul mate. Together, we have gathered a lifetime of beautiful memories, each one is a testament to the love, laughter and commitment we have shared along the way.

Together, we have been blessed to witness our children graduating from high school and college, growing into remarkable adults, starting families of their own and blessing us with the indescribable joy of grandchildren.

As much as we try to control our lives, there will always be surprises. But facing those surprises is easier when you have someone beside you. A friend. A partner, a love story that endures. I am just a woman who bet on her man, and I am thankful every day that I did.

Final Words of Encouragement

To anyone struggling: your marriage is worth fighting for. Let the fight be for understanding, not power. Let it be for love, not pride. Marriage is not about being right, it is about being real, being honest and being committed.

If you are living in a hard season, wondering if your marriage can survive, please do not lose heart. What you are going through may not be the end, it may be the beginning of something deeper, more beautiful.

Marriage is not about staying the same; it is about growing together. It is about learning how to love each other in every season. There is beauty ahead if you choose to keep showing up, keep believing and keep loving.

Dedication

To my husband, thank you for staying, for fighting alongside me when it would have been easier to walk away. This chapter is for you, a testament to the love, and unwavering commitment that carried us through our hardest seasons. I am grateful every day that we chose each other over and over to live and love life together.

To my dear children and grandchildren, in your marriage and relationships, I pray that your faith remains your foundation, guiding you through every joy and every challenge. May your days be filled with laughter that lights up your home, and may you create precious memories that become the treasures of your hearts. Keep God at the center and know that you are surrounded by love and prayers always.

ABOUT DEBBY WOOD

A retired sales executive with a heart rooted in compassion and service, Debby Wood began her professional career as a registered nurse. Nursing laid a strong foundation of empathy and dedication, qualities that carried seamlessly into her successful transition into the world of sales. Over the years, she earned respect and recognition for her integrity, work ethic and ability to connect with people on a meaningful level.

Now retired and living in St. Charles, Mo., she lives with her husband and two COVID puppies. She treasures the slower pace of life and the opportunity to focus on what matters most: her faith, her family, donating time to local nonprofit organizations and meaningful relationships. Her proudest accomplishment is to be married for 40 years to the love of her life. She is a mother of two and a joyful grandmother to four beautiful grandchildren who continue to bring light and laughter into her days. Her favorite moments are often the simplest, gathered around the dinner table, sharing stories and making memories with her friends and family.

An avid traveler, she finds joy in exploring the world with her husband and experiencing different cultures. Whether it's strolling through the streets of a European village or standing in awe before a majestic landscape, she believes each journey is an opportunity to see the beauty of God's creation and grow in gratitude.

Above all, she strives to live a life that reflects her deep faith. Her love for Jesus is at the center of everything she does, influencing how she treats others and views the world around her. With a spirit of grace and a heart full of love, she continues to share her journey with her husband, hoping to inspire others to embrace their own stories, lean into faith and cherish the people God places in their path.

Scan the QR code to watch
a full interview with Debby

Dianne Isbell

CAN'T WAS NEVER AN OPTION

When a dear friend of mine asked me why "I am the way I am"—competitive in everything I do, having to be first, being a perfectionist, constantly challenging myself to excel, rarely relaxing, always serious, surviving and taking action when faced with major hurdles in my life instead of living uncomfortably in the status-quo—I took some time to think about it and came up with several conclusions that surprised even me.

You see, I have been fighting to be "first" since before I was born. I have a twin brother, and I believe it was my goal, even while in my mother's womb, to be born first. And I was. I was born 15 minutes before my loving brother. That was my first competition and could very well have been the impetus for why I would be competitive my entire life.

Secondly, it was my German background and upbringing. My father's grandparents migrated to the United States from Germany, arriving in New York, New York, transversing to St. Louis, Mo., and eventually buying farmland in Illinois, just across the Mississippi in a little town called New Memphis.

My father, one of four boys and four girls, started working on his father's farms at a very young age. Though he finished eighth grade, he was needed to work on the farm full time. He soon met and married a local "city girl" of German descent, who had graduated from high school and business school. Together they worked long, hard hours cultivating one of the family farms—raising soybeans, corn and hay, milking cows and raising chickens and pigs. They also raised me, my twin brother and my older sister and taught us to help others, study hard, work hard, believe in God, be honest, love each other, be respective of others, do the best we could at whatever we did and never lie or cheat.

My siblings and I had chores to do from a very early age. We were taught that you worked to survive. One of my jobs was taking care of the chickens. To this day, I cannot understand why city folks ever want to have chickens, but that's a different story.

I walked across the fields to a one-room school with an outhouse in New Memphis, a town of 100 people with no kindergarten or pre-kindergarten.

By my fourth-grade year, our town and two other small towns consolidated into one school district, and we rode the bus to a school 15 miles away. This is where the next competition in my life came in. The majority of the students in our class now were "city kids," and their parents weren't farmers. I never thought we were poor before that, but that's when I realized we may have been poor in money but not in happiness and values. Nevertheless, I felt I had to prove myself to fit in. I studied hard and got straight A's to prove I was worthy of their friendship and respect. I was probably the only student who loved to diagram sentences on the chalkboard. It was then I decided I wanted to be an English teacher.

Summers were boring, and I drove my parents nuts asking them for things to keep me busy, like painting the picket fence or learning to embroider and sew. I didn't realize it at the time, but I was a frustrated extrovert, and because there weren't a lot of people around the farm, learning new things or doing extra projects helped release my pent-up energy.

I made cheerleader in senior high school, participated in the sextet, choir, National Honor Society, French club, German club, edited the school paper and got an A+ in algebra.

From freshmen year the big topic was where you were going to go to college. My brother's future was already settled. He would help Dad and eventually take over the farm. Of course, I wanted to be like the city kids and go to college. But when I brought up the subject with my parents, they suggested I take typing and shorthand like my older sister, take the required tests and get a secretarial job at the local Air Force base.

I taught myself to type the summer before my sophomore year with my sister's typing book and an old manual typewriter my mom had to type business letters for the farm. I could already type 90 words per minute the first semester and was moved into Typing II.

My plan was to take all the required classes to get into college but have a backup plan to get hired at the Air Force base by taking all the business classes I could as well. I loved shorthand and set a high school record of 140 words per minute in my junior year.

The summer between junior and senior year, I took and passed what was considered a very difficult shorthand, typing and business exam at the Air Force base. I was immediately hired as a secretary in one of the accounting offices. Three days later a personnel department head told me they had just realized I was only 16 (the federal government's required age for employment was 17). Though they said they were surprised I passed a test many high school graduates could not, I was released with apologies and asked to return when I was 17.

I graduated high school with high honors, was hired at the Air Force base and immediately began taking night classes at the local community college. A lot of my classmates were going away to college, and I felt a little inferior, but pressed on knowing I would get a degree.

My father died when I was 19 from a failed open-heart surgery. My brother took over the farm, and my mother was hired at the Air Force base. She was a powerful example of what a woman can do.

I married my high school sweetheart when I was 22, and we had a son when I was 27. I continued to be promoted into progressively more senior secretarial positions.

A director of protocol position came open on base for a major command of the Air Force with more than 55,000 personnel worldwide. Competition was fierce, but I was selected.

Unfortunately, my marriage deteriorated. Divorce meant I had to move out and start over, but I knew in my heart it was something I had to do, and I did it.

I continued my night classes and graduated summa cum laude from Park College out of Kansas City (now Park University), with a bachelor's degree in social psychology. I immediately applied for weekend graduate school classes at Lindenwood College (now Lindenwood University) in St. Charles.

I did well in my protocol position and continued to be promoted. A new chief of staff arrived during that time who proposed a large reorganization, which included placing me and my staff directly under him instead of the two-star commander. I realized I could not work for him and began considering resigning after 26 years of service.

Still, I had to consider how I was going to support myself and my son if I resigned. With staff judge advocate approval, I founded my first business, Etiquette Plus, and began teaching manners to individuals, corporations, colleges and universities. I also became a weekly etiquette columnist for a local newspaper. In the end, the reorganization was abandoned.

Because of my exemplary performance in hosting local St. Louis community leaders to our command and the base, I was selected to be a participant in the year-long Leadership St. Louis program. During that time, I received my master's degree in management from Lindenwood University with a 5.0 GPA, and was selected for a position in strategic planning in a Department of Defense (DOD) organization on the base. Soon after, I was selected to be a participant in the year-long Department of Defense Executive Leadership Development Program (ELDP). At the end of the year, I was awarded the first-ever Outstanding Leadership Award for solidifying the Chairman of the Joint Chiefs of Staff, Colin Powell, as a first-ever ELDP Commencement Speaker.

The following year, I was selected as the first female special assistant to the commander in the same DOD organization, one of my toughest jobs, but received two more promotions while in that position.

My mother lived with me for the last 6-1/2 years of her life. I was her primary caregiver. She passed away in December 2000. And after 37-1/2 years of exemplary federal civil service, in January 2001, I retired at the executive level from the federal government and received one of the highest DOD civil service awards.

Within two weeks, I was offered a significant position in the private sector in Washington DC with a leading telecommunications company. I accepted, but requested an eight-month contract signing delay. The World Trade Center was attacked that September, and since I could have been in the Pentagon in a contractor capacity, I chose not to move to DC nor to sign the contract.

In 2002, I married a very special former military man. I expanded Etiquette Plus and began teaching little girls' etiquette tea classes. To make it more realistic for my young students, I provided old-fashioned prom dresses, gloves, feather boas, purses and jewelry. I also created Victorian-type tulle hats. The Red Hat Society was taking over the country like wildfire. My older sister asked me to create a red hat for her, then for her friends and local boutiques. A new chapter in my life was dawning, and I founded my second business: HATS by DI-Anne. It wasn't long before I had my one-of-a-kind designs in shops all over the country and was a vendor at the Red Hat Society conventions throughout the country.

A fellow Red Hat vendor then asked me if I would create hats for her new boutique. But in addition to the Red Hat Society colors, she wanted other colors like, white, black, yellow, orange, etc. My hats did well, and I began selling them at trunk shows and on consignment all over the country.

I designed a fascinator and entered it into a contest in New York for New York Fashion Week and won. A photo of me and my design was on the jumbo tron in New York, and I won a three-night stay at any W Hotel in the US and an airline ticket for two anywhere in the continental United States. My husband and I went to New York the following December for my birthday.

That win was the first of many. My designs won at 12 of the annual Forest Park Forever Hat Luncheons, were "Best of Show" at the Naples, Fla. Botanical Garden's annual Hats in the Garden, and Best of Show in Desert Springs, Calif.

In 2016, and again in 2021, one of my designs was selected for a year's display in the Kentucky Derby Churchill Downs Hat Museum. I was also selected as a featured milliner for the Kentucky Derby in 2022, had my designs in their gift shop and was featured in their annual fashion show event.

I was contacted by Lady Gaga's marketing company the following year and asked to create four designs for the roll out of her new perfume, Fame. I have designed for President H. W. Bush's sister-in-law, Diane von Furstenberg, Karlie Kloss, Betsey Johnson and Steve Madden. My designs have been worn at special events all over the world including the Ascot Races, weddings in Spain and Ireland and tea in London and France. I was selected as one of only eight designers to be an in-resident designer in the St. Louis Fashion Fund in 2019, as the St. Louis Visionary Arts Awardee in the Outstanding Working Artist Category in 2022, and have had my designs featured in art galleries in the area.

My son has always been the joy of my life. I founded a PTO when he was in junior high, an After Prom Party when he was in high school, and was designated by the local superintendent and school board as head of Citizens United for Better Education (CUBE) that helped pass a referendum to add more classrooms to his senior high school facilities. I was a recipient of a local YWCA award for excellence and the St. Louis Area Federal Executive Board Award for Excellence.

Although I have had challenges and difficulties in my life, I always forged ahead and did what I thought I needed to do, never really thinking that I couldn't do it, that I would not survive. Did I make some major mistakes or bad decisions in my life? Yes. Did I hold myself accountable? Yes. And did I try to make things right and move forward? Again, yes.

I also realized along the way, that something good always came out of something bad. And though, it may not have been recognizable at the time, eventually a path or answer revealed itself.

I am extremely proud of the fact that a determined young girl who started out in a one-room school house, earned both a bachelor's and a master's degree. She never dwelt on negativity. She knew she couldn't change the past, but made the best of what she aimed for. She was hurt by and hurt some on the way, but was both forgiven and forgave, because holding grudges and getting even is counterproductive and a waste of time—time which could be used for accomplishing something better. She remains driven to be the best she can be. But most importantly, she is extremely proud of her loving son who is a very successful business man. I feel it is important to help others as I have been helped. And I will never stop being me.

I think it is important to learn something new every day and meet new people. I have learned to stay away from negative people and live with those who are jealous of me.

And I will never stop being me.

ABOUT DIANNE ISBELL

Dianne Isbell is a national award-winning and internationally-recognized milliner. She is the founder and creative force behind HATS by DI-Anne. Even as a small girl, she had a love of fashion and crafted designs for herself from her mother's closet. At only eight years of age, her mother and grandmother taught her the arts of embroidery, crocheting and how to use a sewing machine, thus enabling her to sew many of her own dresses and suits for her work career.

Dianne's elegance and craftsmanship are the result of a rich tapestry of influences and accomplishments including bachelor's and master's degrees achieved through night and weekend classes.

While serving in ever-increasing civil service leadership positions at Scott Air Force Base, including director of protocol for a Major Air Force Command, reporting to a two-star general, Dianne launched her first venture, Etiquette Plus. For more than 40 years, she has taught etiquette to all ages and penned a beloved column for the *Belleville News Democrat*.

Retiring in her mid fifties, after a distinguished 37-year civil service career, she opened another new exciting chapter: crafting Victorian style hats for little-girl etiquette teas which soon led to one of a kind couture designs. Under her brand HATS by DI-Anne, Dianne has garnered awards including New York Fashion Week Diet Coke Fascinator; Best Hat at the Naples, Florida's Botanical Gardens Luncheon; consecutive best hats at the annual St Louis Forest Park Forever Hat Luncheons; and featured milliner at the Kentucky Derby with multiple designs selected for display in the Kentucky Derby Hat Museum at Churchill Downs.

Her creations have been worn on global stages from Ascot in the UK to Lady Gaga's Fame perfume campaign. Highprofile clients include Betsey Johnson, Steve Madden, members of President George W. Bush's family, Karlie Kloss and Diane von Furstenberg

Dianne's hats are more than accessories; they are wearable art designed to capture joy and confidence. Based in Belleville, Ill., she meets clients by appointment, and her custom creations grace boutiques, popups, trunk shows, and horse-racing and fashion events across the country.

Scan the QR code to watch
a full interview with Diane

Emily Stahl

WHEN PURPOSE MEETS PASSION

I grew up being known for two things: being creative and for being clumsy. In elementary school, I made friendship bracelets. In high school, I created album art for a friend's band and painted canvasses for fun. By the time I got to college, I still had a passion for art but also wanted to help people. I started as a psychology major with an art minor in hopes of going to graduate school for art therapy. When I was three years in, I took my first graphic design class and fell in love. I had a gut feeling that design was the field I wanted to be in. Instead of switching majors, I added a second degree, which meant I would have to go for six years. This was OK with me because I wasn't planning on graduate school because I found my passion for graphic design.

I mentioned earlier I was known for being clumsy. I was always the klutz of my family and used humor to deal with it. I would trip over things and randomly fall. I would be embarrassed but laugh it off as another good story I could tell.

Fast forward to my last couple of years in college. I went to Southern Illinois University Edwardsville. It has a beautiful campus, but it is very spread out. Walking became harder for me. My hips would be sore. Going up stairs was a struggle, so much so that I would have to rely on the elevators. My older sister had been diagnosed with a rare neuromuscular disorder called Late Onset Tay Sachs (LOTS), so that was always in the back of my mind. It was such a rare disorder, I didn't think there was any way that we both had it. I must just be out of shape, I surmised. I lived on the second floor of a building with no elevator. When I could barely manage those stairs, my mom knew it was time to get tested for LOTS.

Looking back on my life, there were signs. I played sports when I was younger, I would try to practice but I could never jump very high. And running was the worst. Everyone hates running during practice drills, so I never thought much of it. I thought sports just weren't my thing, that I was the creative and artsy one. But after walking across campus to my classes—now barely being able to do the stairs and so needing to rely on the elevator—it was becoming clearer to me as well. I finally went to the neurologist.

In 2016, it was confirmed with testing that I have LOTS. It affects mainly the quadriceps and triceps, as they weaken over time. This was the time I started using a cane, which I of course painted. There was no way I would be caught walking with a wooden cane that looked like a shepherd's staff. That is not my style.

The next couple years were very transformative for me. I graduated college, finally got my first full-time job as a graphic designer for a home décor company, which I still work for to this day.

Once at my annual neurologist appointment, there was a representative from the Muscular Dystrophy Association (MDA) that asked if I would speak at the MDA Camp. She wanted me to talk to the older campers about going to college and finding a job while having a disorder.

Because I was diagnosed in my early twenties, I never went to the MDA camp. Even as a speaker, though, the camp was amazing. It helped me to connect with people like me, people in similar situations as mine. This led me to ask how else I could get involved with the MDA. The representative told me they have an MDA Art & Soul event every year and it was happening in a month. Artists sell their work at the fundraising event.

I always imagined having my own business, even back when I was selling friendship bracelets as a kid. I did freelance projects here and there—such as logos and invitations—thinking that was my business, but it wasn't anything product-based. I rebranded myself as the Emily Stahl Design Co., hand-lettered 10 designs, made copies and decided I would sell prints at the event.

Being my first event with only a month to prepare, it was scary. But I somehow pulled it off. Being able to connect my love for art with a fundraising event for the MDA was a life-changing experience. Not only was it taking me out of my comfort zone, but it has also led me to where I am today. It felt like the universe intervened when I needed it the most. That night, the same MDA representative who told me about the art and soul event, saw my hand-lettered prints and suggested I try to sell them at a shop called The White Rabbit. She told me they were always selling unique items and loved local artists.

After recovering from that first event, I decided to reach out to the shop. I didn't want to go in empty handed, so I created a sell sheet. (A sell sheet is basically a one-page sheet describing who you are, what you do, why a company should sell your products and some examples of your work.) It was the beginning of the holiday season when I brought it in, but it worked. They emailed me on a Tuesday asking if I could pop-up at an event on the coming Saturday. I played it cool and thought, "Sure I can, no big deal," when in reality, I was freaking out inside. But again, somehow, I made it happen. The White Rabbit wound up keeping a few of each design in their shop. Since that first event, I have participated in a variety of events, gotten into multiple shops and have expanded my product line from prints to cards, stickers, pins and so much more.

By the summer of 2019, I had been running my business for a couple of years. As a resident of St. Louis, I was watching history unfold with the St. Louis Blues hockey team. It was round one of the playoffs, and as I was watching the game, I was drawing on my iPad. I lettered "Let's Go Blues" maybe 50 times until I got it right. When they won that first playoff game, I made the design into a sticker and put a poll on Instagram to see if anyone would be interested in buying them. For all three people who answered "YES, I want a sticker," to my poll, I sent a message asking for their contact information for orders when the stickers came in. I had no idea how long the Blues would be in the playoffs, so I did expedited shipping on those.

To my surprise, one of the people responded to my message saying, "I actually work for the Blues. Let me know if you'd ever be interested in doing a collaboration." I think I cried tears of joy. As it turned out, she oversees the promotions and giveaways and is also on the retail committee. Once the stickers arrived, I sent her a ton, because I knew she would know people interested in them. She wanted to meet, but of course I got a little busy since the Blues kept winning and eventually won their first Stanley cup that year. We eventually met, and I have worked on some dream projects with the Blues. I have created art for multiple theme nights, created a line with Lusso Merch in their team store and even had the first and only hand-drawn Blue Note featured on some of the products.

What happens when you work on a dream project with the St. Louis

Blues? You probably have the dream of working with the St. Louis Cardinals, which was on my list of dream projects to do. My plan was to update my website and reach out to them. To my astonishment, they reached out to me on my old, rough-looking website.

We had a meeting set in March of 2020, but it was canceled due to the COVID outbreak, and everything shutting down. It was a long road of back and forth, but I finally got my dream project with them. I designed the art for a youth hat gate giveaway in the summer of 2023. I still haven't gotten in their team store, but MLB has strict rules. I'm not giving up, though. I am just giving it time. A girl can dream.

I also have dreams of working with the Kansas City Chiefs, but it's been complete crickets so far. I am not discouraged, because the worst thing they can say is no. I am going to keep my list of dream projects and my vision board up and hopefully more opportunities will come when the time is right. I may have gotten lucky, but each opportunity also came from research, hard work and time. You have to be patient. None of my dream projects happened overnight. They were all years in the making. I see each opportunity to connect as planting a seed, and I believe the opportunity will bloom when the time is right. You can't be too hard on yourself because nothing happens overnight.

Art has been my outlet throughout my life, but I never knew how important an outlet it would be until I was diagnosed with LOTS. It opened an entire world to me that I never knew existed. I shared a few pivotal moments in my career, but if I never met the MDA representative, if I didn't push myself out of my comfort zone, if I never reached out on Instagram, I would have never met the lady working with the St. Louis Blues.

The universe can lead you toward your destiny. But you also have to make the move to get it. Looking back, having a disorder is hard, but I also wouldn't have my business without it. It has given me the opportunity to grow as a person and to give back. It has given me a sense of community, through my disorder with other MDA families going through similar circumstances and through my business with other small business owners.

I don't get out as much as I used to, but it gives me a sense of purpose to keep moving forward on those tough days. If I leave you with any advice, it would be to chase your dreams, work hard and you never know where life will take you. It may not be your original plan, but it could take you to even greater places.

ABOUT EMILY STAHL

Emily Stahl is a graphic designer, lettering artist and professional creative. With more than eight years of design experience and a soft spot for typography and unique ideas, she draws constant inspiration from her ever-growing library of design books. When she's not designing, you'll find her advocating for her rare disorder, practicing Italian or hunting down the best local restaurants in St. Louis — all in the name of "creative research."

Scan the QR code to watch a full interview with Emily

Evangeline Sutton

TO GLOW, GIRL - YOU MUST LET GO!

It didn't happen in a boardroom.

It didn't happen during a pitch, a closing or a celebration.

It happened on a Tuesday morning, in the quiet of my car, hands gripping the steering wheel, face streaked with mascara and frustration, breath catching in the space between burnout and breakthrough.

I had just wrapped up an event I helped build from scratch, one that saw record turnout success, a real hit. I should've been celebrating.

Instead, I sat parked, exhausted and invisible.

Everyone had thanked me for "supporting." For "helping make the event great." No acknowledgment of leadership. No one recognized me publicly that day as an integral part of the current success or future growth of the organization. Just a pat on the head and a smile like, "Aren't you helpful."

It was that day that something deep in me quieted. Not in rage, but in resolve. That was the day I realized I had to let go.

Not of the dream. Not of the goal. But of the weight I was carrying within myself to make it all perfect. To be perfect. To be "helpful." And "good." And "useful" in the eyes of others.

You have to understand. I was the "fun" but "level-headed," reliable, confident eldest daughter in a wholesome family of 10 children. Seven boys, three girls—and I was one of them. We shared the same mom and dad, and with that, the same shared expectation: if you worked for it, you could have it. My parents didn't just dream of homeschooling and homesteading; they lived it with conviction.

We were raised on acres of farmland, classical education and unwavering training in what was "right" and "good." Chores weren't optional, excuses weren't accepted and quitting wasn't in the vocabulary. We learned to solve problems with our hands, speak our minds with respect and finish what we started.

My parents instilled in us something priceless: a blueprint for tenacity, resourcefulness, character, hard work and grit. They didn't raise spectators; they raised builders.

I launched my first business with my brother when I was 24 out of drive and curiosity. It wasn't glamorous, but it was real: the kind of venture that teaches you to earn every dollar, negotiate every challenge and believe in yourself before anyone else does.

That early taste of entrepreneurship lit a fire in me. It taught me to lead, to build relationships, to take ownership, to create value from ideas, to have a solution for every problem and to carry weight with the belief that if I showed up and applied my energy and soul to work, something meaningful would grow.

Eventually, I segued from that business into a role as chief marketing officer for a fast-scaling automotive group in St. Louis, a great company with great leadership. I'm among the youngest women in executive leadership within the automotive industry, not just in St. Louis, but nationally. Women make up less than 25% of the industry's workforce, and only about 7% hold senior leadership positions. The brand was growing, leadership was solid and everything on the surface looked golden. My future looked bright.

But underneath?

I was frustrated.

Mentally stretched.

How could I grow a future with praise in private; but not as much as a thank you in the public eye. How would I own a company or grow a partnership from my position if I didn't receive that acknowledgement or respect when it mattered? It was my career; but was it assuming of me to expect public acknowledgement of contributions. Why did it matter? Was it ego—or concern that I would be carrying the load of an executive until I was only willing to carry papers to the copier? Silently carrying the expectations of being a leader, a woman, a team-builder, a fixer, a wife, a homemaker, a moneymaker, a daughter, a sister and a behind-the-scenes miracle worker.

Perfectionism was the silent engine that powered it all.

I wasn't allowed to fail—not outwardly.

Not with my family, and certainly, never with my professional face. When the applause came, familial or professional, it rarely had my name on it. I don't need a title; or did I? Did I need growth from within and without?

I remember that Tuesday morning like a snapshot I'll never forget.

The event had gone off beautifully. The business was growing rapidly. I had been involved in every detail: the vision, the branding, the coordination, the communications, the people.But when the recognition came, it was undercut."You do so much no one knows about."

"We're so thankful for your support."

"You always have such a great presence."

Presence? I thought. I was the pusher, working to learn as much as possible in hopes to one day partner or own, giving assistance that was paramount to the business's success—and all I'm labeled is present?

I didn't have the thought to cry. I just sat in the cold leather seat of my BMW, still in the moment, the engine running. Cars passed. People move around me. But something inside me stood up.

And in the silence of that parking lot, I made a decision: I wasn't born to lend a hand.

I was born to lead.

It took me years to admit that what I felt wasn't ego—it was a mix of determination and grief.

Grief for the version of me that kept waiting to be seen, hoping to be acknowledged, bending over backward for a "thank you" that never came. Not as a child; nor as an adult.

And the ache?

That ache wasn't a need for motivation or achievement.

It was an identity. I was still trying to "earn" my seat in rooms I was meant to own.

That was a moment of stark clarity: No more shrinking to stay safe. No more waiting for someone to say it's your turn. It's already yours. Own it.

And to this day, I find this a beautiful part of this chapter in life: Letting go didn't slow me down. It sped everything up. Opportunities came faster. My voice carried further. The people who truly needed leadership leaned in closer.

And the ones who preferred the version of me that served without speaking? They faded. And I didn't chase them.

Because what is waiting for me on the other side of that letting go… was mine.

My calling.

My clarity.

My peace.

The kind of legacy we are meant to build doesn't require burnout to prove it's worth. If you're reading this and you're gripping the wheel too tight… trying to hold everything together… trying to be everything for everyone…

Breathe.

You're not falling apart.

You're not failing.

You're not too young, too blonde or too dumb.

You're being invited into the next version of yourself.

Let go.

There is a certain freedom in letting go. Not living in their best for you, but your own best version of yourself. Knowing that you can give fully because you've let go of what you shouldn't hold.

Not letting go of ambition; but of anxiety.

Not letting go of purpose; but of perfectionism.

Not letting go of your dream; but of the lie that you must suffer to earn it.

Not of your standards; but of the belief that you can place boundaries for what you expect.

Not letting go of the goal; but of the need for everyone to clap while you achieve it.

Let go. And rise.

You were born for this.

And you were never meant to be perfect, only real. You. Truly you. Really you.

If you need permission, this is from one girl to the next—stop asking others and ask yourself.

Now go.

Lead.

Build.

Create.

Reclaim your breath.

Let the world adjust to the sound of your footsteps, fully grounded in who you are. Live fully because the day you let go is the day everything begins. Don't dull your glow; let go and grow.

Sincerely,

Evangeline

ABOUT EVANGELINE SUTTON

Evangeline Schultz-Sutton is a dynamic marketing executive, entrepreneur and business leader with a track record of scaling brands and building impact-driven companies. She currently serves as chief marketing officer at Clement Auto Group, where she leads strategic marketing initiatives for one of the fastest-growing dealership groups in the region. As current co-owner of Mike's Tire & Service and past co-founder of Regenerative Marketing, Evangeline has built and scaled ventures across multiple industries, servicing more than 23 industries in five countries.

Evangeline brings a passion for innovation, growth and leadership. She is a frequent contributor to outlets such as Forbes and Christian Examiner and is deeply engaged in mentoring the next generation of leaders through board service and community involvement.

Scan the QR code to watch
a full interview with Evangeline

Faith Berger

A ROOTED BEGINNING IN DESIGN AND CURATION

Before I ever picked up a paintbrush seriously, I studied landscape design and worked in retail and merchandising. That experience helped shape how I see the world—how people relate to space, form and the things around them.

In 1991, my mother Shirley, and I opened Barucci Gallery in Clayton, Mo. That decision shaped my next 27 years. The gallery became a destination for collectors, designers and art lovers, showcasing original paintings, art glass, ceramics, sculpture, jewelry and custom framing. We represented more than 400 artists from across the country. It was a gift to introduce clients to incredible makers and help designers complement interiors across every category.

For me, it was always about beauty, emotion and connection. Barucci wasn't just a gallery—it was a place to discover new voices and support artists doing meaningful work.

While curating for others, I was quietly sketching and painting in the background—developing my own visual language but keeping it private. I had been exposed to so much talent, I needed time to grow into my own. Eventually, the work just started coming through.

From Curator to Creator

My transition from gallery owner to full-time artist happened gradually—and deeply. After Barucci closed in 2011, I continued consulting and curating for both residential and commercial spaces. I loved collaborating with designers and placing the right piece in the right setting.

But it wasn't until COVID-19 hit, and after I lost my mother and longtime business partner, that I realized something was missing: art in my life. I picked up a paintbrush again—and it felt like coming home. It brought everything together—my love of light, emotion, composition and movement.

Since then, my artwork has taken on a life of its own. My series Atmospheric Realities has become a cornerstone collection, now featured at Neiman Marcus St. Louis. I create abstract, emotionally resonant paintings that explore layers of memory, space and mood. They often straddle the line between landscape and emotion, encouraging the viewer to pause, feel and reflect.

For me, painting is about presence. Awe. Stillness. And sometimes, even healing.

The Art Rug: Redefining Luxury Underfoot

One of the most exciting and unexpected expansions of my work has been The Art Rug. Translating my paintings into functional design came from a desire to make art part of people's everyday lives—literally grounding their spaces in something meaningful.

I launched Faith Berger x The Art Rug, a luxury line of custom, hand-tufted rugs made from New Zealand wool and silk. Each design is based on one of my original paintings and is available in a wide range of shapes, sizes and colors. They're not mass-produced—they're made-to-order, sculpted, signed collector pieces with a turnaround of 10–12 weeks.

The rugs have become a go-to for designers and homeowners who want something truly personal and unforgettable. They've been used in beautiful residential interiors and are available on my website, FaithBerger.com, as well as through collaborations with design houses and architects.

In Fall 2024, I launched the Faith Berger Milano Collection—a sculptural rug line inspired by Italian modernism and mid-century design. These pieces blend neutral palettes with strong linear form. They're elegant, timeless and made with the same artisan craftsmanship I bring to everything I create.

Expanding the Brand: Art You Live With

My business isn't just a studio—it's an ecosystem of beauty. While painting is the heart of it, I've been expanding into product lines that make my art part of everyday life. Right now, I'm developing:

Greeting Cards featuring miniature versions of my paintings—designed to bring emotional connection and visual joy to daily rituals.

Bedding and Home Goods that transform my brushwork into beautiful, tactile textiles.

Limited Edition Fashion, including gaming dresses and wraps printed with my original artwork.

Functional Objects and Licensing opportunities in accessories, stationery and home decor.

Every extension is thoughtful. I only move forward if the product feels aligned with the spirit of my work. My goal is always the same: to create something beautiful and meaningful that people want to live with.

Giving Back: Canvas For Kids

As my business grew, I knew I wanted to use it to give back. In 2024, I founded Canvas For Kids, a nonprofit that brings free art experiences to children (and adults) in public spaces such as libraries and community centers.

Participants get to paint both individually and together, exploring creativity and building confidence. It's not about perfection—it's about expression.

Art changed my life. I want every child, no matter their background, to have access to that same sense of freedom, joy and voice.

We have six events scheduled with St. Louis County libraries, and we're growing fast with the help of volunteers, donations and community support. You can learn more at CanvasForKids.org.

A Modern, Woman-Led Brand

At 68, I'm proof that creativity doesn't fade—it evolves. I manage everything from design to sales to marketing, all while continuing to paint and grow the brand. It's a lot—but it's also my passion.

I'm currently exploring partnerships with licensing agents and national PR firms to bring my work to a larger audience. Ultimately, I'd love to create an object that lives in every home—whether that's a print, a rug, a painting or something else entirely.

To me, art isn't just something we hang. It's something we live with—something that brings emotion, memory and depth into our everyday spaces.

I'm constantly inspired by other women—those who lead with strength, grace and vision. Whether it's a fellow artist, a designer or a community leader, I find energy and encouragement in their stories. That collective spirit of women lifting each other up is a big part of what fuels me.

Where to Find My Work
You can explore or purchase my work at:

Neiman Marcus St. Louis
Two Rivers Stone Boutique
FaithBerger.com
Instagram @faithberger.art and @theartrug
Saks Fifth Avenue Gallery (St. Louis)

I also take private commissions and work closely with interior designers and architects on custom projects for homes and commercial spaces.

A Legacy Still in Motion
From Barucci Gallery to my own studio practice, from canvas to rug, from community to commerce—I've built a career around connecting people with beauty.

I'm not just an artist or designer. I'm a connector. A storyteller. A builder of emotional, functional, soulful things.

And with every brushstroke, every rug, every expansion, I'm still writing this story—one grounded in meaning, movement and the belief that beauty belongs everywhere.

Faith Berger Art Consultants
(314) 550-5920

ABOUT FAITH BERGER

Creating A Legacy Of Beauty, Meaning & Modern Design

My career has been a master-class in evolution—an ever-expanding journey that began in retail and design, matured in the heart of the St. Louis art scene, and now flourishes through my brand, Faith Berger Fine Art & Design. I'm not only a painter; I'm a creative entrepreneur redefining how fine art and functional design intersect.

With a deep love of beauty, a sharp eye and years of experience across disciplines, I've built a brand that bridges personal expression and high-end living—from original paintings to art rugs, greeting cards, home collections, fashion collaborations, nonprofit initiatives and more. My work is rooted in emotion, movement and meaning—an invitation to connect with beauty in everyday life.

Scan the QR code to watch a full interview with Faith

Grace Strobel

BREAKING BARRIERS
A MODEL OF LOVE

The first job I got was working in the lunchroom at a school. It was actually my school, the school I had gone to. The lunchroom was full of kids talking and eating. The thing I loved most about this job was helping people and getting to show my independence and ability.

One day, some kids who were eating lunch asked me for help opening their fruit cups and milk cartons. Those kinds of tasks are harder for me, but I can do them. I loved my job, and I'm happy to help anyone who asks, so I walked over to help them.

I was standing by the lunch table, trying to open a fruit cup, when I realized the kids I was helping were laughing. It suddenly felt wrong. Why were they laughing? What was funny?

Then I realized. They were laughing at me. They didn't need help to open their food at all, they had asked me so they could watch me struggle. I started to feel sick, like I was going to throw up. I felt dizzy. My face went white. The lunchroom was always a loud place, but now all the sounds seemed to mix into a roar. I ran back to the kitchen. The world blurred, I felt the tears well up inside of me and I burst out crying.

When you make fun of someone, it only takes a few seconds. For the kids laughing at me, it was over. For me, it wasn't over.

Back home, I sat on my bed and my mom sat next to me helping me through the pain, letting me rock gently while I sobbed. I tried to stop thinking about what happened, when I closed my eyes, I heard the kids laughing, I could see them pointing at me, like a horrible movie in my head. It hurt so much to remember, but I couldn't stop remembering.

I've always been a positive, up-beat person, but now I felt so much sadness, like there were hands on my shoulders, pushing me down. I kept waiting to feel like myself again, but I couldn't. There was an awful twisting pain in my stomach that I had never felt before. I felt scared, alone and for the first time, I felt hated. A part of me died that day. I wanted to stay in my room forever and never come out.

It took a long time to understand that what happened wasn't about me. There are days when I feel like I'll never fully understand it. Sometimes people are afraid of what they don't know. With the help of my mom, I decided I wanted to make a difference. I wanted to share with students what it is like to have struggles, and I wanted to show how you can change someone's life just by being kind and having respect.

My mom and I co-created #TheGraceEffect, a presentation about overcoming obstacles, treating people with kindness and respect, and living with a disability. I started speaking to schools and within the first year and a half spoke to more than 3,000 students—with the goal of raising awareness and breaking down stereotypes about people with disabilities. While doing research for #TheGraceEffect, my mom and I came across photos of a model with Down syndrome and were inspired to pursue modeling as well.

My parents always taught me to believe in myself and never said I couldn't do anything—so I asked my mom if I could try modeling, she said, "I don't see why not, let's do this Grace!" So, in 2019, she hired St. Louis lifestyle photographer, Trenna Travis, and booked a shoot. Mom released my first photos on Facebook and the photos went viral with more than 220,000 shares from all over the world. It was exciting and the start of a whole new career.

When I was born the doctors told my mom and dad that I would not achieve much. That there were still institutions that would take me and that there was no shame in doing that. They said I would never be able to read or write or even tie my own shoes. But I am here today to tell you they were wrong.

My career started taking off with the help of local St. Louis features. My very first magazine cover was for *Chesterfield Lifestyle Magazine*. When the owner and author of Lifestyle contacted us, we went wild crazy with happiness. Then the *St. Louis Dispatch* did a full lifestyle Sunday five-page feature on me. Since then, I have been featured in *Forbes, Allure, Bella Magazine*, PBS, The Today Show, Good Morning America, Yahoo!, Rihanna's FentyBeauty, Marc Jacobs, Lady Gaga's Kindness Channel and a featured panelist for Louis Vuitton Moet Hennessy and Council of Fashion Designers of America Diversity webinar series. I also have a Wikipedia page.

In 2020, I was given the opportunity to represent Obagi Medical, a major international skincare line and was the first American with Down syndrome to do anything of that stature in representation. I have also represented and modeled for: Rihanna's FentyBeauty, Urban Decay, Crocs, Marc Jacobs, Justin Alexander, Amika, Kendra Scott, Veronica Beard, Revelry Bridal, Selkie, McDonalds and the Alivia Clothing line.

St. Louis has been so good to me. In 2021, I was awarded Women of Achievement for Youth Outreach and Advocacy and in 2022, I was contacted by The Missouri Historical Society to document my achievements by adding seven donated clothing items to its permanent collection.

I've also been given The Albert Pujols Watson Award for activism in making change, What's Right with The Region Award, and The Down Syndrome of Greater St Louis Inspiring Change Award.

Modeling and my presence in social media and society is important to me because I want others like me to be proud of who they are, to believe in themselves and know they can break barriers too. We are not defined by our diagnoses. My whole life I've worked hard to prove my abilities. It can be a constant struggle to be judged immediately and thought of as unable. One of the biggest challenges of having Down syndrome was and is the assumption that I was not capable of doing something, even before I'd been given a chance. People with Down syndrome want what everyone else wants. We want a good education. We want people to believe in us and give us opportunities to succeed. We want to be included, have friends, a good job and to belong.

I am the product of being given a chance to succeed, looking beyond a label and working hard to crush outdated perceptions that people with disabilities cannot achieve much. We are actors, swimmers, models, bodybuilders, artists, musicians, workers, college students, athletes and work extra hard every day to prove outdated stigmas wrong.

Sometimes our biggest sorrows become our greatest achievements. You can make a difference in this world.

ABOUT GRACE STROBEL

Grace Strobel is an inspirational 28-year-old model and speaker with Down syndrome. She has been featured in *Forbes, Allure, Bella Magazine*, PBS, The Today Show, Good Morning America, Yahoo!, Rihanna's FentyBeauty, Brides magazine, Vows magazine, Lady Gaga's Kindness Channel, and a featured panelist for Louis Vuitton Moet Hennessy and Council of Fashion Designers of America Diversity webinar series.

She is the first American with Down syndrome to represent a major international skincare line-Obagi Medical, and has signed for her fourth year of contract representation. Grace has also represented and modeled for: Rihanna's FentyBeauty, Urban Decay, Marc Jacobs, Crocs, Kendra Scott, Justin Alexander, Amika, Veronica Beard, Revelry Bridal, Alivia Clothing line and McDonalds.

Awards: Women of Achievement for Youth Outreach and Advocacy, Missouri History Museum Inductee, The Albert Pujols Watson Award for activism in making change, What's Right With The Region, Down Syndrome of Greater St Louis Inspiring Change.

Scan the QR code to watch a full interview with Grace

Heather J. Crider

PRESENCE IS POWER:
BE WHO YOU ARE MEANT TO BE,
LIVE BOLDLY AND IMPACT PROFOUNDLY

My relationship with my sister Sam was not unlike most sibling relationships. She was four years older than me, and although I would swear her life's mission was to absolutely torture me—tickling me until my nose bled, sitting on me, making fun of me—I still worshipped her. To me, she was everything I believed I was not.

Sam was beautiful, funny, gregarious, creative—the person everyone wanted to be around. I was her shadow. An uncle even nicknamed us "Pete and Repeat" because wherever she went, I wasn't far behind.

Sam was my hero—until she wasn't.

When Sam hit her teenage years, everything changed. She found herself running with the wrong crowd. Addiction crept in—drugs, alcohol, choices she couldn't take back. By the time she was barely out of her teens, violence and trauma had shaped her world. There were hospital visits, emergency phone calls and stories too painful to fully process— like the time her home was set on fire during a drug-fueled argument.

Watching my hero fall was heartbreaking. I didn't understand it at the time, but I was mourning the sister I thought I knew while trying to hold onto the hope that somehow, she could still come back.

Sam had two beautiful boys and a gorgeous little girl, and for a while, we all clung to the idea that motherhood would be the catalyst for her to change. But the addiction's grip was deep. There were new marriages, new hopes—and deeper betrayals. One day, on what should have been a joyous celebration—my very first Mother's Day as a new mom—I received one of those dreaded phone calls.

Sam was in the hospital. She had been beaten so badly by her husband that she was in a coma. She was also pregnant. And she had lost the baby.

I will never forget walking into that hospital room celebrating the life I had just brought into the world, while staring at the brokenness life had inflicted on my sister. I made the hour-and-a-half drive every single day to be by her side. And while I thought I was being a hero, while I thought I was showing up for her in the most noble way, I realize now that my heart was divided.

Because the truth was, in those moments, my thoughts were often about me: my anger, my sadness and my resentment for the life I had to put on pause. I constantly felt the obligation, like I was a servant burdened by loving someone who kept slipping away.

It's a hard thing to admit, but it's important to reveal. Because looking back, I wasn't truly leading with impact. I wasn't showing up as the best version of myself. I was surviving the situation, not transforming it.

Today, after years of doing the deep work—and co-creating the Everyday Rockstar® philosophy with my partner Mark Schulman—I see it so clearly. Impact isn't about being physically present. It's about being emotionally aligned. It's about showing up with purpose, not obligation.

If I had the tools I have now—if I had known how to shift from a have-to mindset to a get-to mindset—I believe I could have made those moments not just survivable but truly meaningful. Instead of feeling trapped by circumstances, I could have honored the sacred opportunity to love her, to support her and to simply be there with my whole heart.

One of the biggest realizations we teach through Everyday Rockstar® is this: It's not about eliminating hardship or pretending life is easy. It's about how you frame your moments.

For example, instead of:

I have to take my kids to school > I get to take my kids to school.

I have to have a tough conversation at work > I get to connect honestly and courageously.

I have to show up for someone hurting > I get to be a part of their healing.

That simple shift—have to > get to—creates more purpose, more joy and far more impact in everything we do.

And the heart of this philosophy is about presence. I realize that time is not infinite and neither are the moments we're given to show up for ourselves and for each other.

Two years after Sam survived that brutal attack, she lost her battle with addiction at barely 34 years old. And with her passing came the second wake-up call of my life—"Someday" is the most dangerous word we can believe in. And "whenever" is a lie we tell ourselves to avoid discomfort.

There were so many conversations I thought my sister and I would have "someday." There were many opportunities for healing I thought would come "whenever" life settled down.' And then the clock ran out.

We think we have more time, until we don't.

As women, we're often conditioned to defer ourselves. We hustle. We achieve. We survive. But quietly, inside, many of us still wrestle with the belief that we are not enough, that our value is tied to how well we perform or how much we please.

Confidence isn't a personality trait. It's a decision. It's about choosing, moment by moment, to believe that you are worthy, before the world hands you permission slips.

And here's what I know now: Impact starts inside. If we want to create change in the world, we must honor the small choices we make right now in our own hearts and minds. We have the choice to speak, even when our voice shakes, and to show up, even when it's messy. We have the choice to believe we are rockstars—not because of perfection, but because of presence.

That's what the Everyday Rockstar® movement is really about. It's not about flashing lights or standing ovations. It's about how we choose to show up—for ourselves, for each other—every single day.

I don't know all the battles my sister fought internally. I only know the little girl she was—the one I adored. And I know the imprint she left on my heart. Even though she's gone, her story lives on, because I carry it forward every time I choose to live boldly, every time I choose presence over perfection and every time I choose impact over obligation.

We don't get to rewrite the past. But we do get to own the story we write next.

And it's about time we did.

It's about time we remember that we are enough. It's about time we trusted our own voices again. It's about time we stopped surviving and started living like the Everyday Rockstars we were born to be—not someday, not whenever, but now.

The world doesn't just need more busy women. It needs more women who are fully alive. And the time is now. All we have is now. This is your moment. Don't miss it.

ABOUT HEATHER J. CRIDER

Grounded and mentored in the most advanced research from the most recognized thought leaders in neuroscience at the world's top institutions (Harvard, Princeton, Yale, MIT, Wharton, Brown, etc.) Heather J. Crider is one of our nation's few certified coaches in both neuroscience and the emerging fields of neuro-performance and neuro-leadership.

With a discerning bias toward a practical, evidence-based approach, industry-leading companies worldwide tap Heather's uniquely honed, highly engaging, neuroscience-based ability to empower overwhelmed professionals to beat burnout, equip leaders with exceptional resilience, unleash brain-powered breakthroughs, deepen human connections, as well as unlock both boundless energy and superlative performance.

On behalf of her global clients, Heather is currently pioneering new research and methodology, serving up the uniquely potent interface of music and neuroscience for optimal (measurable gains in) engagement, performance, and results.

As co-creator of The Everyday Rockstar Performance Leadership Academy, Heather and her global research team have developed a distinctively interactive, AI-enabled and practical brain-based approach that measurably reduces stress, while enhancing emotional intelligence, performance and focus at individual, group and organizational levels.

Heather has been a sought-after keynote speaker and thought leader at conferences and associations for 20-plus years, is the author of "Believe In Yourself More Than Your Grandma | Unleash Your Superpower Through Simple Neuroscience," released in 2024, and hosts the Go Reflect Yourself Podcast. As a neuroscience coach and neuro-practice pioneer, Heather has appeared on numerous podcasts and webinars and has been featured in Forbes, Yahoo Finance, Brainz Magazine and Thrive Global.

Scan the QR code to watch
a full interview with Heather

Heather Kirchner

CHASING THE GLOW:
MY JOURNEY FROM CORPORATE AMERICA TO PURPOSEFUL ENTREPRENEURSHIP

There's a moment in life when you realize you're no longer willing to trade your energy, your time or your peace for a job that doesn't light you up anymore. For me, that moment seemed to come gradually. Then it happened all at once.

After months of feeling drained by the grind of late-night calls, endless meetings and the constant demand to do more with less, I found myself looking at our young kids one day and thinking, "They're growing up too fast and I'm missing too much–and for what?" It wasn't that I didn't enjoy working hard; I've always been someone who gives 110% to everything I do. But I started asking myself: If I'm going to work this hard, why not do it for something I'm truly passionate about, something that brings me joy and something that gives me the opportunity to give back to a community that I love?

It was a combination of things that led me to take the leap; watching my children grow faster than I could keep up with, and feeling disconnected from the impact of my work as well as the kind of perspective-shifting loss that reminds you life is fleeting and precious.

I realized it was time to bet on myself. It was time to build something that aligned with my values—family, wellness, community and purpose.

Last September, I stepped away from corporate America. I was grateful and fortunate to be in a leadership role with great compensation and benefits, but I was killing myself day in and day out to build someone else's legacy. It was terrifying and liberating all at once. I didn't have every detail mapped out, but I knew the direction I was going. I wanted to create something meaningful, something that empowered others and something that I would wake up energized about every day. It's probably the biggest bet I've made in my life, but I decided it was time to push the "I believe in me" button.

Fast-forward to today. I'm so proud to be pouring my energy into goGLOW St. Louis—our flagship location in Rock Hill and one of the brand's first franchise locations in the country. It still feels surreal to say that out loud! Yes, there are hard days and unexpected challenges, but those become easier to work through when everything is on the line.

From Tech to Tans: Following the Spark

If you had told me a few years ago that I'd be running a sunless tanning studio, I probably would have laughed. My background was in technology. I spent the majority of my career helping passionate founders grow and scale their Software as a Service (SaaS) businesses. For a time, I loved it. I met so many incredibly intelligent people and learned so much about what it takes to build something from the ground up. I loved the grit, the grind, the long nights and the early mornings. But even more than that, I learned what kind of businesses and people light me up.

For me, it was always about the founder's fire. I was drawn to businesses led by people who were wildly passionate, who cared deeply about their customers, and who insisted on building something excellent. These were non-negotiables for me. So were a strong product-market fit, a service that people raved about and a team culture built on respect and heart. I didn't know it at the time, but I was already laying the groundwork for what would come next.

I am a fair-skinned girl, and I burn in the sun the second I step outside, however I feel more confident when I'm tan. During my high school and college years for events and dances, this meant laying in tanning beds until I was burnt and had color.

Fast forward to about a year ago I was diagnosed with basil cell carcinoma, a form of skin cancer which was likely caused by my tanning bed use. I had a chronically dry spot on my upper lip which just wouldn't heal and led me to a dermatologist. While I was so thankful that the cancer and margins could be surgically removed, this really made me evaluate a lot of things about my life. With the cancer being on my face and much larger than I thought, it was more involved than a typical Mohs surgery and brought with it a surprising lack of confidence, caution and frustration post-surgery. It was this experience that led me to want to do better for myself and future generations. I was convinced there had to be a way to give people a healthy, natural looking tan. Enter goGLOW!

When I first experienced goGLOW as a client, I was hooked—not just on the results, but on the mission. As a wellness enthusiast and someone who has undergone multiple surgeries to remove skin cancer, I'm hyper-conscious of what I put on and, in my body, and am a huge sunless tanning advocate, particularly for the younger generations. The goGLOW experience checked every box. Our patented technology eliminates harmful chemicals and overspray. Our solutions react with your natural skin oils for a personalized, natural glow and our vegan skincare line supports healthy, radiant skin without compromise.

It was beauty meets science meets soul, and I knew almost immediately that I had to bring this to St. Louis.

Building a Business, Building a Life

Opening our Rock Hill location has been a whirlwind—in the best way. It's been the perfect combination of all the things I love: pioneering a brand-new market, creating a culture that energizes both clients and team members, and building something that my family is proud of. Every day, I get to lead with intention, mentor rising stars and take bold swings, all while giving people a product and experience that genuinely makes them feel good in their skin.

What's even more fulfilling is how deeply involved my family is in this journey. My kids talk about "mommy's business" with a kind of pride that brings me to tears regularly—not to mention while writing this. They help fold towels, greet clients and tell anyone who will listen about how cool goGLOW is and what I'm doing (even though I'm not sure they know what a spray tan is just yet). Watching them learn that they can dream big, take risks and build something of their own someday is the real win.

And then there's Aaron—my husband, my rock, my biggest cheerleader. He's the kind of partner who shows our kids what it means to love fully and support unconditionally. None of this would be possible without him, and I'm endlessly grateful for the way he shows up for me, for our kids and for our dreams.

The Power of Community and Connection

One of the most unexpected joys of this journey has been the way the St. Louis community has shown up for us. From day one, we've been met with open arms and overwhelming support. There's something truly special about this city, especially for small business owners. People want you to win and believe there's enough success to go around for everyone. They'll spread the word, leave glowing reviews and tell their friends. People like this are the flames that fuel the fire of our business.

I've also been lucky to meet and learn from so many powerhouse women and entrepreneurs along the way. When we get together, one of the first things we always ask each other is, "How did you get here?" And while the answers vary, the common thread is always "courage." At some point, every single one of us took a leap. We got tired of waiting for someone to give us permission and decided to believe in ourselves.

That's what I hope people take away from my story—not that it's been easy, or perfect or done without fear, but that it's possible. You don't have to have it all figured out to take the first step. You can pivot, and you can evolve to write your own story.

Leading with Heart – Always

My leadership philosophy hasn't changed much, whether I'm running a team in tech or running a custom spray tanning studio. Historically, I worked with a majority of male tech leaders who often told me I was "too nice" but at the same time couldn't believe the results I was always driving. I believe in doing the right thing, always. You can still push people to the limit without being aggressive and demanding. I believe in treating people with respect, setting high standards and leading by example. If you focus on your team, your clients and your community, the business side tends to fall into place.

At goGLOW St. Louis, we're not just building a brand. We're building a culture. A space where people feel seen, celebrated and empowered—where they leave feeling better than when they came in, not just because of how they look, but because we made their appointment the best 20 minutes of their day.

What's Next

This is only the beginning. We've got big dreams for goGLOW in St. Louis—with plans for additional locations and a growing team of talented, passionate people. But no matter how big we grow, I never want to lose sight of the "why."

I left corporate America because I wanted more—more presence with my family, more alignment with my values and more connection with my community. And I found it right here in our first little studio in Rock Hill, surrounded by glow, grit and so much gratitude.

So, if you're standing at the edge of a big decision—if you're feeling pulled toward something new, thinking there may be more for you—listen to yourself. It might be scary and messy, but it might just be the beginning of everything you've been waiting for.

ABOUT HEATHER KIRCHNER

Heather Kirchner is a go-to-market strategist and entrepreneur with a passion for sunless tanning and clean beauty. She spent most of her career as a leader in software and technology, and recently left her role at FoodStorm (acquired by Instacart) to open goGLOW, a custom airbrush tanning salon in Rock Hill. She cites the move as a compilation of all the things she loves most about business, from pioneering an industry, to launching a product in a new market, creating a positive and energizing culture and mentoring staff—not to mention setting an example for her young children.

As a wellness fanatic and someone who has undergone surgeries to remove skin cancer, Kirchner was inspired by the goGLOW experience, drawn to details like patented technology that eliminates harmful chemicals and overspray during the service, proprietary solutions that react with the natural oils on your skin and a vegan skincare line to support your glow. Bringing a better product and better outcome to St. Louis residents is the catalyst for this veteran corporate businesswoman to continue chasing her entrepreneurial dreams by opening the Rock Hill goGLOW location in her hometown – with more St. Louis locations to follow.

Scan the QR code to watch
a full interview with Heather

Jamie Vann

A COLORFUL PATH

Growing up in St. Louis in the 1980s was exactly what people might imagine when they talk about a great childhood. T-shirts and shorts cut from jeans I grew out of, layers of Coppertone, climbing trees, playing soccer in the yard, riding bikes and jumping ramps made from two, used paint cans and a piece of plywood. We caught butterflies by day and fireflies at night. We had barbecues with baked beans and corn on the cob for supper and popsicles or Hostess cupcakes for dessert. We spun our vinyl of Elton John, Linda Ronstadt, Three Dog Night and Jim Croce on rotation. Life was simplistic. It was timeless. And it opened the doors for my big dreams, vivid aspirations and an even bigger creative spirit.

From a young age, I believed the world was full of possibilities and I wanted to explore all of them. With a box of Crayola crayons in one hand and a head full of ideas for the next project in motion, creativity came naturally to me. I was always learning and growing, wanting to do the next best thing.

My world was a place where creativity wasn't just encouraged, it was inherited and often times challenged. Whether it was Dad building something in the garage, Mom sewing items for her next craft show, my gram drying flowers in tins of silica sand or weaving grapevine wreaths, or my art teacher, who believed that art class was more important than math, I was lucky to be surrounded by people who made things happen while educating others along the way. Their influence and instruction, in the form of a comment or a question for me to reflect upon, stuck with me. It was a continual stream of learning and growth. It shaped how I saw the world, what I believed was possible, how to differentiate myself from the rest, and most importantly, not just how to think, but how to think creatively with intention. Whether I was putting together a make-shift lemonade stand in my front yard with my brother, cutting elaborate collages out of old *Better Homes & Gardens* magazines and rubber cementing the patterns of words and phrases onto layers of construction paper, or painting themed-characters on the backside of the cheerleaders briefs for Fall Festival, my creativity was continuous and the attention to detail in my work was fierce.

As I got older, that same creative energy turned toward serial entrepreneurship. By the time Prince was telling everyone to party like it was 1999, I wasn't just partying, I was building a colorful life for myself. Business after business, idea after idea, I kept chasing that feeling I loved as a kid—the thrill of making something out of nothing or repurposing something deemed useless by one person and giving it a new life for someone else. Seeing others get excited about the end product was the validation I needed to fuel new and lofty ideas. Some worked. Some didn't. Yet the continuation of learning through mistakes and successes was key.

In my twenties, I thought entrepreneurship was mostly about independence, about building something of my own. But even back then, something deeper was pulling at me. It wasn't just about success or recognition. I wanted to create businesses and spaces that meant something, places where people felt welcome, valued and respected. I wanted to make life, for others, a little brighter, a little more colorful.

As a entered my thirties, I turned to reading to continue to grow and learn. After reading Simon Sinek's "Start with Why: How Great Leaders Inspire Everyone to Take Action," I realized I knew my "why," I just couldn't articulate it. Before I could fully put my life's purpose into words, much less a full sentence, it took years of trial and error—winning battles, losing races and lots of mentoring and business coaching guidance. Through tough conversations, deep questions and must I admit, a handful of adult beverages, I had massaged my life's purpose, my why, into a clear and concise sentence: to bring value, create fairness and foster inclusion in the lives of others.

Finally, understanding and being able to share my why felt like finding the pot of gold at the end of a rainbow. It gave meaning to all my successes and failures. It made sense of the choices I'd made and of the deep-rooted belief that if I worked hard, stayed positive, and treated human beings with dignity, respect and kindness while never comprising my good name, things would work out. Guided by this formula served me well. Through school, through early jobs and friendships, through my entrepreneurial ventures, I found success more often than not. Of course there were bumps along the way, but overall, I trusted in a simple philosophy: work hard, don't burn bridges, stay true to your good name and never quit.

Being a serial entrepreneur with a visionary mindset and a servant heart to bring value, create fairness and foster inclusion in the lives of others, created an opportunity to build something bigger than most thought possible. When asked why, I simply answered, quoting John O'Leary, "Why not?" So, in true Jamie fashion, I accepted the challenge to create the second, fully accessible amusement park for people of all abilities including our veterans, in St. Louis, Mo. It may seem crazy, to some. But for me, it was a series of steps and processes accompanied by millions of learning and professional growth opportunities built on relationships. My schooling taught me that businesses were built on relationships and connections and in my mind, what could connect people more than an initiative to bring about inclusion through education, employment and entertainment to an underserved demographic that doesn't discriminate?

At the time, this project had been compared by sheer size, cost and attention to detail to Disney World, yet like every other business plan I had worked through, I couldn't complete steps 3, 4, or 5 without completing steps 1 and 2 so, I jumped right in. It was creative. It was challenging. It was a struggle. It was rewarding. It was beautiful and it brought out the absolute ugly. Over eight years, there were personal and professional sacrifices and successes: 60-plus-hour weeks, time lost with my family, awareness built for the disabled community, no paycheck, lots of event planning and execution, two nonprofits up and running, lots of networking and peopling, hundreds of thousands of dollars raised, dozens of verbal commitments given and an overall emotional roller coaster.

But there came a time when hard work, unbeknownst to my belief, understanding and past experiences, just wasn't enough, when doing the right thing didn't guarantee the right outcome. There came a season when everything I had built personally and professionally with my team was ripped apart. At first, I fought with everything I had. I threw all my energy into believing a truth that was simply a lie. I kept telling myself that the betrayal was a simple mistake, that all would be resolved "Friday." Yet that Friday never came.

For the first time, creativity, persistence and grit—the gifts I had been born with—weren't enough. I couldn't work harder to fix what was happening. I couldn't outthink or outrun the outcome and the pain it caused so many, especially me. I had to sit with it. And in case you didn't know, creative souls don't sit still well so… I struggled. In my struggle through the stillness, I came to a very hard realization; I had allowed my identity as a human being to be intertwined with the project I had given nearly a decade of my life to, and I was embarrassed. I was ashamed. I felt I was a failure to myself, to my husband, to my children, to my community and to God. Once I had acknowledged it, I had to find a new way to move forward. So, I leaned hard into my tribe—God, family, true friends, mentors and my business and spiritual coaches. I prayed until there were no words left. I searched every inch of my soul. Then I prayed some more. I cried, waited and I trusted.

The recovery wasn't graceful. It wasn't quick. It was worrisome and messy but, in the struggle, it was holy. Most days I could get out of bed but not off the couch. Instacart became a staple, because leaving my house and potentially running into someone I knew, was too devastating to endure. Healing wasn't a straight line. It wasn't clean or easy. But little by little, I started to understand the colorful path I was now on. I realized, as a child of God, He knew me better than anyone, and His path is better than anything I could dream up. I trusted that God knew for me to rebuild, I needed to trust Him, and I did. The lessons I was taught on being still were plentiful and profound. One in particular was that God "speaks" to me in images not sound, because I am a creative soul and a visual learner—a life-changing realization that became so obvious when I was still and trusted Him wholeheartedly.

It also taught me to allow myself grace, to be more patient with myself and with others. It taught me that my worth isn't tied to my achievements, or my resume or bank account. It's tied to how I show up for myself and others when things are hard. It's about who I've helped along the way and how I made those I interacted with feel. It taught me that it's okay to not have all the answers. Sometimes, the best thing for me is to simply stay in the arena, keep showing up and trust, even when I can't see the progress.

Changing lifelong, engrained beliefs is also a process. I had always believed strength meant avoiding pain. I believed success meant always completing the goal, always moving forward. I came to realize that I was wrong because real strength is earned. After months of working my way out of the colorless life situation I had found myself in, understanding that real strength is in choosing to keep going when you want to quit. In choosing to keep learning and growing through painful moments and in letting the hard things shape you into someone wiser, kinder and more compassionate.

Over the duration, I developed resilience. I built deeper relationships, forged through vulnerability. I found clarity about God's purpose for me that my pride had blurred. While I wouldn't have chosen the bleak, colorless, lifeless eight-year path that was abruptly uprooted, I certainly wouldn't change it. Wisdom is gained through a combination of knowledge and experience.

Today, my path is bright, clear and illuminated with every color imaginable—a vibrant story of survival and triumph. There are bold, joyful colors representing my successes and the happiest memories. There are dark, somber colors representing my most trying and traumatic times. And there are muted, in-between shades for the ordinary days that matter just as much. Every color is important. Every color has its place. I've come to believe that it's in our response to life's challenges that our true colors are revealed.

My eight-year journey less traveled taught me one of the most important and powerful truths: No Grit. No Pearl. I will continue to challenge myself to learn and grow as a wife, mother, friend, member of my community and as a child of God. I feel more sound and secure in who I am and where I am going than I have in more than 10 years. Please know, my hardship is not my whole story, nor is it yours. Adversities are just chapters, not conclusions. Brokenness is not an ending; it's simply the beginning of something new and grander than originally imagined. And grit—the quiet persistence, the stubborn hope, the choice to keep moving forward—is what creates a brilliant and beautiful pearl (of life). The life I have today—full of richer experiences with my husband and children, deeper connections with those true friends and the meaningful work I am excited to be apart of—is better than anything I could have planned for myself. It's not perfect. It's not free from struggle or challenges. But it's authentic. It's colorful. It's me. I'm finally on the right path, and I'm grateful.

ABOUT JAMIE VANN

Self-motivated game changer with 20-plus years of experience spanning the nonprofit and private sectors, leveraging a data driven servant leadership approach to amplify impact, create awareness and foster missions dedicated to growth, inspiration and leadership.

Relentless relationship builder, strengthen relationships with community leaders, government officials, donors, nonprofit players and communities, harnessing a comprehensive strategy that unites philanthropic vision with corporate insights, community relations savvy, government affairs know-how and public affairs diplomacy.

Achievement-driven problem-solver, exceeding client, donor and diverse stakeholder expectations by surpassing revenue and fundraising goals, channeling emotional intelligence, creativity, attention to detail, business development, strong public speaking skills and client relationship management expertise to soliciting, building relationships and growing ROI.

I am a servant leader fulfilling my core belief: to bring great value and create equality, fairness and inclusion for others. Having more than 20 years of experience as a "get-it-done" serial entrepreneur, I founded, co-founded, and successfully run six businesses, two being nonprofits. Having advised half a dozen business professionals and nonprofits in all aspects of business growth and inclusion within the workforce, it is said that I have a gift of inspirational masterminding that translates to empowering said leaders, in their field, by reigniting a positive mindset, goal clarification and brand development.

My professional experience includes being a catalyst for pioneers in the inclusion environment. As president and founder of nonprofit, Spirit of Discovery Park, it was my role to be "the voice of the community" as I was helping serve and raise awareness for that is far too often overlooked and underappreciated. Drawing from my past experiences in the community relations and sales fields, I have been able to contribute additional change for the greater good by co-founding the nonprofit, St. Louis Blues Blind Hockey Club and the for profit, Greenhouse at SoDP. Collaboratively, these three entities have altered the disabled lens, in just a little more than eight years, for the best; something that makes me truly proud.

Currently, I am carrying out my God-given talents with St. Louis-based nonprofit, Operation Shower, while sharing my time and value with for and nonprofit entities through woman-owned business, Brailo Sales & Service. Offering a variety of services and products, I plan to keep helping others help themselves as long as I can.

Scan the QR code to watch
a full interview with Jamie

Jennifer Q. Williams

FROM CHAOS TO CLARITY -
A JOURNEY OF PASSION, PERSEVERANCE AND PURPOSE

The Spark of Organization

I was the kid who found joy in the neatness of a well-organized space. My mother often recalls how, even in middle school, I would spend hours arranging my closet by color, season and fabric. This love for order and structure wasn't just a phase. It was the beginning of a lifelong passion.

As I grew older, I pursued a degree in communications and public relations at Saint Louis University, envisioning a career in public relations. However, life had other plans. A friend on the West Coast was opening a custom closet franchise in St. Louis and said he thought I'd be a perfect fit. I joined the venture. And it was there that I discovered my true calling. The idea of transforming chaotic spaces into organized sanctuaries resonated deeply with me.

In 1991, at the age of 25, I made a bold decision to drop out of graduate school and venture into the world of entrepreneurship. Armed with a vision, a passion for organization, and a willingness to take risks, I founded Saint Louis Closet Co. I had no savings, no collateral and barely any experience in the industry. But I had determination and a dream.

Building from the Ground Up

Starting a business from scratch is akin to assembling a puzzle without the picture on the box. There were moments of uncertainty, fear and doubt. I remember approaching banks for a startup loan and being turned down repeatedly. They questioned if a young woman could succeed in the construction industry. It was disheartening, but I refused to let their skepticism define me.

Finally, a bank officer took a chance on me and approved a Small Business Administration (SBA) loan. With that support, I began my journey. The first year was challenging, but we made $236,000 in sales. It wasn't much, but it was a start—a testament to the power of perseverance.

Over the years, Saint Louis Closet Co. grew. We expanded our services, hired dedicated employees, and built a reputation for quality and reliability. But growth came with its own set of challenges.

The Recession and the Road to Resilience

In 2006, I made a significant investment. I purchased a 30,000-square-foot building and invested $6 million in renovations and new equipment. Just six months after moving into our new space, the 2008 recession hit. Sales declined, competitors closed their doors and I feared we might be next.

But giving up was never an option. We tightened our belts, cut unnecessary costs and doubled down on customer service. Slowly but surely, we climbed back and emerged stronger than ever. The experience taught me invaluable lessons about resilience, adaptability and the importance of a supportive team.

Balancing Business and Family

Being a woman in business is challenging. But being a mother of two while running a business is a delicate balancing act. When the COVID-19 pandemic hit, it threw everything into disarray. My children were home from school. My business was operating under new safety protocols. And the world seemed to be on pause.

But instead of succumbing to the chaos, I embraced it. I woke up earlier to get my daily walks in, kept my kids focused on the blessings they had, and revamped my business to operate within the new guidelines. It was exhausting, challenging and at times overwhelming—but it was also a reminder of the strength and resilience within all of us.

Giving Back to the Community

Through all the ups and downs, one thing remained constant: my commitment to giving back to the community. In 2020, I launched "Closets for a Cause," a program where money, volunteer time, and necessary items are donated to local charities. It's my way of showing gratitude for the support I've received from my community and helping those in need.

Whether it's providing winter coats to the homeless, supporting a local school or offering a helping hand to someone going through a tough time, I believe in the power of community. And I believe that when women support each other, incredible things happen.

Lessons Learned and Words of Wisdom

If there's one thing I've learned on this journey, it's that success isn't about avoiding failure. It's about embracing it, learning from it, and using it as a steppingstone to greater things. As Maya Angelou once said, "People will forget what you said, people will forget what you did, but people will never forget how you made them feel."

So, to all the women out there dreaming big, working hard and making a difference, keep going. Your story matters. Your journey matters. And together, we can build a world where every woman has the opportunity to shine.

Thank you for joining me on this chapter of my story. I hope it inspired you, made you smile, and reminded you that no matter where you are in your journey, you are not alone. Keep going. Keep growing. And never forget, the best is yet to come.

ABOUT JENNIFER Q. WILLIAMS

Jennifer Q. Williams is the founder and president of Saint Louis Closet Co., a locally owned and operated custom closet company in St. Louis. Since 1991, she has been dedicated to transforming spaces and lives through organization. Beyond her business, Jennifer is deeply committed to giving back to her community, supporting local charities and empowering women in business. She is also the founder of Jenny Q, a lifestyle brand focused on helping women navigate the challenges of balancing work, family and personal growth.

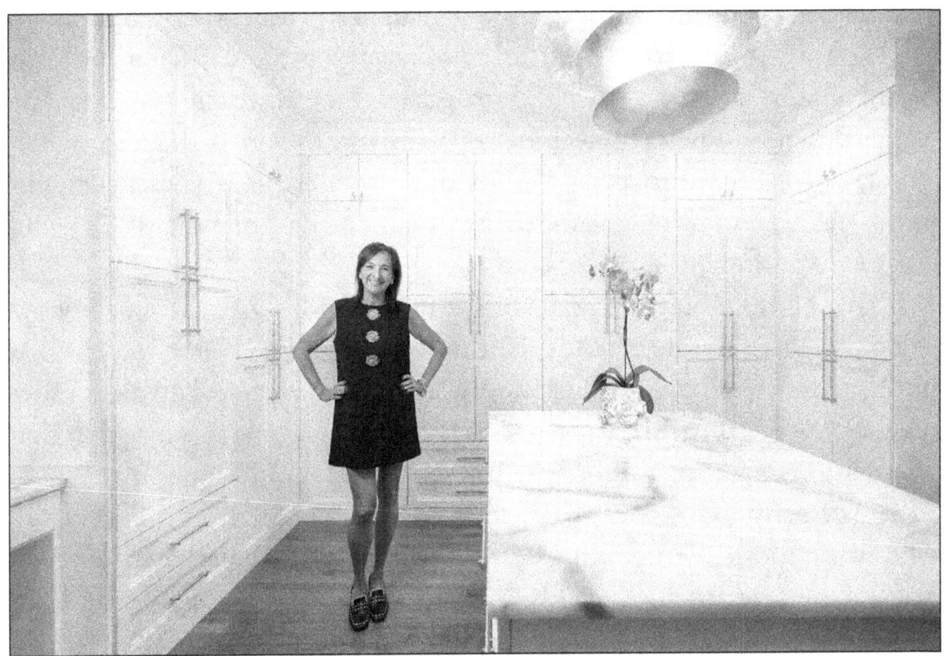

Scan the QR code to watch a full interview with Jennifer

Jessica Cooke

A LOVE LETTER TO MY DAUGHTER

When you become a mother of a daughter, somehow you seem to share a heart. It begins to beat inside both of you the day she is born. A mother wants to guide her child, to protect her, to teach her all of the things she never knew, to keep her from any of the hurts she felt.

You reflect on your own childhood and believe that you just might have a chance at raising an amazing woman one day, one that is like you, but so very different, too.

I have had the pleasure of having a mother who was there for everything. And she is still there for me through all of life's victories as well as its challenges. And her mother was the same. So, when my own daughter was born, it was my turn to be strong, fiercely devoted and to add to that wonderful generational motherly influence.

I was finally in a career that I loved. I was married and raising a son who was almost 2 years old. Life was good. We had purchased our first house. I was advancing quickly in the company I worked for, and my husband's career was booming.

But then, I began to feel ill. At first, I brushed it off, thinking I had a lingering virus. However, as the weeks passed, my symptoms got worse—much worse. And I wondered: "Was I sick from our recent vacation out of the country? Did I have a new allergy? Was I pregnant?" Not one, not two, but three pregnancy tests were taken at different times. A trip to the doctor was warranted. They asked me all the same questions I had already asked myself. They ran blood tests and scheduled additional testing.

My work was expanding and over several meetings, it had been decided that I would assist in opening a new location. My boss and I were inside her office when a voice came over the intercom: "Jessica has a phone call on extension one." Not knowing that the doctor's office was on the other end, I picked up the phone. (This was 2002. We didn't have cell phones.)

"Jessica," the nurse said over the phone, "no need for further testing other than to set your appointment with your OB-GYN. Congratulations, you are pregnant." I guess out of shock, the first words out of my mouth were, "It's Cooke with an 'e'." I was sure they had called the wrong Jessica Cooke, as Jessica Cooke had completely ruled out pregnancy already with the number of tests I took. I heard laughter and the reassurance that, yes, they had called the right number for the right person, and I was definitely pregnant. Now the only question was: "How far along was I?"

Once I was sure that I was pregnant and had closed my mouth from the shock of it, I was overcome with excitement and could not wait to run into my husband's arms and tell him and my son that our family would be growing. I finished the day at work noticing my boss' door was shut the rest of the day and other management was coming and going.

Fast forward through my growing belly bump, the location opened and no more talk about me assisting was mentioned. I brushed it off, as I didn't think much of it until later. But now I know why.

We decided not to find out the gender of baby number two, as we decorated the nursery with John Lennon's "Imagine" baby line of pastel animals and the mobile that softly played the tune.

Baby number two was scheduled to arrive at the end of June. But this baby was eager to meet the world. And on June 1 at 3 a.m., my water broke, and the contractions came hard and fast. I still tell my husband today that I swear that day at 3 a.m. was the only time I have ever witnessed him drive that slow and hit all the stoplights along the way. We were supposed to drop my son off with my mom, and as we approached her exit, I screamed: "No time!" My husband kept driving, and it was a good thing he did, because by 6 a.m., my 8-pound-15-ounce baby girl was tucked in my arms. She was the most beautiful baby girl I had ever seen. And just like me, she was born with one bent ear, and on the same side as me. Her perfect pout made my heart melt.

I took 12 weeks off work. At the very last minute a sweet assistant administrator for the company told me about the FMLA act. I did not know about the law and had already been preparing to go back to work in six weeks. We relied on my income as well as my husband's to make ends meet, and I carried the health insurance. But in the end, even 12 weeks felt like merely a long weekend, as she was barely sleeping through the night. She was born with thrush, jaundice, blocked tear ducts and was already on her second ear infection. I had been to work during this time for payment of my portion of health insurance and couldn't afford any more time off anyway because we needed the insurance. As much as I dreaded sending her to daycare and leaving her side, I knew I had to get back to work.

I did return to work and soon began to get into my "working mom groove" of having a toddler and an infant. I worked Saturdays and Sundays, so I could be home two days during the week, not only for the kids, but because we could not afford daycare five days a week at that time.

The holidays soon approached—an extremely busy time in the pet industry. I was a salaried employee, and oftentimes I was expected to work 12-hour days or to cover shifts to make sure everything was taken care of for the entire day. I was even on call 24/7 at times or had to leave in the middle of the night to cover shifts which sometimes lead to my working two shifts back-to-back. I didn't mind this at the time, as I knew what I had signed up for and I loved my job. I was prepared to balance this, and I thought I could handle it now with two kids. Wrong. I was exhausted.

Once on an extremely busy day with an overwhelming workload and no end in sight, I heard over the intercom: "Jessica, you have an urgent phone call on extension one." My heart sank, probably because I still had PTSD from the last urgent phone call. In 2002, if you got a phone call at work, something had to be urgent, and no phone call was always better than any phone call.

It was my kids' daycare and the voice on the end of the phone was shaky as she explained that my daughter had been fussy but also seemed to be having a very hard time breathing. She wanted us there as soon as possible. I knew my husband was at an appointment hours away, so his going was not an option. My mom was too far away at her job and could not get there. I approached my boss and explained the situation and said my mom and husband were unavailable. I could see the look of disappointment on his face that I would leave my team at a time like that. I decided to call a friend to go pick up my daughter and my husband or mom would meet her at the hospital when they could. I went back to work after this was arranged and I felt sick to my stomach that I was not going to be there.

Soon after, I walked up to my boss, my purse in hand, and told him that I had to go and make sure my daughter was alright. I said I was meeting my friend at the hospital and that I would be back after my daughter was settled. He responded: "You may not have a job when you get back."

As I started to leave the parking lot, tears rolled down my face. I was terrified of losing my job. I questioned whether I was doing the right thing. I felt like I was letting my work down. But then I began to question why I had been put in a position to choose between my daughter and my job in a time of crisis. I was a great employee. I was a great mom. Why did it have to be one or the other?

When I arrived at the hospital my daughter was being treated for RSV. She was asleep with an oxygen mask over her tiny face. And then I knew I had made the right decision. She would need to stay the night. My husband soon arrived, and as I had promised my boss, I went back to work. Before long, I would be back at the hospital to be by her side.

When I walked back into work, it was if I had never left. No one even acknowledged that I had returned. I felt a strong need to tell my boss that my daughter had RSV and that she did need to go to the hospital, that she was staying the night, and that I would be heading back there after my shift.

The next day, I was written up with a warning. I don't know if it was pure exhaustion, but I was numb. I had no emotion as I listened to him explain the why of the write-up. It was clear at that moment that no matter how I shined at that company, no matter how hard I worked, they would expect me to choose my family second. That was a deal breaker for me. As I signed the write-up a ball of fire built inside me. I literally felt like that flame was going to shoot out through the pen as I wrote my name. It was at that moment that I decided I would never be made to feel like I had to choose between my daughter and my career. And I haven't since that day 22 years ago.

Within six months, I opened Yuppy Puppy Pet Spa. I became a business owner, but I was always a mom first. Don't get me wrong, as a business owner, I have put in more hours than I ever would have as an employee, but I did it with my kids by my side, and I wouldn't have done it any other way. My sixth year in business, we welcomed baby number three. And this time, it was on my terms, not a boss' terms.

I have gotten to attend every special school celebration, sports game, dance recital, homecoming, prom and high school graduation—all because of a time in my life that I had to choose which direction I would go. And I chose my kids.

My daughter has grown up, literally side-by-side with me at Yuppy Puppy Pet Spa. She was in a pumpkin seat for my first grand opening. She was covered in pink paint, as she helped me expand, when she was in grade school. She started to learn to groom dogs by my side on summer break during junior high. She has gone to award ceremonies with me and my staff. She celebrated her 18th birthday the day I opened my second location. She works at the front desk now, at 22 years old, as she studies for her nursing degree. She has heard me tell the story of how my business started and has seen the hard work that it entails.

Now that she is a woman and will one day be a career woman and a mother of her own family, I'm confident that she will know she can have a fulfilling career and be a great mom at the same time, because her mom did it. Through my example, I have molded her into a strong woman with core values and beliefs that she knows she should never have to compromise for anyone else, no matter how scary things may seem. She can do it, because her mom did it.

My business has been a love letter to my daughter. For 22 years, I have watched her grow right along with my business, through the highs and the lows that life has thrown at us, but always by each other's side, like I promised her the day she was born.

ABOUT JESSICA COOKE

Jessica Cooke is a nationally recognized entrepreneur, nonprofit leader and lifelong animal advocate. She spent 22 years building The Yuppy Puppy into one of the most celebrated pet care brands in the country—earning honors such as Coolest Pet Place in America, the Champion for Children Award, Small Business Owner of the Year from the US Small Business Administration and numerous local awards for excellence in business and community impact. With a heart for rescue and a passion for service, Jessica now leads Yuppy Puppies Forever Rescue, a nonprofit dedicated to giving dogs a second chance at the loving homes they deserve. Her leadership has touched thousands of lives—both human and canine—while inspiring others to lead with compassion, courage and unwavering vision.

Today, Jessica is embracing a new season of life—focusing on her farm, creative passions and future ventures that combine beauty, nature and community in meaningful ways.

Scan the QR code to watch a full interview with Jessica

Jillian Tedesco

THE ENCOUNTER THAT CHANGED MY LIFE

When I look back, certain seasons of my life stand out—mostly the struggles, the times I was barely getting by. But it was through those very struggles that I discovered my purpose and grew in character. From walking away from a toxic relationship and a failed business partnership to launching a nutrition program from my home, I learned resilience the hard way. I pushed through financial uncertainty, anxiety and self-doubt, fueled by a deepening faith and an emerging passion for food and helping others. With the support of my now-husband, Jason, and a whole lot of grit, I turned personal pain into a powerful mission.

Looking back, I can clearly see God's hand in every season. I remember the moment I truly encountered Him—it changed everything. It happened just a few months after the falling out with my business partner, when I walked away from the business entirely. I didn't even know people actually did that—just quit and leave it all behind! But that surrender opened my heart to something bigger.

I remember the first lesson God revealed to me while I was reading about why Jesus died for us: that Jesus forgives our sins—no matter what we've done—and loves us unconditionally. This forgiveness can't be earned; it's a gift, freely available to anyone who chooses to receive it. God not only forgives us, but He also offers to be our refuge, our safe place in the middle of life's mess.

As I was reading this BOOM—the conviction hit me! WWJD, literally? I was supposed to forgive my former business partner, if I wanted to have love and peace in my life. I had to learn to let go, and Jesus was a perfect example. I prayed and journaled about it. God, help me, how do I forgive someone who screwed me over, took my money, isn't going to pay me back? Blah, blah, blah. Poor, pitiful me. I wrestled with it. If this was the way to peace, a step toward forgiveness and relinquishing anxiety, how was I to do it by myself? How was I supposed to just let go and forget? I prayed and prayed that God would change my heart. I couldn't forgive that guy that fast without God's help. God doesn't promise that bad stuff won't happen, but what He does expect is for you to ask Him for help. He wants you to repent and humble your hardened heart to Him.

The next day, on my way to work, I drove past my former business partner's car. Our eyes connected, and I felt an intense energy. I hadn't seen him in months, but the day after I prayed about him, I encountered him. Later that evening, he texted me. We both said how sorry we were for everything that had happened. We wished each other the best, and I remember smiling. I was so blown away by our apologies. A huge weight was lifted off me, and I could feel the joy of forgiveness. Call it what you want, but I call that an answered prayer. That was the first experience of my spiritual relationship with God, of my prayer being answered. And that allowed me to redirect my energy toward positivity and healing, away from resentment.

I continued to read and study with renewed focus. At my new job, another gym, I worked with a man named Matt, whom I now believe was an angel in my story. I also believe God places these people in our lives to help when we want to walk in His direction. Matt was a Christian, and he and I covered the front desk at the gym together. He was confident in his faith, something new to me, and I was intrigued. I opened up and shared my story with him, how I was working my way out of a bad place. He shared his story, too. It was very dark, but it eventually led to him finding his spiritual way with God. His vulnerability was humbling and gave me added hope. He encouraged me to keep reading and seeking, specifically telling me to read the Gospels, the first four books of the New Testament.

Let me preface by saying that picking up a Bible is overwhelming. I didn't have much of an understanding of the Bible. It doesn't make sense if you have no guidance. The Old Testament is 39 books of law, wisdom, history and prophets. The New Testament is 27 books about Jesus and His followers, but it refers back to the Old Testament, so it's super confusing to a new reader. Over the years, it starts to make sense—the characters, their roles, and the lessons they teach comprise stories that are beyond valuable. It has been my favorite text to study, and it is the first place I go for personal development.

The Gospels—Matthew, Mark, Luke and John—are about the story of Jesus Christ. Starting with Matthew, I read about Baby Jesus, Bethlehem, and the three wise men who rode on camels. I was in denial. Three guys on camels ride miles across the desert to see the newborn King, in the middle of nowhere, based on prophecies, following a bright star and bringing gifts of gold, frankincense and myrrh? This is so farfetched! I thought. I closed the Bible and went straight to Google. I stayed up well into the early morning, plagued by curiosity and doubt.

Matt encouraged me to continue seeking because that is what God wants us to do. When you don't have a good understanding or commitment to the word of God, it's easy to dismiss it as false or unrealistic, as you don't have the whole story—and it's a big one, for that matter. You definitely have to commit to unpacking this miraculous story to understand the message it contains. But it's easier not to, right? I was so curious, but I wasn't sure I wanted to be all holy yet, like a pastor or Bible thumper. I had to put down my notions and look for myself. He had answered my first prayer, and I didn't doubt the relationship my mother had with Him. I just hadn't experienced it for myself.

That weekend, I went shopping at the farmers' market. After purchasing food, I walked through a section where farmers and artisans were selling their products. I stopped to purchase natural, homemade soaps. A hundred different varieties were arranged in a beautiful display, and I was overwhelmed with choices. The young girl working the table—she was maybe 12 years old—stared at me. She wore bib overalls and had dirty hair.

I said to her, "There are so many different soaps and smells—I can't pick. Do you have a favorite one?" I will never forget the way she responded, as if she herself was a messenger.

She distinctively stared into my eyes, and I felt unsteady. She was so young, yet she made such surprisingly strong eye contact. Reaching over the counter, she picked up a bar and held it in front of her face, never breaking eye contact with me. "This is my favorite soap," she stated, "frankincense and myrrh."

My mouth dropped, my eyes opened wide, and I felt my heart beating. Maybe it's a coincidence, I thought. Then, I looked beyond the display. The sunlight shone under the awning, directly on my face. I squinted into the warm light. The hair on my arms stood up, and I felt God Himself shining down on me, saying, "I know you are seeking me, and I know you are doubting me, too, but I am real, and I hear you, Jillian, loud and clear." It was no coincidence. And I'm sure you've already guessed—I bought the dang soap!

I went home and journaled about my experience. I couldn't quite believe that I'd had two God experiences in the same week. It was overwhelming yet exciting. I didn't know what to do or think next. Holy cow, could the real God be speaking to me?

The following week, I was working with Matt at the gym. After I filled him in on what happened, he smiled and said, "God will answer you if you seek Him."

Later that day, I was running the front counter, making smoothies and checking people in, when a woman I didn't know walked up. She looked to be about 45, with blond hair and a meek presence.

"Are you Jillian?" she asked timidly.

"Yes," I replied.

"You have been on my heart lately," she let out.

Not knowing the woman, I was very taken aback. She'd turned white like a ghost, but she proceeded to explain how hard it was for her to tell me this. And I was thinking, Who are you and why are you trippin'? It was awkward. She looked so sincere, almost as if she was giving me a message on behalf of someone else but didn't know why. She tried to maintain eye contact but kept looking down nervously. Then she slowly reached over the counter, put her hand on my forearm, and said, "God wanted me to tell you that everything is going to be OK." Then she left. I never saw her again.

Mind you, Matt saw the whole thing go down. After the woman left, Matt smiled a big smile and approached me, laughing with joy. He stated, "You think that was hard for you to hear? Do you know the courage it took her to listen to God and pass that message along to you? She was obedient to God's plan."

I stood there, frozen in shock. A human being I did not know told me that God had talked to her—about me. I wasn't sure how I was supposed to process that. I'd never experienced anything like that in my life, nor has God since contacted me like he did that woman. Do I selfishly wish he would? All the time! It would be a powerful and amazing experience. But that short interaction was my miracle, and it's a big part of my story.

After that experience, I started feeling relief from my fear and started to trust God more. I was able to let go of myself a bit. I let Him worry about what was next, and I focused on what I loved. It was freeing. As a result, I committed my life and my new work to Him. To this day, the choices I make and how I live my life are based on my spiritual foundation. I believe in my spirit that my business is God's business, and I'm just following His plan. I believe God cares more about my availability than my ability, otherwise He wouldn't have chosen me for this task.

I continued praying and journaling about what I was supposed to be doing with my life. I loved to cook, and I knew I was meant for more. I felt the permission and support to do what I do best—serve others (pun intended) by helping them eat better and leading with passion. I wanted so badly to help my clients overcome their most challenging hurdles: time and a lack of knowledge about healthy eating. The need was clear. So I came up with a solution.

I created a service to help my clients eat better and alleviate stress—premade, chef-inspired meals for a healthy lifestyle. I started cooking to help people, but in return, it helped me more. I started dreaming about what I deeply wanted, to focus more on food and less on training. Could I go to culinary school? I knew there would be a ton of work involved, but that excited me. This was the most pivotal point in my life. God swooped in and said, "I got you. Trust in me, and follow your passion. Do the work, and walk in faith." So I turned the page. I continued my practice of being with Him and followed my dream.

My transition from training to cooking full time would take three years. I knew I would have to keep my day job as a trainer, attend school at night, and launch my concept on the weekends if I wanted to do it all. At that point, it didn't bother me that I basically had three jobs—trainer, student and weekend chef. I had so much joy wrapped up in the birth of this concept and I never looked back.

Today, fit-flavors has seven locations, and the impact we're making on people's lives—and in our community—continues to grow. This business is still God's business, and I'm just doing my best to follow His lead. If you're feeling stuck or unsure of your next step, I encourage you to lean in and let Him guide you. He always shows up.

ABOUT JILLIAN TEDESCO

Jillian Tedesco is a chef, mother, author and the founder of fit-flavors, a meal prep company in St. Louis dedicated to creating high-quality, balanced meals that inspire healthy lifestyles. A graduate of Le Cordon Bleu, Jillian brings her culinary expertise to everything she does, from crafting innovative menus to educating others on the benefits of quality nutrition. As the host of the podcast Owning the Wait and a published author, she shares her journey of faith, growth and leadership, encouraging others to embrace grace and pursue excellence in every aspect of life.

Scan the QR code to watch a full interview with Jillian

Kelli Risse

TRUSTING THE NEXT RIGHT STEP

I didn't wake up one day, toss my grade book in the air, and declare, "That's it, I'm outta' here!" My decision to leave teaching wasn't impulsive or loud. It was honest, discerning and deeply intentional. I spent 15 years in the classroom, most of those years teaching first grade, and I genuinely loved it. First grade is where the magic happens. You watch kids transform from sounding out words to reading, writing and solving problems with confidence. I was the teacher with high expectations and a soft heart. Strict? Absolutely. But my students knew I cared for and believed in them.

For many years teaching filled me with joy, but slowly that joy began to fade. Themes gave way to test prep. Creativity got squeezed out by compliance. Teaching became less about sparking growth and more about standardized testing. Still, one truth remained: Great teachers find a way to show up, adapt and lead through change. I did, too. But in the quiet spaces, there was a nudge I couldn't ignore. A question that lingered longer each time it surfaced: Is there another path for me?

While still teaching, I followed that question into a side-hustle, a plan B business through a direct sales company in health and wellness. Like most first-time entrepreneurs, I didn't start with a polished business plan. I started with passion, a community and an audible library overflowing with business books queued up at 1.5 speed, because apparently, success sounds better slightly faster. It was my first step toward something new. It was a new way to help others and earn additional income. But more than that, it was a taste of freedom, and once you see what's possible, it's hard to unsee it.

I didn't go into teaching for the money. The real paycheck was watching students discover their voice, confidence and abilities. But over time,

I couldn't ignore another reality: No matter how much heart, time or leadership I gave, there was little recognition, beyond a paycheck. And that didn't reflect the weight of the work. In a profession where advancement was tied only to years served and not impact or effort, it became clear the way I was wired to grow, lead and be recognized wasn't going to be fulfilled in that system. With this business, I saw a path where my impact and growth could actually shape my future.

I wasn't reckless or impulsive. I didn't storm out with a resignation letter in one hand and a business plan in the other. I was intentional. I chose a one-year leave of absence, a runway for the future I was beginning to envision, a safety net that gave me space to explore a new direction without closing the door completely. Some might say I should have "burned the boats" and just walked away. I didn't. But deep down, I also knew I wasn't returning.

On the last day of school in May of 2015, I cried like I always did at year's end. But this time, the tears weren't only for my students. They were for the season I was completing. I packed up my classroom quietly. A few close friends, amazing women I still adore, made brownies and hosted a small goodbye. All those years of showing up and giving my best, and as I walked out those doors, life at the school kept moving. It was business as usual. But for me, it wasn't just the end of a year. It was the closing of a chapter and the beginning of honoring what was next.

That summer looked normal enough, filled with vacations, time with my kids, and working my side-hustle. My husband was my biggest champion. My friends were supportive, though I could sense the concern tucked behind their smiles. My financial planner friend didn't sugarcoat it. "You're crazy," she said. "You're walking away from retirement, stability and a guaranteed income." I understood her point. I knew exactly what I was choosing to leave behind. But I also knew what I was choosing to walk toward.

There will always be outside voices questioning your choices. What matters more is how well you know your own. For me, the decision was rooted in faith and the belief that this new calling was meant to be honored, even when the path ahead wasn't fully mapped out. I kept listening and discerning the next right step. And every time I asked, God kept showing me the next door to walk through.

At first, I leaned fully into the direct sales business I had already started in health and wellness. It felt like a natural extension of who I was, because I was still educating. I was still helping people. It was just in a new way. And for a season it worked. But the more I served others, the clearer it became that the real transformation wasn't happening at the surface level. The real work was deeper beneath the habits, choices and stress.

When I discovered coaching, something in me recognized the alignment immediately. I pursued certification and launched my own LLC. But I didn't stop there. I earned my advanced coaching certification and also completed a year-long, five-certification Neuro-Linguistic Programming (NLP) training. It wasn't because I needed more credentials, but because I believe to lead others through transformation, you must first be willing to do the work yourself. And I had done the work.

My work evolved over time and my mission became clearer. I wasn't called to offer quick fixes or surface-level solutions. I was called to help clients create sustainable success so they could break free from burnout, people-pleasing and self-sabotage. My role was to guide them from being overworked, overwhelmed and overstressed, to performing at their best by doing what matters most, not doing more. I understood what it felt like to be caught between high expectations and quiet exhaustion, between doing everything right yet still running on empty. I recognized the pattern because I had lived it. I also knew it could be broken.

Building a business didn't come with a guaranteed paycheck or a perfect plan. There were lean months, scary investments and times when the money I brought in went right back into the business by way of branding, websites, coaching, taxes, training and travel. There were moments of wondering if or when the payoff would come. But I didn't build my business on wishful thinking. I built it on trust, alignment and consistent action. There were questions, of course. They weren't questions rooted in fear, but in responsibility and discernment: Is this the right next move? Is this aligned with my mission? When uncertainty showed up, I didn't spiral. I anchored myself in the same practice that has always guided me: prayerful leadership, listening, aligning and trusting the next right step.

My years in both teaching and direct sales taught me valuable lessons about leadership and business, even though it wasn't my long-term fit. Every step served its purpose and prepared me for what came next:

coaching, speaking and writing. Helping others align with their purpose and lead themselves well has shaped me, too. It's fueled my growth, strengthened my leadership and stretched me in the best ways. With each season of growth, the questions that once held me back began to lose their grip. When they did show up, I met them with clarity, grace and self-leadership. I couldn't imagine myself back in the classroom. I knew I was exactly where I was meant to be.

And then 2020 happened. I watched my former colleagues navigate a world no one was prepared for: virtual classrooms, kids in pajamas, overwhelmed parents and teachers stretched beyond their limits. And still, teachers did what they always do. They showed up and gave everything they had. I knew exactly how I would have responded. I would have poured my energy, heart and resources into those kids and did whatever it took to make sure they were OK. I also knew the cost it would have had on me: exhaustion, overextension and trying to hold it all together for everyone else again. I would have been physically, mentally and emotionally depleted.

But this time, I wasn't there. And for the first time, I felt a deep, unwavering clarity. No matter what happened in my business, I would never go back. That was my true "It's About Time" moment. It did not happen the day I left the classroom, but the day I fully owned the life and the work I was called to build in this moment. It wasn't because the path was easy or because I had every step mapped out. I was no longer willing to settle for what wasn't aligned, even when staying might have felt safer.

Some defining moments arrive in a flash. Others unfold through small, repeated choices. For me, it wasn't one bold leap. It was the courage to keep choosing the next right step until the questions quieted and clarity took center stage. Through each season of uncertainty, I listened, aligned, refined and kept going. I didn't move forward by accident. I moved forward by faith, support from a new community and self-leadership. I stayed grounded in the work, the calling and the truth that I wasn't walking this road alone. Success, I've learned, isn't about control or waiting for perfect conditions. It's about faithful, steady courage and the willingness to continue to show up, to be discerning and to lead yourself well.

Since then, everything has shifted. I began showing up in my business with ownership and certainty. I created executive coaching packages, stepped onto paid speaking stages and launched my four-book series, "Succeed with Ease," to help high achievers become peak performers and create success that's sustainable and aligned. I moved from classroom walls to professional development stages and from parent-teacher conferences to leadership trainings. Along the way, I stepped into leadership roles, built boundaries and uncovered more about how I'm called to lead.

Today, I lead high achievers toward sustainable success by helping them become peak performers without burnout, pressure or overwork. This is the work I'm called to do and I'm fully here for it. I didn't burn the boats or make a reckless leap. I made intentional, aligned decisions. I kept choosing the next right step. I kept trusting the journey and the One who guides it. Because trusting God, I've learned, is the highest form of leadership. It's what helps me release the need for control, stay aligned and create space for ease, creativity and growth.

Every day, I renew my commitment to listen well, lead well and trust well. And when uncertainty tries to creep back in, I return to the same question that has guided me this far: What's the next right step? This is how I lead. This is how I live. This is how I choose to succeed with ease. Because ease isn't about avoiding hard work or obstacles. Ease is about alignment. It's about leading yourself so well that even in the hard moments, you move forward with clarity, courage and conviction.

ABOUT KELLI RISSE

Kelli Risse is a peak performance specialist who empowers individuals and organizations to avoid burnout, retain top talent and maximize performance for sustainable success. With a unique blend of neuroscience, communication strategies and emotional intelligence expertise, Kelli delivers transformative results that help her clients succeed with ease both personally and professionally.

Kelli holds certifications as an emotional quotient consultant, 8 factors of engagement consultant, neuro-linguistics programming

trainer and practitioner, and advanced transformational coach. As a stress mastery expert, Kelli is dedicated to helping clients navigate challenges, build resilience, and thrive under pressure.

Kelli is the CEO of Winning In Business, host of the *Winning In Business* podcast and international best-selling author. Her compelling insights and practical strategies have earned her features on ABC, NBC, FOX, CBS and numerous online media outlets. As a professional speaker, Kelli is known for her engaging and relatable style. She inspires audiences to adopt actionable strategies that lead to lasting success and well-being.

Kelli is expanding her impact with the launch of her new book series, *Succeed With Ease*. This transformative series includes principles and tips to master mindset, focus, energy and connections—empowering business owners and professionals to achieve peak performance without compromising their health, happiness or personal fulfillment.

As a champion for success and well-being, Kelli collaborates with organizations through keynote speaking, workshops and executive coaching to create high-performance cultures that foster innovation, collaboration and growth. Her mission is to guide professionals and teams to rise above stress, maximize their potential and achieve extraordinary results.

When she's not working, Kelli enjoys playing golf with her husband and two adult sons, connecting with her community and continually pursuing ways to help others *win in business* and in life.

Scan the QR code to watch
a full interview with Kelli

Laura Hettiger

JUST SHOW UP

Just how far would you go for a chance? Not metaphorically, but literally, how far would you actually go?

I know exactly how far I would go: 3,000 miles accompanied by 29 rejections.

As a journalist, you need tough skin. You must be willing to ask the tough questions. You need to be comfortable being uncomfortable. You need to show up.

That is what I did when I landed my first job in television news. I showed up.

And that is what I did again when I got my second job in television news. I showed up.

Let's start at the beginning.

Growing up in a small town in Southern Illinois, my life did not revolve around the news. A photographer never visited my school. We never saw a reporter in my town. The only time my hometown of Flora was mentioned on any report at all, was if it was scrolling across the screen on a "news ticker," because we were under a tornado watch.

My family did not turn the television on in the morning. There really wasn't a need to turn it on in the evening, either. And on the rare occasions that I saw my parents watching a newscast, never once did I think, "That's what I want to do when I grow up!"

But I always liked knowing things. I was curious. And I was resilient.

As a little girl, I would regularly go up to strangers to talk to them about what they were shopping for or what they were doing. Some people would ignore me. That taught me a valuable lesson: "Never count the nos. All you need is one yes."

Being told no has never scared me. However, looking back at a potential opportunity and thinking, "What if?" is terrifying.

That is why I applied to my dream school. That is why I sought out a dozen internships and landed seven. That is why I pursued my favorite sorority. That is why I tried out for the University of Illinois Cheerleading Team.

And that is why I decided that instead of focusing on all the nos I would likely get in my life, I would seek out just one yes.

That was my mission in February of 2011. It was a mission that forever altered the course of my career and my life.

I was an excited 23-year-old from Illinois with a fresh master's degree in broadcast journalism. I sent resumes and my reel on a DVD to more than 50 television stations all over the country: everywhere from Tucson, Ariz.; to Odessa, Tx.; to Newport News, Va.

While I waited to hear back from all the news directors I had pitched myself to, I substitute taught Spanish at my local high school. Few things are more humbling than walking the halls you once traversed with your friends—and occasionally made fun of—than being a sub for a foreign language in which you are not fluent, and all while living with your parents.

In between my substitute jobs, I constantly checked my email and my mailbox. Fortunately, I never got any rejection letters. In fact, I never heard back from anyone at all. Not one, single television station replied to my inquiries.

I realized rather quickly that I was not going to find my elusive "yes" through the mail, digital or otherwise. That is when I decided it was time to show up and ask for a job. And that is exactly what I did.

I packed my car full of suits, resumes and the few DVDs I had left and set out on a "Find a Job Road Trip."

Over the course of one work week, I showed up, unannounced, to 30 separate television stations. Every ABC, NBC, CBS and Fox affiliate from Memphis to Tupelo, from Birmingham to Huntsville, from Gainesville to Savannah, from Charleston to Knoxville—I hit up all of them.

There was no email asking if I could come. No call ahead asking if the boss was there. I simply drove myself to all those television stations with one question: "Can I have a job?"

Out of the 30 stations I visited, I had face-to-face interactions with bosses at 26. Most of them were men who had been in the broadcasting business for decades. All of them commented on how rare it was for someone to just show up. After all, that is not how things are done. And to my favor, I was just naïve enough to not know that's not how things are done.

After driving 3,000 miles alone, I finally got my one "yes." When I walked into the lobby of the NBC affiliate in Charleston, S.C., the receptionist told me the News Director only met with people who had an appointment. I assured her that if she would simply call him, he would want to meet with me. I was not naïve about this, however. I just had a feeling that I was going to work at this particular television station. After scanning me up and down, she made the call.

The news director came down. He met me but informed me he could only give me five minutes. I told him I only needed three. More than three hours later, that Southern news director took a chance on a Midwestern girl, making her the newest reporter in The Holy City.

So showing up not only showed my first boss how far I would go to get a story, but it showed me who I am and who I could be.

Showing up taught me courage. It taught me persistence. It taught me resilience. It taught me how to think on my feet. And it taught me that if you want something in life, you literally have to go get it. Nothing is owed to you. Everything is earned.

Reporting for 15 months in Charleston also taught me how much I missed home. It showed me that if I was going to have the life I really wanted, I needed to show up in St. Louis.

So that is what I did in the summer of 2012. I showed up at KMOV-TV in downtown St. Louis and asked for a job.

And just as I had discovered on my first "Find a Job Road Trip," people do not just show up to television stations in the Show Me State. But I did.

A boss would later tell me that he and a few managers got together to discuss my tactic and my potential. They all agreed that I would work at a television station in St. Louis simply because of my grit. They had to decide if they wanted that girl with grit on their team or on their competition's team. Within a few days of showing up, I became the newest reporter at Channel 4.

During my dozen years of working in St. Louis, I have shown up for some of the biggest moments in our area's history. I was on the ground in Ferguson when the unrest broke out in the wake of Michael Brown's death in 2014. I was on Market Street when the St. Louis Blues proudly paraded the Stanley Cup through downtown in June of 2019—their first-ever National Hockey League (NHL) championship. I turned my kitchen into a working television station to continue broadcasting during the COVID-19 pandemic. I have interviewed mayors and police chiefs. I have talked to people on their best and their worst days.

And I have seen what could happen to a child who does not have someone encouraging them to show up. Fate had me show up at a homicide in North St. Louis on a crisp fall morning in 2014. The victim's body was still in the street as children were waking up and making their way to the bus stop. They heard the gunshots. They saw all the police officers. They had to walk around the crime scene. In that moment, I looked at those kids and I knew it was my time to show up for someone else.

It took some time to figure out how to do that, but then, a few months later, an email showed up in my inbox telling me about The Little Bit Foundation. The local nonprofit is dedicated to breaking down barriers to learning for kids across the St. Louis region.

As I clicked through the Little Bit website, I knew I had to use my voice and my position in the community to show up for these kids. But first, I had to show up in front of my boss to ask for a chance: a chance to create an event that not only raised money to help these students, but an opportunity that would give them a chance to run in a race, to earn a medal and to hear: "You did it!" and, "Good job!" and, "I'm proud of you!"

Laura's Run 4 Kids benefiting The Little Bit Foundation is now in its eighth year. Together, we have raised more than half a million dollars for kids in St. Louis.

When the race starts each year, I get emotional thinking about how life can feel like a race sometimes. You know you are supposed to put one foot in front of the other over and over and over, yet you can easily get sidetracked. You can feel down, out of energy or even get hurt. Life does that to us each day.

But then as I see kids making their way toward the finish line each year, pumping their arms, pounding their feet and smiling, I am so proud of them for simply showing up and trying.

Now, 14 years into my career, I am still showing up. I am still trying.

I am no longer naïve, but I still have a lot of grit. I am still unphased by being told "no," and I am still terrified of looking back and thinking, "What if?"

I have learned that to be a woman in 2025, you have to believe in yourself. To be a professional in 2025, you have to be persistent. To be a mom in 2025, you have to think on your feet. And to build the life you want in 2025, you have to show up, go get what you want and make it happen for yourself.

As I move forward into the next phase of my life as a married mom of two, I pray that I am teaching my own children the importance of showing up and figuring things out for themselves. I pray that I am teaching them to be resilient and to use their own talents to help others.

And I pray that when the time comes for them to show up for themselves and for others, they do not fear the word "no;" rather, they run after their own elusive "yes."

ABOUT LAURA HETTIGER

Laura Hettiger hosts Great Day St. Louis and My St. Louis Live on First Alert 4. The Flora, Ill., native lives in the St. Louis area with her husband, Dr. Mark Gdowski, and their two young children.

Laura is passionate about helping others and serves on the Board of Directors for the Saint Louis Crisis Nursery and The Little Bit Foundation.

Scan the QR code to watch a full interview with Laura

Lena Johnson

THE A WORD

A brand-new gift from God arrived two weeks late at 8:07 a.m. on a cold, January day in 2017. My husband was the first to hold him, and just as he named him Matthew Michael Johnson Jr., our son wailed out in protest, as if to say, "No thank you. I don't like that name." Everyone in the operating room laughed, and we were filled with a joy we had never known. We brought him home and fell in love—hard.

As Matt and I tried to settle into parenthood and figure out how to care for this perfect creation, we quickly realized that this miracle we had been handed would bring more love, fear, challenges and tests from God than we ever could have imagined. We were in for a storm—a beautiful, yet frightening and miraculous storm.

Parenting, we quickly learned, was not for the meek. By day 10, our little bundle had decided that living on the outside was not for him. He had already made the message quite clear by prolonging his arrival, and now it was obvious—he wasn't having it. Colic can present with many symptoms, and he had them all. Sleep? No thanks. Breast milk? Not unless it was gluten and dairy free. Soothing? Not a chance. Car rides? Not unless you want vomit everywhere accompanied by constant screaming.

"What did we just get ourselves into? Was this normal?" I sadly asked myself. That question would easily become the most terrifying and painful question I had ever asked. I was so eager to become a mother and had felt sufficiently armed with my nursing background that was supposed to have made this chapter of life easier.

The first year of parenting is supposed to be beautiful, not traumatic, right? I knew this would be hard, but sheesh, I wasn't ready for this. I asked myself, "How do we navigate this?" We just started our marriage the year before and were still learning how to love each other, and now we have a child who challenged us to our core.

As a pediatric nurse, I was familiar with how to care for sick children who were afflicted with all kinds of medical problems. But it wasn't until I had a child of my own, that I understood the gravity of having the sole responsibility for another human being—a human who not only made living our day-to-day lives so difficult, but a human who we would die for, I mean literally die for. I wanted to see him happy, always. Yet, he was rarely content. And some days, I felt like I was drowning.

My neuroticism was strong, and my identity was slipping. I was struggling to find peace. We were holding on for a miracle and were trying everything we could to make this baby happy. We saw specialists, went to chiropractors, changed formulas and even tried scary procedures to correct his lip and tongue tie. (Lip and tongue ties occur when the tissues connecting the lip or tongue to the gums or floor of the mouth are too tight or thick, restricting movement and potentially affecting feeding, speech and dental health.) Our marriage started to suffer, and we quickly realized that this might shake us at our foundation.

By age two, Matty, as we called him, showed signs of speech delay and developmental differences that I knew were not typical. Mother's intuition was guiding me now, and the good Lord told me to attack. All I knew was, I had to act.

We started our journey with First Steps, a therapeutic program designed for developmentally delayed children aged 0-3. Still in denial, I thought, "I'll just get him evaluated to rule anything out. What will it hurt?" Well, he qualified for assistance. We started the program, and I got to work.

I immediately had him seen by the Washington University's Child Psychiatry Division. I wanted real answers. But I knew. My heart knew. My soul knew. I'll never forget that day when the doctors all gathered into a room to utter that word, the word that I feared more than any other word, the "A" word. I collapsed into my chair, feeling complete and utter despair, pure hopelessness. I began to cry.

The female neurologist looked at me and said, "Oh no honey, you don't understand. We need him. He is wonderful. He is essential in our world, and we can't live without people like Matthew. He is perfect." Wow. Something just shifted. I had never heard that before. I had never been asked to consider this perspective. Could she be right? Is this going to be OK? Is my son going to be okay? We were about to find out that he would be more than, "okay." He would be our teacher. He would show us the meaning of life itself.

Again, God was showing me the path and as with many journeys, the only way out is through. It was now March of 2020, and the pandemic hit the world, leaving no one unaffected. As horrible as COVID was, God showed us a silver lining that year and we used the time at home to our advantage.

I was blessed to be able to stay home with Matty, but now we had a new endeavor—his baby brother. COVID was now allowing Matt to work from home too, which was essential to meeting the demands of Matty's therapy and parenting two children under 3 years old.

Matty was approaching school age, and it was time to have our adorable little boy evaluated once again to see if he qualified for services through the school district. By now, we had done more than just a little therapy. We were doing hours of speech, language and occupational therapy every day, in and outside of our home. We even signed him up for a special medical program that provided intensive ABA (Applied Behavioral Analysis) therapy, which is designed specifically for children diagnosed with the "A" word. I was throwing myself into research and was now operating on the principle of, "We won't regret doing too much, but we could regret not doing enough."

We were rocking and rolling. Matthew was progressing at a rate the therapists had never seen. We saw miraculous gains and he showed immense progress. In fact, he was responding so well to the massive amount of intervention that some therapists even questioned his diagnosis. We had participated in so much therapy that the school was telling us that he was falling right on the line of meeting criteria for an IEP (Individualized Education Plan), and because of his improvement, we may not qualify for help.

So, wait a minute. We go above and beyond to help our son and the interventions are working, and your data now indicates that he's done, that he falls in the middle, in the gap? Just as he was about to start elementary school, the school district punishes us for doing our jobs as parents? I said, "Oh no. I don't think so." The gap is where children fail. It's where they fall through the cracks. The margins are where the system loses its effectiveness. I've watched this play out so many times with other families, families who have no idea how to advocate for their child and are at the mercy of following a complex and turbulent path, with little to no support. I would not let this happen to our precious son. He deserved the best. I was now a mother on a mission.

God was revealing my purpose—to show others how to speak for their precious children who couldn't speak for themselves. I would fight like hell to get my son the attention and help I knew he would need through his years of primary education, or at least through preschool. I understood the urgency of getting him help during his most formative years. I also knew that once these years pass, it can be too late to make an impact.

I spent months calling and emailing superintendents, the bosses of superintendents and every doctor and therapist I could to get to advocate for us. By now, I had written a novel on my son, a dissertation that outlined his entire life, that laid out a detailed timeline from the day he was born, to clearly illustrate his need for assistance.

My persistence paid off. God was showing me something new—that my love for my son could move mountains. Matt and I were learning that the only people who would decide his fate were us. It made us stronger—more resilient. If we could do this, we could do anything. The only people who would advocate for this little person we loved, was us. God trusts us this much, eh? Turns out, yeah. He sure does. We were now understanding what our true power was, what God's true power was.

After months of battling the school district, we had success at last. My son finally got his IEP. That qualified him for special services at school. We picked our family up and moved to a new county, where we would take our IEP and use it in a district that would truly deliver the resources he needed and support us as a family. We had a fresh start. Matthew was growing into a wonderful little person. He was brilliant, unique and to know him, was to love him.

We were learning that our son, could do so much more than we gave him credit for. He was excelling in all areas of development, and while we marveled at our first born, the doctors were curious to find out more about our special boy. Man, were they surprised at their discoveries.

Matty was entered into a worldwide genome sequencing database. This program is designed to compile a DNA collection to determine any genetic patterns they might find with others around the world with similar traits. As it turned out, Matty was one of a kind. He had a unique gene deletion on one protein, of one letter, of one gene that had never been seen before. Only six people in the world had this particular gene affected, but only he had this one letter out of place. It didn't even have a name.

They were chomping at the bit to see him in the office. I can remember the geneticist waiting at the door to get his eyes on my child. You see, the others around the world that had this gene affected were severely sick. They had short life spans and suffered greatly. So, when they saw my child, they were in shock. They measured every finger and every toe. They dissected him as if he were some medical miracle. Because he was.

The medical world could offer zero explanation and only tell us this: "Whatever you are doing, keep doing it, because your son is perfect." This was so eye-opening for Matt and I. Not only did this new information give us validation, but it affirmed the power of our Lord. My son was not a child with a disease. He was and is a true miracle and a precious gift.

The "A" word is just that—a word. It means nothing to us now. This label that I was so fearful of was merely a pathway. A pathway to freedom. Isn't that what faith is, after all—the trust that you are free?

Our journey has shown us that our son cannot fit into a box. He is made in the image of God, and only God will define him. We don't use the "A" word in our home. Matty doesn't have any idea that he carries this label because it is simply irrelevant. We choose not to live in fear. And for our family, to identify with this word, keeps us in fear. We don't have any idea where Matty will end up, but we do know it will be some place beautiful. We know that our son can do anything. He is an amazing person who has his own unique path. He will continue to thrive because his father and I will continue to stop at nothing to see that he has every possible resource and every ounce of love we can give.

Matt and I started our marriage with little purpose—two young, selfish people who did not understand true love. We understand it now. Love can be defined very easily. It is sacrifice. If it does not involve sacrifice, it cannot be love. Our son continues to inspire us, and we don't know where we would be without him and his brother. Life would have little meaning without these two. We now understand the power of love and have relied on this revelation to keep us hanging on. After almost a decade of marriage, we still have struggles, as every marriage does. But we can now look at each other and say, "Look at what we did. We made that. We made these completely unique little individuals who are happy and thriving." And that, my friends, is our purpose. The grandness of what we've accomplished is how we measure our success.

Matty is now 8 years old. He is the smartest kid I know. He does not require any special education or special services and is a bright second grader who loves school. This child who once worried us when he wouldn't speak, now needs to be told to be quiet. He is kind and shows empathy like no other. He loves learning about science and computers and exemplifies goodness. He enjoys life to the fullest. He is the most beautiful soul I know, and I'm honored to be his mother. I can't wait to see what he does in life. But one thing is for sure, he won't do it because he has autism. He will do it, because he is Matthew.

"For You formed my inward parts; You covered me in my mother's womb. I will praise You, for I am fearfully and wonderfully made; marvelous are Your works, and that my soul knows very well."

– Psalm 139: 13-15

ABOUT LENA JOHNSON

As a Missouri native, Lena has enjoyed living her whole life in the heart of the Midwest and currently resides in southern Missouri, where she publishes her community magazine, *Parkland City Lifestyle*. Inspired by her dear friends, Kelley Lamm and Gordon Montgomery, this longtime nurse learned she could make a larger impact on her community by sharing beautiful stories highlighting locals. She enjoys everything about her small community, where her and her husband Matt raise two young sons. She also enjoys a regular visit to the city, where she gets her fix of fancy dining and metro culture. She loves spending time with her family and attending church on Sundays, while running an Airbnb, raising chickens and baking sourdough at her historic home in downtown Farmington. She loves to teach line dancing and attend fitness classes with her girlfriends. Lena is the quintessential Missouri gal: a country girl who loves a taste of the city life. From float trips, campfires and barbecues to cocktail parties, pro sporting events and galas, Lena attests to "having it all" here in the Parkland.

Scan the QR code to watch a full interview with Lena

Megan Wilson

A BLANK PAGE

A blank piece of paper, a blank canvas, a blank wall in my home or even a blank screen on a computer, all scream for something to be created.

The first mark, the first brushstroke or the first thought can be the hardest to make. I know it has been for me. But if all the weight is put in one move, one brushstroke or one profound thought, we may miss out on what several marks, brushstrokes or thoughts may bring. All of the actions together, in whatever way they are presented, add a depth, dimension, texture and a fullness that you will never get with just one motion. I believe that can be the truth with how each of our stories unfold. Every detail matters, even the hard, the unexpected, the twists, the turns and everything in between. Those first marks may not make sense, but you keep going, you keep layering, you keep creating and something beautiful comes to life if you stick with it.

As a child, I always found joy in coloring, painting, drawing and everything in between. I would often be found creating for hours at a time. From the time I was a little girl, I've loved thinking outside of the box and challenging myself to create something completely different than anyone around me. It may be my stubbornness shining in all of its glory, or it could be a gift that was being developed and stretched from a young age. All of those moments as a child investing in creating whatever was in front of me added up to become a foundation on which I have grown and have fine-tuned my skills as the years have gone by.

As a visual person, I can often see a finished product in my mind before making that first hint of a design. You would think that having the ideas before starting would make the process that much easier to execute. But I can fall into the trap of doubt, overthinking and impostor syndrome quickly. "I'm not good enough," and "I'm not qualified," or "That idea will never work," and "There are so many people that could do it better," are thoughts that flood my mind even after years of experience. This has been a battle that I've had to face and overcome with each creative challenge. Being able to create, though, is a talent that God has given me, and it is my responsibility to share it and not keep it to myself.

Sometimes our greatest strengths can be our greatest weaknesses, and we can get in our own way. At least I have, and it is something I have to continue to develop and grow in.

Although stepping out as an artist has often been more of a battle of the mind for me, I am continuing to embrace this and gain confidence every day. I have tried my hand at several different art mediums and in many different areas, but I have struggled sticking with things. Despite this struggle, God has given me some incredible opportunities to step into, and they've almost all started with a simple conversation.

A conversation is a risk. But it gives you the opportunity to stretch yourself, be vulnerable, commit to new things, ask questions, learn, be curious and step into new opportunities that would never happen otherwise. A conversation allows you to put yourself out there and not stay on the nice, comfortable sidelines. You can't guarantee that the outcome of a conversation will be good or bad, but you will never know what could be if it was never even started. I am continuing to deepen my understanding of the power found in conversations. Not only is dialogue with others impactful, but having friends and a community surrounding you, speaking life into your gifts and talents, is vital and can help build courage and confidence along your journey. There have been several friends who have believed in my gifts, and God has used them to bring new opportunities to me to create.

Becoming a children's book illustrator has been a result of both a conversation and friends connecting me with the right people at the right time, and I am forever grateful. I always thought it would be amazing to illustrate a children's book, but never knew how to go about it or even thought that it was something I could accomplish. But God knows your heart's desires and interests without your having to speak them out loud.

Taking someone's manuscript and making it come to life was something that I didn't know I was fully capable of. But after the initial connection with the author and the support and encouragement surrounding me, I was able to make it happen. The stirring and pondering over each page to come up with something that would grab the attention of the reader was challenging in a creative way I hadn't stretched myself before.

It was not giving all of the story away, but just enough that the reader couldn't wait to turn the page. I was able to bring more than just illustrations. I brought in the creative gift that God has given me to give it a unique twist with things that include hand lettering, word illustrations and hidden easter eggs throughout the book. These are intentional details that the common eye wouldn't just notice, and a color palette that could draw people in.

Having the opportunity to make a vision of a manuscript come to life through illustrations was not something I took lightly, and it became a new space where I found joy. I could not have done this on my own, and it is surreal to know that a character that was only described through words on paper now has color, personality and has been used as a tool to encourage thousands of people all over the United States to lean in and shine in their gifts. It's not about me at all, but it makes me want to continue to create so God can use me as a vessel to encourage others wherever they are.

Illustrating my first children's book, "Rosie Finds Her Shine," brought confidence and excitement about what other illustrations I could tap into. This led to illustrating more children's books, including "Night Magic" and "Anabeth's Question About Heaven," which included authors from New York to Missouri and down to Georgia. This project opened my eyes to so many other possibilities that are out there. You really don't know what you don't know until you push yourself to do new things.

My curiosity grew to what other opportunities might be available, and as my circle of influence continued to expand and I challenged myself to start more conversations, I was given the opportunity to use my gifts to design, curate and decorate an 1871 historic building that had been renovated into a boutique hotel. It may not have been drawing out characters on pages or designing layouts with a manuscript, but I was able to take everything that I collected through my creative background and attack this project with intentionality that executed all of the details for a guest to walk in and not only have a place to stay but also a place to soak in the history of the building.

People can enjoy the different color palettes, the original artwork hanging on the walls, the painted murals, a custom scent that welcomes you at the door, carefully selected furniture found in antique stores from all over the state, and details that offer a truly unique experience when staying at the inn.

For me, creating something from nothing is such an exciting opportunity to stretch my mind, to share my inspiration and to create an experience that may impact someone in a way I will never know if I don't step out and make it happen.

I have found my calling to use my artistry to create as those opportunities and challenges come along. It may not have always come easily to step out and face my fears. It hasn't shown up in a nice tidy box with a pretty bow that is always predictable and consistent, but there is still beauty created and purpose with every project. And each project might be a little different—from illustrating pages in a book, walls in a hotel, or whatever might be waiting for me around the corner—but they have deep meaning that I have grown to appreciate.

Looking back, every blank space—whether a page, a room or even a moment of hesitation—was an invitation, an invitation to begin, to trust that even when I didn't feel ready, the act of starting would shape me.

Creativity isn't about having it all figured out. It's about showing up again and again, with curiosity and courage. Each project, each conversation and each step into the unknown has reminded me that we are all artists of some kind, shaping something out of what seems like nothing. So, start the conversation. Make the mark. Say yes before you feel ready. You never know what masterpiece is waiting on the other side.

ABOUT MEGAN WILSON

Megan Wilson is an artist that brings a creative twist to everything she touches. Her desire and heart behind creating is to bring joy and encouragement to others through her art. She has illustrated several children's books that include whimsical hand lettering and hidden easter eggs throughout the book to leave a reader with an experience of wanting to come back and read the book over and over again. Megan has not only brought words on a paper to life through art, but she has also been a part of renovating a historic building that has turned into a boutique hotel that is a one-of-a-kind experience with original artwork, handpicked antique furniture, custom color palettes and intentional details throughout. Currently, you will find Megan teaching art full time to both elementary school and advanced high school students at Clopton Schools located in Clarksville, Mo. She lives with her husband and four children in a rural town north of St. Louis. As she pours into students to encourage the next generation in fine arts, her desire to continue her creative endeavors alongside her students remains a priority. She can't wait for her next creative opportunity to make another project come to life!

Scan the QR code to watch a full interview with Megan

Monica Adams-Quentin

THE AWAKENING:
FINDING STRENGTH AND PURPOSE
WHEN LIFE THROWS YOU OFF COURSE

Where do you go in your mind, your spirit and your heart when all of your childhood dreams fall apart? How do you respond to the paralyzing words that you may not live? My dreams of changing the world through medicine, health, fitness and healing athletes came to a crashing halt when the words: "You have a massive blood clot" came out of my doctor's mouth in 1990.

I start with this realization because in the journey of your life, there is often an awakening—wherever you met the turn in the road that catapulted you forward. I'm not saying the journey will be easy or that you will know immediately what your purpose is. I am saying when you pay attention to your gut instinct and the whispers from your guiding source, you start to realize the path is always being laid out in front of you. The question is, do you follow it or do you resist?

To a child, an obstacle course brings with it excitement and a mental challenge that, when completed, brings a sense of fulfillment and reward. As adults, we hear obstacle and form an automatic aversion in our minds, as if one thing thrown in our path creates a stopping point with no possible detour. The reality is there will always be forks in the road. It's how you mentally confront your obstacles that sets you on the course for success or failure.

I chose to accept the path that was laid before me and greet it head on as if to say, "Bring it, and I will accept it, and I will multiply the possibilities of the role I play in changing the world."

As I take you through my story, allow your heart and soul to open and hear your own story playing out. You may have picked up this book and believed your ending had already been written. My hope is that you will go back to your stopping point and find that your journey is only beginning, and that there are endless opportunities of where the fork in the road will lead you.

Wherever the walk of life has taken you, or what you've gone through, the truth is, we are all on this journey together. And through the twists and turns in the road, we will navigate our way through the storm and come out a better version of ourselves.

Big Dreams

From an early age I knew I wanted to go into medicine and health and fitness. I was an extremely active child, involved in dance, gymnastics, cheerleading, soccer, softball and basketball. I was never pushed by my parents. Instead, I was guided to be the best I could be at whatever I was pursuing. I have never known a life of slowing down. I woke up then and still do, with a sense of vigor to attack the world and give it all I have.

I was fortunate to play soccer at a collegiate level. I attended a small university on a soccer scholarship in my first year. The town and academia didn't interest me, but I am glad that stop happened on my journey, because it showed me that sometimes a slower paced life is needed to allow you to appreciate the time just before everything takes off. I listened to the whispers from above instead of ignoring them. I transferred to the University of Missouri-Columbia and was elated with every day that brought me closer to my dreams of helping athletes heal and get back in their game.

I enrolled in the sports medicine program with an even greater dream to become an orthopedic surgeon. I could smell, see and taste the life that I was going to lead. After all, it is what I had set out to do when I was only seven years old. My mom would tell you that when I set my mind on something, there is no one that can stop me. That's what I thought too.

My time at MIZZOU was short-lived, yet it is the most profound turning point in my life, outside of losing my father only five years later. A devastating blow would happen only three short weeks into my time at the university, yet it will always be where I go for strength when I feel I can't do something, or when someone tries to block my vision. I had no idea what was coming would throw me on a path to change the world. God wanted me to lead here on Earth through His words, His vision and the story He wanted for me. It would confirm my thoughts that I am one of His chosen.

The First Fork In The Road

Let me set the tone for what would eventually be the most pivotal moment of my life. Excitement was building for our first collegiate game in September of 1990. I had injured my back in practice, and I knew I had to get the injury under control or face losing my opportunity to be the starting goaltender. I went to the chiropractor, had X-rays taken and was told to slow down, or face having long-term injuries reappearing later in life. The injury was pretty extensive but not enough to make me miss practice or set my mind for our first game.

I recall the morning before everything came crashing down. I was set to go to my physics class that morning, but I was in such excruciating pain that I called my mom (who was 3 hours away) asking if she could come get me and take me home to see our family chiropractor. I hoped he could get me healed and back to fulfill my dreams. I told her I was going to stay at the dorm and miss class. My normal 20-minute walk to class had become so arduous due to the pain, that the time it took to get to the building had almost tripled. My mom said to ice my back and try to relax and that she would be driving up after she got off work.

As each minute passed, I became more and more anxious. The pain was only getting worse and the anxiety started to kick in. Yet I didn't understand why. I must have called her asking when she was coming five times that morning, as it felt like days had passed from the first call I made. I had no idea a ticking bomb was forming inside of me.

The pain got so bad that my final call to her was to tell her I was calling 911 and taking an ambulance literally across the street. By this time my legs had started swelling, and eventually my right leg was too tight to straighten. It seemed every second brought a new obstacle.

This news sent shivers down my mom's spine, because my pain tolerance is high. For me to suddenly shift gears and want to go to the hospital made no sense to anyone. My guide from above was done whispering.

This was a smack in the face to get to the doctor. I made that call and within seconds sirens were blaring and across the street I went to finally get some answers.

In 45 minutes, an acting physician would see me and dismiss me. He diagnosed me with "a pinched nerve that was cutting off circulation." Although I was new to my studies in medicine, I knew this wasn't medically possible. The doctor couldn't get a pulse in my ankle. My legs were cold and tight. But none of this seemed to concern him. I felt like I was on Candid Camera.

He told me I could leave, although I couldn't walk. So, he wheeled me out to the front of the hospital hoping someone would be there to pick me up. My best friend was there as my ride or die. She was there to help calm my mind and my spirit and transfer me to the next part of my journey.

The Pivotal Point Of The Journey Shows Itself

My mom and boyfriend were 3 hours away and drove separately to come rescue me, scared for what they were hearing and eventually seeing in me, but not wanting to show their fear. Everyone knew something had to be very wrong but were puzzled by the dismissal from the hospital. They also didn't want to break my spirit as they could tell I was hell bent on getting back to my classes and on with my life.

We made the trip home, and as I sit here writing this, I can feel tears form, as I witnessed my mom, my true hero in life, make that long drive up to be with her baby only to selflessly tell me I could drive with my boyfriend and she would follow us back home. She is always so giving and always there to rescue her children. Mom, I wish I had driven with you that day as I can only imagine what was going through your mind. Maybe God and you had to talk and you needed silence to prepare you for what was coming. Whatever the reason, I thank you from the bottom of my heart for always being there to help calm me.

The next morning we went to our family chiropractor, who was the most amazing physician I have ever known. His excellence in his field was matched by his candor and soothing ways of healing you from the inside out. He saw me that day, and you could tell in his eyes he knew something far beyond a back injury was wrong. In fact, he diagnosed exactly what would eventually be my fate but did so just by sight.

The smartest thing my doctor did that morning was not adjust me for fear something greater was forming inside of me. He followed his own gut instinct. Every move made by every person that was thrown into this story allowed for this to be written and to hopefully help you slow down enough in your own life to help you on your journey.

I went home that day and got in the jetted tub to help ease the pain that continued. What happened when my mom went to pull me out of the tub stopped her in her tracks. A massive lump had formed on the inside of my leg on top of the swelling that had increased in my legs.

None of us saw the signs of what was really wrong with me, because we had believed what the doctor in Columbia, Mo. had told us. The chiropractor, in a field that many traditional doctors laughed at, nailed the diagnosis just from gut instinct and his own intuition.

The lump that formed in my leg sent my mom screaming for my dad to pack things up and take me to the hospital again. A 60-picture cat scan was taken, and they chose to admit me since at this point, they didn't know what was causing the pain, the swelling, the lack of a pulse in my ankle or the coldness you could feel in the temperature change on my skin. There were so many signs that, at this stage of my life, make me say, "Really? How was this missed by so many?

The next morning the doctor came in and said they still didn't know what it was and would keep trying to figure it out. But we may never know. No sooner did he leave my hospital room then he came sprinting back to the room telling me not to move. The next words would change my life forever.

Here Is What I Learned From That Life-Altering Experience

I was raised in a very Christian household, and while I had a wonderful relationship with God, this experience took my faith to an entirely new level. It is so true that God would never have us go through something so horrific without being by our side to carry us through.

I believe we have to endure challenges to understand that we can grow stronger and make it through anything. The earlier we realize that ultimately we are not in control, and that he is and learn to lean on him for guidance, the clearer our path will be. I promised Him if he saved my life that I would forever speak kindness and change the world on a grand scale led by his example. I want to be remembered for this phrase when I am no longer on this earth: "The greatest rewards in life come from the most uncomfortable walk."

*This story continues in a book I will be releasing. So be sure to follow TheRealMonicaAdams.com for a launch date and to hear how it would lead me to a field where I would come into your homes for the next 30 years and tell stories of hope and positivity and motivate you to be all you can be!

ABOUT MONICA ADAMS-QUENTIN

I want to thank you for allowing me a seat in your home, whether through radio or television, for the past three decades. It's been an honor to entertain and inform St. Louis for a great majority of my life. At the age of 19, I was told I was a miracle patient after suffering the largest blood clot in medical history. In surviving that ordeal, I knew I would focus on dedicating myself to making an impact on this world. Since then, it's been my goal to change lives through health, wellness and storytelling. I am now even more inspired to affect this world like never before, and I invite you along on this journey with me! I look forward to meeting you, and to challenging you to discover your full potential.

Business Resume

Monica Adams is the host and executive producer for her highly successful talk show "The Real Monica Adams Show" which is seen daily LIVE on multiple platforms. Monica and her team are getting ready to celebrate 500 shows in less than two years. Prior to her launch in 2023, Monica was a news director in radio for WIL, KDHR/KHAD and KJCF/KTJJ for 12 years. She hosted a health and fitness show on KMOX radio in St. Louis for eight years. While on radio, Monica also served as an assistant sports director, covering the St. Louis Blues, Cardinals and Rams. Additionally, Monica was part of a CMA award-winning morning team for WIL country radio, for eight years. She then transitioned to television in 2005, working for FOX affiliate KTVI, and holding roles in traffic, entertainment, fitness and health, and reporting. Monica most recently served as the morning anchor on KSDK television, the NBC affiliate in St. Louis. During her time there, she created two successful series, one known as "Monica's Motivational Moments" and "Monica In The Metro," producing, writing and editing pieces covering all aspects of wellness both during and after the pandemic. She also started her own entertainment pieces, which aired from 2000-2022, where she showcases current movies at the box office, highlighting A-list actors.

Monica has written extensively for Travelhost and Streetscape magazine, covering many lifestyle pieces and showcasing many facets of St. Louis and its history. She is a proficient host, reporter, writer, producer and anchor, and has also shot and edited many of her own pieces.

Monica is generous and extremely charitably minded; working with multiple nonprofit organizations, she has served as a brand spokesperson, motivational speaker, emcee and auctioneer for almost 30 years. She has been honored with multiple awards, including the Missouri Broadcaster's A.I.R. awards, and has been part of Emmy collaboration wins numerous times, for both FOX and NBC.

Outside of broadcasting, Monica is a personal transformation specialist, having studied sports medicine and physical therapy, and holding multiple certifications as a personal trainer and wellness specialist. Monica has been a personal trainer for 26 years, designing programs for several corporations, while also holding private events where she teaches her own Transformation Journey Program. She has worked as director of Wellness for Essence, Esse Healthcare and Innovare Healthcare, designing programs for seniors and specially designing programs for an orthopedic surgeon, serving as his main rehab trainer.

Monica has a passion for style and design, and enjoys serving as a design and wardrobe consultant, specializing in men's fashion. She worked with Bachrach Menswear for seven years and is now with Bespoke in Clayton, Mo. She has recently released her new women's clothing line called "Know Your Value by Monica Adams." It features athletic wear and classy, trendy business apparel.

Personally, Monica is married to a Lieutenant with the St. Louis County police and is a big supporter of all of the first responders. She and her husband have three dogs they have rescued, they love to travel, have a deep appreciation for the arts, are big foodies, and love to give back to the community, together. Monica has most recently taken up piano lessons and looks forward to pursuing music in the coming years.

Scan the QR code to watch
a full interview with Monica

Nicole Newkirk

POOLSIDE WITH A PAST:
FROM SURVIVING TO DESIGNING THE DREAM

I never saw it coming—not the darkness, not the despair, not the moment I stared at my reflection in the bathroom mirror, tears blurring the once-familiar face staring back at me, silently praying for a different life. Before that moment, it all began like the perfect fairytale.

He was magnetic, intoxicating and charming in a way that made people simply gravitate toward him. A natural salesman, he could sell sand in the desert. From the beginning, he showered me with gifts, extravagant gestures and promises of a life most people only dream of. Weekend getaways turned into romantic vacations, and whispered confessions of love soon gave way to a huge glittering diamond on my finger. It was a whirlwind—a fantasy world he created with the precision of a masterful con artist. One of his favorite lines was, "You're the best sale I've ever made." Back then, I used to laugh. I believed it was a compliment. But looking back, those words carried a weight I didn't yet understand.

We were married within a year.

It wasn't until after the marriage papers were signed, and the door was shut on my independence, that his mask started slipping. Cracks began to show in the seemingly perfect exterior of the charismatic, loving man I thought I had married. Words turned sharp. Arguments spiraled into manipulation. I was not just his wife. I became his possession. And when manipulation wasn't enough, his hands spoke the words his mouth couldn't.

The first time he hit me, I convinced myself it was a mistake, an anomaly. He apologized, gave me a new Chanel purse and promised it would never happen again. But it did. It happened again and again. With every apology, the contents of my closet grew a little more until it overflowed with luxury items.

The lies I'd tell and the bruises I'd hide on my body became nothing compared to the bruises to my spirit.

I was trapped in a prison invisible to the outside world, chained to his unhealthy "love" full of anger, abuse and control. He was convincing, brilliant even, and he knew exactly how to keep me tethered. In the depths of the nightmare, there were fragments of light—threads I wouldn't see clearly until much later.

My ex-husband was relentless in his drive for success, not just for himself but through me. He pushed me to learn business strategies, sharpen my negotiation skills and master the technical intricacies of AutoCad and 2D and 3D design renderings. Though at first it felt like another layer of control, the lessons would eventually become my means of escape.

I threw everything into the work. Growing our business and visualizing outdoor spaces became addictive, as my business and design skills improved. For a time, it distracted me from the harsh reality of my marriage. But over time, a painful truth began to settle in. No matter how much success the business experienced, no matter how much of my heart and talent I poured into it, it was not mine. He claimed ownership of everything we created.

I was 27 years old and beginning to think about the future, about becoming a mother. But that thought alone broke me open. It wouldn't just be my life he would destroy. The idea of bringing a child into the cruelty and control I experienced was unbearable. I couldn't allow an innocent, precious life to endure the chaos and violence that had become my reality.

Somewhere in the mix of love for the future I wanted, and anger for the life I had been denied, a deep realization struck me. That realization ignited a spark. I began crafting a vision, a meticulous and bold blueprint to reclaim my freedom. I visualized a fresh start—a life full of happiness, connection and independence—wherein I could reconnect with my family and friends, those relationships he had worked so calculatingly to isolate me from. I wanted to rebuild myself and my life and share it with a child, free from the shadows—a life I was always meant to live.

Even as the condescension and cruelty escalated and the abuse persisted, a quiet revolution began to take root within me. It was as if a heavy curtain was being drawn back, granting me a glimpse of the existence I was meant for—a life imbued with elegance, self-respect and limitless potential. Every demeaning word tested the limits of my tolerance, while every attempt at control sharpened my determination to reclaim my narrative. This awakening was profound, almost indulgent, as though I had been ushered into an exclusive realm where I was no longer a prisoner of his distorted world, but instead, the sovereign curator of my own extraordinary story.

This decision wasn't easy. But it was the turning point. Light began to shine into the cracks of my life, and though I was terrified of what lay ahead, I knew I couldn't stay in the darkness any longer.

Starting over wasn't just a step. It was a mountain I had to climb, one painstaking step at a time. I began planning in secret, quietly building the foundation for my next chapter. I bought essentials—anything I thought I might need to stand on my own once I finally broke free. Each small act felt like its own rebellion, a quiet promise to myself that my future would someday be mine again.

I sought out a counselor who specialized in abusive relationships, someone who understood the complexities of dealing with individuals with narcissistic and anti-social personality traits. Those therapy sessions became a safe-haven for me. Counseling allowed me to step back and see my life from an outsider's perspective who was trained to deal with the difficulties I was going through. It gave me clarity, strength and the tools to understand myself in ways I never had before. Therapy became a lifeline, drawing me toward an unshakable sense of self-worth. To this day, I passionately advocate for seeking guidance from a professional who specializes in the challenges you face. That choice redefined my life in unimaginable ways, serving as a testament to the power of healing and personal growth.

Still, I knew I couldn't do it alone, and I'm forever grateful for the unparalleled blessings of the support system in my life—my incredible parents, supportive brother, cherished family and loyal best friends. They stood by me with unwavering strength and unconditional love, guiding me through one of the most challenging and transformative chapters of my journey.

My first big step toward freedom came on a day most people associate with love. On Valentine's Day, while others exchanged cards and roses,

I sat with my divorce attorney and signed the petition to be filed the following week. That moment marked the end of a relationship built on control and the beginning of a life of freedom, where I could finally breathe again.

But leaving was only the beginning. The road ahead would test me in ways I could never have imagined. This was an incredibly hard time for me, one that forced me to be ruthless and make decisions, some of which I am not necessarily proud, to protect myself and my future. I locked my ex-husband out of our bank accounts and pushed him out of our business, which was solely in my name. It was a painful, calculated move, but a necessary one to reclaim control over my life. With him out of the picture, I continued to run the business on my own, pouring every ounce of my energy into it to keep it afloat.

Many of our employees stayed loyal to me through the chaos that followed.

My ex-husband refused to go quietly. He vandalized job sites, sabotaged projects and even created a competing company with a nearly identical name. He added unauthorized materials to my vendor accounts, racking up debts in my name. He maxed out my credit cards and did everything in his power to destroy me, convinced I would crumble under the weight of it all. But he underestimated me. He never dreamed I would be strong enough to leave, much less to thrive.

With every attack he launched, I pushed back harder. I survived the sabotage, resolved the financial messes and kept selling jobs, one by one. Each new contract I signed, and every project I completed became a victory, not just for my business, but for me. Leaning on the skills I had cultivated during my marriage—business strategies, creative problem-solving and razor-sharp negotiation—I found my stride. Design was no longer just my job. It was my passion. Imagining serene, beautiful spaces for others to share and create memories in with their families and loved ones, gave me purpose. Each design I created felt like a piece of me finding its way back home. Every success, no matter how small, reminded me that I had not only survived, but I had reclaimed my life using my skills, hard work and determination.

Love was the last thing I wanted or even thought possible after everything I had been through. But sometimes, the most beautiful things find us when we are not looking. But there he was—my "Pool Boy." I like to tease and call him that, but the truth is, the label does not capture the depth of who he truly is. Beyond the playful nickname, he became so much more than I could have imagined. His presence was like a breath of fresh air breaking through the heaviness of my past and reminding me of the beauty life still held. With his unwavering belief in me, he inspired a courage I thought I had lost forever. He taught me to dream again, to see possibilities where I once saw walls. He was not only my partner but my constant source of encouragement and the spark that reignited my passion for living fully and authentically—the one God knew I needed.

This wasn't a relationship built on dependence or control. It was a partnership of equals. It was everything my past had not been—full of balance, mutual respect and unwavering support. Together, we created a life rooted in laughter, adventure and living for the present. There were no games, no manipulations, no contests for power or wealth—just a genuine connection that celebrated joy and freedom. He reminded me that love, in its truest form, can be empowering, liberating and extraordinary.

We embarked on unforgettable adventures together, moments that felt like dreams. For the first time, I tried surfing. My heart was racing as the waves carried me forward. We hiked for hours, wandering through lush trails that led to hidden waterfalls. Hana, Hawaii, will forever be imprinted on my soul. A destination unlike any other, it is breathtaking and sacred, alive with beauty and spirit. It was as though the universe had whispered its secrets to us there.

It wasn't long after that unforgettable adventure that we received the most incredible news—I was pregnant with our beautiful daughter, Hana Jaymes. Her name, a tribute to that magical place, felt predestined. She was a part of me long before I held her in my arms—a wish I had quietly carried in my heart for years. The moment she entered my life, everything aligned. She became my light, my reason, my everything. Being her mother is a gift beyond measure—a joy so profound. It is, without question, my proudest accomplishment.

That chapter of my life, unplanned yet divinely orchestrated, became my greatest blessing. Through love, adventure and the power of motherhood, I rediscovered who I truly was. No longer defined by my struggles,

I felt unstoppable—thriving, happy and more alive than I had imagined possible. Together, we had unknowingly manifested Hana, and she was the most beautiful expression of everything we shared and everything I dreamt of becoming.

Becoming parents to our incredible daughter and building a business alongside my fiancé and lifelong partner has been a truly remarkable journey. It's been a path defined by growth, resilience and an unwavering shared vision. Over the course of 11 years, what began as an adventurous love story, blossomed into something extraordinary—a beautiful family, a flourishing business and a partnership filled with profound meaning and fulfillment. Although our story isn't one of fairy tale perfection, it is a testament to hard work, mutual respect and the relentless pursuit of shared goals.

Our relationship thrives on passion and laughter, but it works because we challenge each other, grow individually, forgive and adapt to life's challenges. Together, we have built Oasis Pools, a luxury swimming pool and outdoor design company, and along the way, learned what it takes to balance the demands of business, parenting and friendship.

Outside of Oasis Pools, I began to feel a pull toward a more personal endeavor—one that allows me to share my voice in a different way. I have launched Not Your Average Life, a lifestyle brand rooted in the belief that luxury is not just about money, but about a mindset—a way of seeing the world and creating beauty, joy and abundance right where you are. For me, luxury is about taking control of your life and curating a space that feels rich with meaning, intention and high-vibrational energy. My mission is to inspire others everywhere to step into their power and realize they, too can craft a life that feels undeniably beautiful, rewarding and uniquely theirs, redefining luxury and showing others that they have the strength and originality to design a world beyond their wildest dreams.

Looking back on my journey, I can see that every scar, every tear, every challenging obstacle was part of a greater version of myself. I am no longer the broken woman crying in the bathroom mirror. I am a survivor, a business owner and a mother with a story worth telling.

But this story isn't just about me. To every woman who feels trapped, every woman who has questioned her worth, every woman who sees no way out, I need you to hear this.

You are stronger than you realize. The fire you think has burned out is still there waiting for oxygen. You do not have to have all the answers. It starts with a single prayer, a single decision, a single step forward.

And if you take those steps, no matter how small, you'll find that your darkest moments don't have to define you. Those cracks where the light comes in are your foundation. And from that foundation, you can build something extraordinary—a business, a dream, an empire, a life that is yours and yours alone.

ABOUT NICOLE NEWKIRK

Nicole Newkirk is an award-winning swimming pool and outdoor living space designer, known for blending luxury with functionality. As the co-owner of Oasis Pools and the visionary founder and CEO of NYA Group (Not Your Average Pool Girl), Nicole has been delivering unforgettable designs that capture the heart of outdoor living for more than 15 years. Her achievements include being named Pool Nation's Top 25 Pool Builders, earning the prestigious 2024 Pinnacle Award from *Luxury Pools and Outdoor Living Magazine*, and recognition on *Pool Pro Magazine's* "30 Under 40" list. Showcasing her achievements in a field where women remain underrepresented, her work has graced platforms like the *Landscaping Network*, *Clayton City Lifestyle magazine*, *Ocean & Home*, and numerous other publications throughout the years.

Breaking barriers in a male-dominated industry, Nicole's dedication to research, knowledge, and an unwavering commitment to her vision has set her apart. With an education from Webster University and proficiency in design and AutoCAD, she has demonstrated that expertise and elegance can coexist seamlessly. Through her passion for outdoor design, Nicole has created spaces where families can enjoy lasting memories in a beautifully designed space.

With Oasis Pools and NYA Group, Nicole continues to transform poolscapes to breathtaking outdoor retreats offering clients a VIP experience that redefines poolside elegance. Nicole's philosophy embodies the idea that swimming pools are not mere water features but the focal point of an unparalleled lifestyle. Luxury is not a privilege but a lifestyle choice. Nicole continues to thrive in the world of outdoor living, creating bespoke experiences that redefine what it means to be poolside.

Scan the QR code to watch
a full interview with Nicole

Randi Naughton

THANKS DAD

Growing up as the fifth child in a family of seven, I definitely had to work harder to get what I wanted. When you're lost in the shuffle of a blue-collar family of nine, things are not handed to you.

When I was as young as 12, I was earning money babysitting and picking fruit and vegetables on local farms. It wasn't much money, but it sure taught me what hard work really means. In my teens, I worked in restaurants as a waitress, then later as a bartender. These were some of my favorite jobs. You will never work harder to earn your money than in those types of jobs. I enjoyed the work immensely and developed skills that would serve me for a lifetime.

When I turned 16 years old, my father told me that I was now responsible for my own lunch money and my own school clothes. After some griping that it wasn't fair—as would be expected from a teenager—I happily accepted that challenge. He once told me a person doesn't deserve anything unless they work hard for it. I believe my father's sage advice resonated with me powerfully throughout my career. When I moved to St. Louis, Mo. with my husband in the late 1980s, I had some radio and television experience from my time in Buffalo, New York.

I started hitting the phones and sending letters even before we moved back to the Midwest. By the time I got to St. Louis, I had a part-time radio job already lined up. I was also quite the pest as I consistently contacted television news directors looking for even a part-time gig.

Eventually, my pestering paid off. After being told time and time again that the news director was in a meeting and he couldn't talk to me, I finally got a call.

I got that part-time gig with St. Louis' KTVI Chanel 2 as an entertainment and lifestyle reporter in 1992. At the same time, I also worked part-time at KYKY-98.1 FM radio.

In 1994, when the U.S. Olympic Festival was being hosted by the city of St. Louis, and KTVI was one of the gold sponsors, I saw a chance to elevate my game—no pun intended. The KTVI sports staff was short-handed at the time. So I went into the news director's office and said boldly, "Let me be a sports reporter to help cover the Olympic Festival. You need the help."

The boss had only known me as the lifestyle reporter, so he asked me if I had ever reported on sports. I said no, but told him I had played numerous sports in high school. I had run track and played volleyball, basketball, tennis and softball. I also told him what a huge sports fan I am (another thing I can thank my dad for), and that I'm a very curious person. I explained to him I would just go to the sporting event, find out what's going on, and report the facts.

He hired me. And that's how my sports broadcasting career began. I took my dad's advice into that office with me and asked for what I wanted. I thought, "What is the worst that could happen?" And he could have said no. But he didn't. They were short-handed at the time and I saw it as an opportunity.

I believe that moment was the catalyst for my long broadcasting career. I was named a sports reporter and eventually KTVI's weekend sports anchor in the early 1990s. At the time, I was pretty much one of the only female sports reporters doing this in a medium to major market.

Today, female sports reporters are everywhere. And I love it.

I went to Spring Training. I went to the NHL playoffs. I went to Super Bowls. I covered the World Series. I was in the dugout. I was in the locker rooms. I carried equipment for the St. Louis Rams in the Dome at America Center Convention Complex. I experienced the daily grind.

I saw some amazing historic sports moments, but I was there for the everyday grunt work also. Yes, it was hard work. But I loved it.

My time as a female sports reporter in the early 1990s did not come without some pushback from some of the male reporters in the market. Yes, even from my own newsroom, I heard pretty much everything you could hear regarding women in sports broadcasting. What does she know? Why is she here? She doesn't belong. In a market like St. Louis that is so deeply rooted in sports traditions, there were people who acted like I was invading their turf.

Well, being a sports fan—and doing my homework regarding teams, transactions, rosters, standings, etc.—I took pride in immersing myself in all of it.

I heard it from the viewers as well. "You should be reporting on more female sports because you're a female." Well, it doesn't work that way. One time, I remember I was sitting in an airport waiting for a flight, and a man saw my media credential for the St. Louis Rams on my luggage and asked whether I was a cheerleader. I quickly corrected him and said, "No. I am the sideline reporter during games." I got the eye roll, the shoulder shrug. So he decided to test me on the team and asked me about players, positions and numbers. I handed him the Rams media guide and proceeded to name most of the roster, their positions and jersey numbers. His eyebrows raised at my knowledge and that I had passed his "quiz." It was a light-hearted moment, but one that I enjoyed nonetheless. I'm not going to lie—I thoroughly enjoyed schooling that guy.

I never let any of that bother me during my days in sports journalism as I also considered that a challenge. I had seemingly more to prove. Any mistake, even a small one, would be amplified. I'll always be proud of my time covering sports. I remember one time I was traveling with the Rams to Buffalo to cover the game there. I was on the phone with my producer working out satellite coordinates for live shots. My father overheard all of this. He was an old-school kind of guy and really didn't know much about that world. He was a little bit taken aback by my conversation with the producers back in St. Louis as he overheard the game plan for coverage. He just looked at me and said, "Wow. I'm proud of you." That's a moment I won't forget.

I reluctantly transitioned out of the sports department to Fox 2 News in the Morning in 1999 and stayed on the air in that time slot for 23 years.

The schedule consisted of getting up literally in the middle of the night at around 1:30 or 2 a.m., stepping in the door at work between 3 and 3:30 a.m., checking scripts, producing segments, having my hair and makeup done and then being on the air anywhere between 2 to 4 hours a day. I would sign off the air when it was only 9 a.m. Then I'd take a couple of hours to prepare for the next day and be home by 1 p.m. Bedtime was around 7 p.m.

I had to turn down many dinner invitations and evening events because of that schedule. As grueling as it may sound, I will say it was the best schedule I could ask for as a working mother. My daughter and I went to bed around the same time every night. I was able to make every parent-teacher conference, every practice for after-school activities and every major milestone. I believe that being there for her so consistently is one of the reasons she and I are very close to this day.

Many of the viewers who followed me over the years watched my daughter grow up. She is now married with a wonderful husband and a great career. Some people say we not only look alike, but I definitely see her drive and determination in the work she does, not only in her job as a property manager for a St. Louis company, but as an equestrian as well. She has been riding horses since she was 11 years old, and she has such a competitive and driven spirit. Her father is a former professional athlete, so I think she got her competitiveness and drive from both of us. I definitely see glimpses of me in her. I could not be more proud of the woman she has become.

One night, in the winter of 2022, I was driving to work in the middle of the night, and I was doing the math. I realized I started at the station in 1992 and here it was 2022. Holy cow—30 years! That's a long time and a really good number. I decided it was time to step away from that and leave my television job in July of 2022.

Today, I enjoy being the host of my podcast "More to Say with Randi Naughton." It is a variety-type podcast where we have interesting conversations with interesting people. My guests range from sports figures to authors to people in the entertainment world and change-makers. This allows me to fulfill my curiosity and learn a lot of new things—like how to navigate a podcast and everything that comes with it, for example, maintaining social media and heavily promoting it. I'm not great at it yet, but I think I'm making good progress. I've always loved to learn and grow, and this platform is the perfect space for that.

I also work part-time on talk radio, and I am also continuing to run my voice-over and narration business from my home recording studio. You can hear my voice on commercials, web tutorials, video games, movie dubbing, audiobooks and phone systems all around the world. I have some great clients and we have maintained wonderful relationships.

I've recently revamped my website, RandiNaughton.com, with everything you need to know about me and what I'm up to.

So, I'm not really "retired." I'm just doing lots of other things differently. Not having to maintain a morning show schedule is allowing me to do many things that I was previously restricted from doing.

Those who know me may also know that I'm a huge animal lover. I've worked with numerous animal charities over the years and all of my pets have been rescued. In fact, I rescued a mini horse who came from an abusive situation and who was in terrible shape. He was malnourished and had a terribly infected eye injury. I rescued him and got him the medical attention he needed. Unfortunately, the veterinarians could not save his eye, so it had to be removed. That's where I came up with his name: Uno. Today, he visits parties, community gatherings and senior homes through my business called "Uno to Go." It's adorable to watch kids have a pony painting party. Uno loves it, and the interaction with this amazing little guy brings smiles to so many faces. Uno has his own Facebook and Instagram pages as well.

I'm also always snapping photos of birds, animals and nature.

I very much love to cook and feed people. For some reason, chopping vegetables has such a calming effect on me. It's a simple joy, but one I truly treasure.

I made so many friends in my 30 years on the air at Fox 2. Working in radio and television 10 years prior to that rounded out to a nice number of a 40-year career.

I firmly believe that my father's advice to a then-16-year-old—to make your own money, ask for what you want, be relentless and work hard—was such an important contributing factor to the success I had in my career. Even though I no longer get up in the middle of the night and deliver the news in the early morning, that drive that my father instilled in me is still there today. And I've passed it on to my daughter.

Some may say I retired. But retired doesn't mean shutting it all down. My energy and drive are not retired—I'm just doing something different. Who knew that that advice from my dad so many years ago would help lead me to such a wonderfully enjoyable career and the energy and drive I still maintain today?

Thanks, Dad.

ABOUT RANDI NAUGHTON

Randi Naughton began her broadcast career in sports in the 1990s before moving to the AM anchor desk at FOX 2 News where she spent 30 years delivering the topics of the day. She has interviewed countless celebrities, sports figures, authors and prominent members of the community. While she has stepped away from the news desk, Randi continues to run her own voiceover and narration business with clients worldwide and recently launched a new podcast – "More to Say with Randi Naughton: Interesting Conversations with Interesting People."

"During my 40-year broadcast career, I have honed my skills to make it a more casual, easy conversation, rather than an interview," said Naughton. "I feel like I can talk to anyone. I was always limited to short interview times on TV…three minutes or less. This gives me a chance to do a deep dive in conversation with my guests and let it breathe."

For more information about Randi Naughton, the podcast, and her other talents, visit RandiNaughton.com. Follow her on X, Instagram, Threads and TikTok.

Scan the QR code to watch a full interview with Randi

Sarah M. Glasser

FINDING PEACE THROUGH PURPOSE:
MY JOURNEY TO CREATING YENOLOGY

Life has taken me on an incredible journey—one filled with passion, purpose and unexpected turns that have all led me to where I am today. I created YENology as a space where wellness, luxury and community come together. More than just a boutique, YENology is an extension of my experiences, values and desire to help people find peace in their own way.

But to understand YENology, you must understand how I got here—how an early fascination with language and culture evolved into a career in family law and later into cannabis advocacy, eventually blossoming into a business built on wellness, intention and heart.

A Strong Foundation: Childhood and Early Curiosity

I was incredibly fortunate to grow up in a loving and supportive family. My parents gave me every opportunity to explore the world, both academically and personally. They nurtured my curiosity and taught me that it was not only OK to follow my passion but important to do so.

One of the first turning points in my life happened in sixth grade when my grade school offered Chinese as a foreign language. It was unusual, different and unique, and I jumped at the chance. That decision ended up shaping so much of my future. Learning Mandarin not only challenged me intellectually, it also opened the door to a new culture and way of thinking. I was fascinated with Eastern philosophy, art and especially medicine. There was something incredibly balanced and thoughtful about the traditions I was just beginning to explore.

In high school, I had the opportunity to travel to China—an experience that solidified my growing passion. That trip marked the first time

I encountered traditional Chinese medicine and holistic approaches to health. I saw the use of herbs, acupuncture and energy-based healing in ways that were very different from the Western medical model I'd grown up with. I didn't realize it at the time, but that early exposure to Eastern wellness would echo throughout my life.

A Passion Deepens: Studying Abroad in College

I went on to attend Washington University in St. Louis, where I majored in East Asian Studies. My goal at the time was to pursue a career in international or immigration law. But before heading to law school, I had one more opportunity to study abroad—this time through a Duke University program that placed me in Beijing and Nanjing for six months.

This immersive experience expanded my understanding of Eastern culture in ways that books alone never could. I gained a deeper, more personal appreciation for Eastern philosophies and healing traditions, particularly how they are woven into everyday life in subtle, powerful ways. While I didn't yet fully engage with practices like acupuncture, acupressure, or medicinal teas, this time in China planted the seed. I was introduced to the concepts and observed how seamless wellness was integrated into daily routines. It wasn't just an approach to illness—it was a lifestyle of balance and prevention.

It wasn't until years later, after law school and while navigating fertility challenges with my first son, that I truly began incorporating these practices into my own life. That's when I turned more intentionally to acupuncture and herbal supplements as part of my personal wellness journey. But the reverence and curiosity began during that formative time abroad, a chapter that would ultimately shape my perspective on healing and wellbeing for years to come.

A Legal Detour: Family Law and Domestic Violence Advocacy

My original plan was to continue to law school and pursue a career in international or immigration law, building on my East Asian studies. I enrolled at the University of Tulsa College of Law with that goal in mind. But life, as it often does, had a different plan for me.

While in law school, I randomly signed up for a Domestic Violence Law class. I had no idea at the time how pivotal that decision would be.

That single class shifted the entire trajectory of my legal career. I realized that I wanted to work in family law, specifically helping women and children facing domestic, emotional and sexual abuse. The calling was immediate and powerful—I knew this was the type of law I was meant to practice.

After graduating, I returned to St. Louis and began practicing family law. I dedicated myself to supporting vulnerable families during some of the most painful periods of their lives. I also joined the board of Woman's Place (now part of YWCA), where I worked for eight years to help survivors of domestic and sexual violence.

Through this work, I learned that law isn't just about rules and regulations about empathy, advocacy and empowerment. These values became central to everything I did.

A New Curiosity: Cannabis

By 2016 and 2017, discussions about medical marijuana legislation were heating up in Missouri. I knew that legalization was coming, and I wanted to be informed—both for my clients and for myself. So, I started attending cannabis law seminars and educational events in California and Colorado. I wanted to know how new legislation would impact family law, but I was also intrigued by the plant itself—its history, its healing potential, and the immense legal complexities surrounding it.

Through those early seminars, I met some of the trailblazers in the cannabis industry—people who were shaping policy, building businesses, and advocating for access and education. I was inspired. When Missouri officially passed its medical marijuana legislation in November 2018, I knew I wanted to be part of the movement.

I joined a team and began working on applications for cultivation, manufacturing and dispensary licenses. The process was intense, expensive and competitive. We didn't win any licenses, which was disappointing at first, but ultimately freeing. That experience helped me realize that my passion wasn't just about winning a license, it was about using my knowledge to educate, advocate and help others understand the value of this plant.

In 2021, I was part of a group of women that founded *We Are JAINE*, Missouri's first women's cannabis business organization. As co-president for three years, I helped create a platform for women in cannabis to connect, support one another and build careers in an emerging industry.

I realized that my passion wasn't just legal or professional. It was personal. I wanted to help change the narrative around plant medicine and alternative forms of healing.

Giving Back Through the Arts and Advocacy

Even as my career shifted, I never stepped away from giving back to my community. In addition to serving on the board of Woman's Place, I spent four years on the board of the Saint Louis Ballet, chairing multiple gala events and supporting the arts in our city. I've always believed that business and service should go hand in hand. Whether I'm donating a relaxation gift basket to a local silent auction or hosting a wellness workshop at my boutique, giving back is embedded in everything I do.

In 2022, I was honored to be named one of St. Louis' Most Influential Businesswomen by the *St. Louis Business Journal*. That recognition meant a lot, not because of the title, but because it reflected the years of work, care and intention I had poured into my career and my community.

The Birth of YENology

YENology was born from everything I've learned and experienced—my passion for wellness, my years of legal and advocacy work, my commitment to empowering women in business, and my belief that everyone deserves access to high-quality, intentional products that support their well-being.

I envisioned a space where all those values could come together—a place that celebrates beauty, healing and meaningful connection. I wanted to create more than a boutique. I wanted to build a sanctuary space where people could explore thoughtfully curated items that nourish both body and soul, and where conversations around identity, self-care and personal growth are always welcome.

That vision became YENology.

YENology is a reflection of my life's journey. Inside, you'll find a curated selection of luxury accessories, wellness tools, original art and high-quality hemp-derived products, each chosen not just for its form or function, but for the intention and story it carries. Every product is there to enhance your everyday rituals and support a more grounded, connected way of living.

The name itself—*YENology*—was inspired by the word *yen*, which means a deep craving or desire. To me, YENology represents the craving for something meaningful: for calm in chaos, for authenticity in a world that can feel superficial, and for connection in an increasingly disconnected society.

It also represents my enduring respect for Eastern philosophies and traditions. The "ology" is a nod to study, depth, and inquiry—because this space is not just about products, it's about learning, sharing and transforming.

What Makes YENology Different

YENology is more than a boutique—it is a feeling. From the moment someone walks through the door, my goal is for them to experience a sense of calm, beauty and authenticity. Every detail, from the scent in the air to the music playing softly in the background, is intentionally curated to encourage guests to slow down and truly be present.

I want people to feel welcomed, not sold to. To feel seen, not rushed. I've carefully selected every product with the same level of attention I bring to all areas of my life, choosing items that speak to wellness, ritual, intention and aesthetics. The result is a collection of goods that support both inner and outer well-being—whether it's a beautifully designed smoking accessory, a healing tincture or an original piece of art.

But what really sets YENology apart is the experience. I believe that retail can and should be immersive. YENology is a space where people can engage with products in a meaningful way—learning about their origins, their uses and how they might enhance someone's daily practice of self-care. It's also a space where connections thrive. Many visitors don't just come to shop; they come to ask questions, share stories or simply be in an environment that feels nurturing and elevated.

I also believe strongly in community engagement. That's why I host unique events—from elevated art nights to plant medicine education sessions, yoga sessions to wellness workshops. These events create opportunities for people to come together in a safe and open-minded space. They allow us to explore healing and creativity in the community, rather than in isolation.

YENology is also proudly inclusive. I work with women-owned brands, collaborate with local artisans and uplift voices that have traditionally been underrepresented in wellness and cannabis spaces. It's important to me that the boutique not only reflects my personal journey but also serves as a platform for others to grow and thrive.

YENology also supports individuals in the cannabis industry, as well as first responders and veterans. We provide special pricing and extend extra care to those who serve, advocate and work on the front lines of change and healing. Giving back is not an add-on—it's embedded into the values of this business.

Looking Ahead

As I reflect on how far I've come, I feel both grateful and grounded. The path that led me here wasn't always clear, but it was deeply purposeful. Each chapter—whether in the courtroom, a classroom, a boardroom, or a boutique—has shaped how I show up in the world. And as I look ahead, I carry with me the lessons of those experiences, using them to guide what comes next.

My vision for YENology is ever-evolving, but the core mission remains the same: to create a space where wellness, luxury and community come together with authenticity and intention. As the boutique grows, I want to deepen our impact—offering more educational events, expanding collaborations with values-aligned brands and continuing to curate experiences that spark curiosity and connection.

I want YENology to be a place where conversations happen—about healing, about plant medicine, about mindful living, about the ways we care for ourselves and others. I want it to be a space where people feel inspired to try something new or reconnect with something old, whether that's a ritual, a philosophy, or a piece of themselves they haven't accessed in a while.

I also want to continue supporting women in business. It is extremely powerful when women come together to share resources, lift each other up, and challenge the status quo. That spirit of collaboration and empowerment lives at the heart of everything I do. YENology is an extension of that ethos, and I'm excited to continue building relationships with other women-owned and mission-driven brands.

Personally, I feel a strong pull toward storytelling—both my own and those of others. I've learned that when we share openly and honestly, we create permission for others to do the same. I want to be someone who listens deeply and leads with integrity.

The beauty of this phase of life is that I no longer feel the need to choose between my passions, they all have a place. My legal training, my interest in Eastern healing, my advocacy work, and my entrepreneurial spirit all exist in harmony. YENology is the embodiment of that integration—a physical and energetic space where all the pieces come together.

In Gratitude

If I've learned anything through this journey, it's that following your intuition is rarely easy, but it's always worth it. There were times when I doubted myself, moments when the path forward felt uncertain, and seasons where I had to take bold steps without knowing where they would lead. But every time I honored what felt true to me—even when it meant taking a risk or starting over—it brought me closer to the life I was meant to create.

YENology is my way of bringing all that truth into form. It's my offering to others who are seeking calm in a noisy world, beauty in the everyday and community in a way that feels real. It's a place for the curious, the creative, the healing, the hopeful. Whether someone is coming in to shop, to connect or to simply take a breath, I want them to leave feeling a little more grounded than when they arrived.

To my family—thank you for being my constant. To my parents, your support has never wavered, and I'm so grateful for the foundation you gave me to grow and explore. To my husband, thank you for being my rock—your unwavering support, thoughtful listening, business insight, and belief in me make it possible for me to pursue my passions. I truly couldn't do this without you. And to my three beautiful children, thank you for loving me through the long days, the late nights and the moments when I'm tired and stretched thin. I hope that through this work, I make you proud and show you what it means to follow your heart.

And to those who walk through the doors of YENology, whether for the first time or the 50th—I see you, I'm grateful for you, and I hope this space offers you exactly what you didn't know you needed.

This is more than a business. It's a love letter to everything I believe in thoughtful living, radical compassion and the idea that healing and joy can exist in the same breath.

Thank you for being part of my journey. Here's to continuing it—together.

ABOUT SARAH GLASSER

Sarah is a licensed attorney who began her legal career practicing family law in Missouri. In 2017, she pivoted her focus to cannabis law and supporting the passage of medical marijuana legislation in the state. She is now the founder and owner of YENology®, a boutique in Frontenac, Mo. that blends luxury, wellness and community. YENology® offers thoughtfully curated gifts, artisan smoking accessories and plant-based products, all designed to support intentional living and holistic well-being.

A graduate of Washington University in St. Louis with a degree in East Asian Studies, Sarah immersed herself in Eastern culture and herbal medicine, including a transformative study abroad experience in China through Duke University. She went on to earn her Juris Doctor from The University of Tulsa - College of Law, where she centered her work around women's health and wellness, volunteering with local domestic violence organizations.

Sarah served on the board of Woman's Place for eight years, advocating for survivors of domestic and sexual violence. In 2021, she co-founded Missouri's first women's cannabis business organization, *We Are JAINE*, where she served as co-president for three years, helping grow a supportive and empowering community for women in the industry.

She also dedicated five years to the board of Saint Louis Ballet and chaired several of its annual galas, combining her passion for the arts with her commitment to community involvement.

In 2022, Sarah was named one of St. Louis' Most Influential Business Women by the *St. Louis Business Journal.*

Her greatest passions include her family, women's health and empowerment, holistic wellness and supporting the arts.

Scan the QR code to watch a full interview with Sarah

Sarah Guldalian

WHEN IT ALL FALLS APART

Women are nurturing by design. We care, and that is a beautiful thing. Yet, there is more to care for than we have the capacity to give each day. With many of us in the sandwich generation, we care for the generations on either side of us—growing kids, aging parents, even grandchildren— as well as our spouses.

If that wasn't enough, we are also in the prime of our careers with most of the aforementioned people counting on us. And let's not forget about the clients and employees who rely on us too. How could we? The number of messages we get daily would never allow us to forget. **We are giving a lot.**

In my late 30s, I came face-to-face with my limits. I had run hard for several years, starting and scaling a business, while we built our beautiful family. At first, the work was exhilarating. I was driven by mission—to be a light in the marketplace. I started out vibrant and confident, and exciting things happened, admittedly more quickly than expected.

Fast-forward a few years, and I was in a much different place, a darker place. I felt like I was balancing a house of cards, at any time, with one gust of wind or even a subtle breath, everything I'd worked for could come crashing down. After a while, I became like a statue with an outer shell adorned by awards and accolades, an impermeable veneer, but I felt hollow within, often frozen by fear.

From day-to-day, I didn't know if I could live up to being "me." Some days, I even felt my organs quiver from anxiety. Yet, no one could know. I felt I had to stay strong for everyone else, no matter how I felt inside.

While I bore a large weight of responsibility, control felt like an illusion. I felt out of control of the many dynamics, opinions and expectations swirling about. Some voices were particularly loud, and I felt like I was living in a pressure cooker with the dial ever-increasing.

I had adopted unhealthy paradigms to press forward, like, "Never let them see you sweat," and, "Fake it 'til you make it." Over time, I convinced myself that, as long as I appeared to have it together, I was good. But deep down I knew this was not a sustainable lifestyle.

I would hide in the bathroom for a few moments just to catch a deep breath, but my life was so busy and responsibilities so great, that even then I may hear a knock on the door to answer a call, fix a problem or sign documents. If I was honest, I feared I was shortening my life by living this way, but I also feared what might lie on the other side of surrender. Fear was the central theme of my life.

I had ceased to be the joyful, light-filled person I once was. She seemed long gone. I was living to keep everyone happy but no one seemed happy, especially me. I had lost myself and didn't know where to find me again. I tried retracing my steps to better times but it felt too late. So, here I was, having given all I had to give, but it didn't matter, because everyone and everything depended on me. I lived on little sleep and tons of coffee. The only thing I felt I could control was food, so I did.

As it turns out, you can hide your pain from others, but you can't fool your body. Stress has a way of catching up with you, and I felt broken. I visited my doctor, who gave me two options: Take these new prescriptions, all for stress-induced ailments, or change my lifestyle to let my nervous system rest, but I didn't see a way out. And I fought it as long as I could.

One day, the balancing act was up, and the house of cards fell. I wasn't strong enough to keep it all together. And, when it did, I came to my breaking point. I was in utter shock. It was hard to make sense of all I had lost, especially relationships I thought would always exist. I was crushed. I hid away so no one would think of or talk to me to stop the barrage of questions.

How could I answer their questions when I had so many of my own, like, "How did this happen?" and "Who am I now?" My identity had been so tied to my position that I no longer knew who I was. I'd given everything I had, and it wasn't enough. I felt disqualified from life.

One morning, I felt crushing sorrow. I decided to take a drive so my sweet family wouldn't see me cry. And I thought I might spot something that would remind me of who I was before this. I needed help. I needed direction.

I thought back to a time in college when I experienced a similar emptiness. I then had a personal encounter with Jesus, and Jesus absolutely changed my life. He healed my heart and filled me with the light I'd set out to share when I started this journey. I knew He was my only hope now in this moment, as well.

I realized that it had been some time since I'd heard His voice. While I knew He was with me, I didn't slow down to listen. I had given more power to the squeaky wheels in my life, making idols out of humans. In doing so, my fear had grown louder than anything.

While many people had left my life now, I knew God never would. Even in this dark moment, I knew He still loved me. Though I could hardly feel a thing, I still believed every word in the Bible. In the book of Deuteronomy it says, "The Lord himself goes before you and will be with you; he will never leave you nor forsake you. Do not be afraid; do not be discouraged."

I knew Jesus was the answer now just as He had been before. I had come to the end of myself and needed His help. I needed to surrender my heart, these broken pieces, and let Him fix me. I had to quit trying to control everything and surrender my life to Him. There was no other way.

I found it difficult to speak now. (If you know me, you know how odd that is as I am marked for being loud and gregarious.) In a barely audible whisper, I said, "God, please help me. I've lost myself. I don't know who I am or what to do." He answered.

In that moment, I truly felt God's presence all around me, like the warmth you feel as a little girl when you're crying and your dad hugs you. It was a phenomenal experience for me, someone who now often felt alone with a nervous system that would not calm. I felt His love fill me up. I also sensed Him encouraging me to speak words He was depositing into my heart in this moment.

Sensing it was a turning point for me, I picked up my phone to record these words. My voice was shaky, but I knew these words came from a different source; from a place of power and confidence that was not my own:

"I have called you to encourage and to inspire and to evangelize to the world. Do not forsake the calling I have called you to."

These words from God's heart broke a lie I had been believing; that I was too far gone to be used by God. You see, when I had set out on this journey years ago, starting my business, my guiding Bible verse had been Matthew 5:14, that says, "You are the light of the world." But my light had since dimmed as I got away from my light source: Jesus. I had wondered if I was disqualified from my God-given calling, however, here He was reaffirming it. I am called to shine.

In this moment, He reminded me of why and how He created me and revealed that my value is not tied to what I can accomplish. My worth is not defined by my performance, salary, weight or title. In fact, judging myself by the world's standards is what snuffed out my light. Instead, He showed me that He is my source of light and power. When I plug into Him, I can inspire those around me.

These words have since formed my personal mission statement, now framed in my office, which says, "I am called by God to encourage, inspire, and evangelize to the world through my gifts." [To evangelize to the world simply means to share the good news about Jesus.] To this day, when I feel lost or confused, I play that voice memo and it reminds me of who I am and how far God has brought me.

In this pivotal moment, I was revived and knew I had to make changes to avoid returning to survival-mode. Moving forward, I must drown out the other voices so I could hear His voice louder than any other. I had to follow Him and Him only. No more putting people on pedestals. He, and only He, is the Lord of my life.

In the Bible, God says, "I will give you a new heart and put a new spirit within you; I will take the heart of stone out of your flesh and give you a heart of flesh" (Ezekiel 36:26). This is what He did for me. He turned stone back into flesh.

Instead of covering up my faults, I began to appreciate that I can do nothing on my own, but with God guiding me, I can do all things. I was to be totally and utterly dependent on Him, fixing my eyes on Him above all else.

Healing was a process. I had to change my habits to protect my peace, quiet the noise, and listen for His direction. That meant spending more time with Him than anyone else. I want to share the habits I adopted that I employ today:

I find I am freshest and also most sensitive the first hour of my day. My mood for the day is established here. I used to wake up at 3 a.m., look at my bank account, and immediately crack into work. And, I won't lie, I have had to retrain myself several times since. However, I now start with <u>Jesus</u>. I make Him my priority, because I need Him! He brings me peace!

I make my coffee, sit in my chair and open my Bible App to read the Verse of the Day and the daily devotional. I meditate on a few verses to better understand their meaning. Then I talk to God or even write Him a letter. This can be a helpful way to pray. And I feel Him there with me.

I have also added time in my schedule to take care of myself: to go to counseling, to journal, and to focus on healthy eating. And we always attend church. This is not to fulfill any scorecard but because I so enjoy worshipping Jesus, who is worthy of all my praise, as well as learning more about the Bible, and forming deeper connections with others.

Just as I needed to create healthy habits, I knew I needed to break up with bad habits to truly be free. This was much more difficult for me, because I had been lacking boundaries for years.

First, I set boundaries with myself. I would no longer start my day by checking my texts, emails and bank account. I also had to identify unhealthy relationships and dynamics and learn ways to guard my heart. In fact, as God healed my nervous system, He showed me what to say to people and when not to answer. And, instead of giving my day to dissecting their words, I learned to focus my attention on what the Bible says about me: who God says I am.

Mainly, I could no longer say "yes" to everything. Knowing my family is my priority, I began to reserve my energy for them and for the calling God has placed on my life. I no longer give my energy to man-made expectations which utterly drain me. After all, my identity is a mom, wife and daughter of God before I am anything else. So, I respond to work when I'm working. I also avoid shows, music or even people who rob me of peace.

Ultimately, what I have come to realize is that this is my life, the life God has given me to steward, and my responsibility is to steward it well. I always have the choice to say "no" to anything that gets in the way of that. Any time I feel someone putting pressure on me, especially in areas that are not my responsibility, I just say "no" or back away. I don't live to please them. I live to please God.

Maybe you have found yourself in a similar situation. I want to encourage you to cry out to God. It's easy. Just say, "God, I need your help." Get a Bible. Start in the book of John. Start talking to or writing letters to God. Put Bible verses up around your house to remind you of who you are in Him. And remember that you don't have to figure it all out, because God has it figured out for you. You just have to trust Him.

"Trust in the Lord with all your heart and lean not on your own understanding; in all your ways submit to him, and he will make your paths straight" (Proverbs 3:5-6).

ABOUT SARAH GULDALIAN

Sarah Guldalian is an award-winning writer, marketer and producer of 25 years with an expertise in creating and expanding brands. She is recognized for championing faith-based organizations, who are spreading the Gospel of Jesus Christ through their platforms, and for cheering on other women in business.

Sarah found success, winning Telly & AVA Awards, by founding and serving as executive producer for advertising agencies Rhino Hyde Productions and Top Notch Brand Company. Prior to starting her companies, Sarah worked for International media organizations, ABC, Warner Brothers, Emmis Communications and Lutheran Hour Ministries.

More than anything, Sarah identifies herself as a Christ-follower, wife and mother. She also feels incredibly proud to serve as executive director of The Rooted Sisters, a Christian business women's network across the country.

Scan the QR code to watch
a full interview with Sarah

Sarah Hayek

A JOURNEY OF RESILIENCE AND SUCCESS

Humble Beginnings

I was born into a world that was full of love. My mother, a single parent, worked tirelessly to provide for my brother and me. She was my first hero—the embodiment of strength and determination. Her sacrifices were the structure of my childhood, filling our small home with warmth and laughter, despite the hardships we faced. I remember the evenings when she would return home exhausted from work, yet still find the energy to help me with my homework or listen to my dreams.

Growing up, I learned the value of hard work and perseverance from my mother. Watching her navigate life's challenges instilled in me a sense of resilience. I understood early on that life wouldn't always be easy, but with determination, I could do anything I put my mind to and carve my own path.

Graduating Early And Moving Out

As I reached my teenage years, my desire for independence grew stronger. At 17, I made the bold decision to move out and take control of my life. It was a leap into adulthood that was both thrilling and terrifying. Armed with a strong sense of purpose and a drive to succeed, I graduated high school early, ready to embrace the world beyond my hometown.

The transition was not without its challenges, however. I juggled part-time jobs while managing my studies, but the hustle only fueled my ambition. I was determined to make a name for myself. I was determined to find my dream.

Meeting My Husband And Pursing My Passion

Shortly after moving out, I met my amazing husband. He became my biggest cheerleader, supporting me through every step of my journey. His unwavering belief in my potential gave me the confidence I needed to pursue my dreams. Together, we navigated the ups and downs of life, always lifting each other up.

With my husband by my side, I enrolled in a cosmetology program. It was an exhilarating experience that opened my eyes to the art and science of beauty. I immersed myself in learning everything I could about hair, skin and makeup. The more I learned, the more I realized that I wanted to specialize in something that would allow me to express my creativity while helping others feel beautiful. I was on the fast-track graduating the program three months early while being in New York at The Wella Studio. I had earned the trip by hitting the highest service/retail sold competition.

After obtaining my cosmetology license from La James International Cosmetology College, I began my first stylist job at KJ & Kompany, where I poured my heart into my work. Owned by my first mentor Keith Blum, it was where I quickly discovered my niche for color and cuts and offering the best for my clients.

Starting A Family

As my career began to flourish, my husband and I decided to start a family. We welcomed three amazing boys who became the pride and joy of our lives. Balancing motherhood with my career was a challenge, but my husband and I made it work. Our home was filled with laughter, love and the chaotic energy that only children can bring.

A New Challenge

Just as I was settling into my new role as a mother, my world was shaken by the news of my mother's breast cancer diagnosis. The woman who had been my rock now needed me to be strong for her. It was a painful reminder of life's unpredictability. This experience deepened my appreciation for the fragility of life and ignited a desire within me to help others who may be facing their own battles.

My mom has been cancer-free for 11 years, but she had a lengthy recovery. She endured a double mastectomy and had plastic surgery for reconstructive implants. After the surgery, she got an infection. It took a good two years for everything to settle down and for her to be able to feel comfortable. She is incredibly strong, though, and made it through.

With the testing available today, I was able check my own risks for cancer. Now I know that it is in our hereditary genes.

I proceeded to have blood work done and tested positive for BRACCA 2. I found out when I was 38. I had a full hysterectomy at 40 to remove the risk of ovarian cancer and minimize the risk of breast cancer. This of course put me straight into menopause, but it was worth knowing I was being preventive.

Building A Career

A new job opportunity was brought to my attention; I applied and boom in the blink of an eye, my career was just elevated to the next level as I accepted the position of field education trainer with Proctor and Gamble. I continued to build my career as I focused on a five-state territory, leading in salon education for some of the largest salons in the country. I soon advanced into a national education manager role covering a 22-state territory and overseeing five of my own field education trainers. I poured my heart into my work. My dedication paid off, and I began to earn a substantial income, reflecting the years of hard work, late nights and sacrifices.

As my career progressed, I was fortunate enough to travel some of the most beautiful places in the world—Barcelona, Madrid and Puerto Rico to name a few—while immersing myself in diverse cultures, teaching and working alongside some of the top leaders in the hair industry.

These experiences were transformative. I attended conferences and workshops, learning cutting-edge techniques that built the skill, knowledge and experiences to make me who I am today.

Each destination enriched my understanding of beauty and the artistry of hair. I found inspiration in the unique styles and approaches of different cultures, which I integrated into my work. Collaborating with industry leaders not only expanded my skill set but also fostered connections that would last a lifetime.

Settling Back Down And Opening My Own Salon

After years of traveling and gaining experience, my husband and I decided it was time to settle back down. In 2020, amidst the chaos of the COVID-19 pandemic, I took the leap and opened my own salon. It was a time filled with uncertainty, but I was determined to create a sanctuary for beauty and empowerment. The salon quickly flourished, becoming a hub of creativity and luxury.

It was during this time, through a friend, that I discovered Hair Lingerie founded by Kiara Bailey. I fully embraced the luxurious, high-end hair extensions, recognizing the growing need to help women struggling with thinning hair—whether due to health issues, hormonal changes or simply the natural aging process. I was passionate about helping women feel empowered and extraordinary.

I became fascinated with the transformative power of luxurious hair and how it could enhance a person's confidence and change their entire look. It only fed my passion to ensure that each client left my chair feeling beautiful and empowered.

Caring For My Clients And Leading A Strong Team

As my salon grew, I focused on creating a nurturing environment for my clients as well as expanding by moving into a larger space to add stylists to help grow my vision. I care deeply for my clients and want to ensure that each one receives personalized attention and exceptional service. I've built a strong team of stylists who share my vision of empowerment and excellence. Together, we fostered a culture of creativity, support and growth.

Leaving A Legacy

As I reflect on my journey, I can hardly believe how far I've come. From a young girl raised by a single mother to a successful salon owner, mentor and globetrotter, every challenge has shaped me into who I am today. My husband's support and my children's pride in their mom continue to inspire me, and I carry their spirits with me in everything I do.

Now, as I look to the future, I am filled with excitement and determination. I plan to continue to grow my salon and create even more opportunities for aspiring stylists. My goal is to leave a legacy that empowers others to pursue their passions and celebrate their own beauty.

Life may have thrown its challenges my way, but I've learned that resilience and passion can lead to incredible success. I am committed to living my story authentically and empowering others to do the same. The journey is far from over, and I can't wait to see where it leads next.

ABOUT SARAH HAYEK

With 26 years of experience in the hairdressing industry, Sarah has dedicated her career to transforming and enhancing the beauty of her clients. Sarah's journey has taken her around the globe, where she has honed her skills and embraced diverse techniques that reflect the latest trends in hair fashion.

As the proud owner of a full-service luxury salon, Sarah specializes in providing exquisite celebrity backed hair extensions tailored to each client's unique style and preferences. Sarah's commitment to excellence and attention to detail to ensure that every client receives personalized care and stunning results.

Sarah believes that hair is not just a style but an expression of individuality, and she strives to create an environment where everyone feels valued and beautiful. Whether you're looking for a complete transformation or a subtle enhancement, her passion for hair and dedication to her craft guarantees a luxurious experience.

The Red Beauty Salon
30W Hwy D
New Melle, MO 63365
www.theredbeautysalon.com
(636) 888-0255

Scan the QR code to watch a full interview with Sarah

Dr. Stacey Collins-Dixson, Ed.D.

COMING IN TO MY OWN

The phone notification lit up the dark room. It was a Saturday night, and the glow from my husband's phone lit up the room as we slept. I looked across his sleeping body worried—what if it's important? He had come home late that night, drunk, and passed out in the bed. This had happened before, and it was happening more frequently in recent months. My mind was frantic—who is needing him at nearly midnight? Is there an emergency? If so, he can't even deal with it in this state. I opened the phone so I could formulate a plan on how I could deal with the issue on my own, and I saw it: a message on Snapchat from the kids' pediatrician. "I miss you, Love," it stated, "I'm glad you had fun tonight."

I was a year into my doctoral study, and nearly 20 years into my marriage to a man who wields considerable power in our small community. I had four children, a full-time job, a couple of little side hustles from home that gave me a bit of extra money and a full load of classes as I worked toward a doctorate so that I could earn enough money to be able to drop the side job. My husband had a business that we bought and built together. The nature of his business required frequent absences as well as continual and unpredictable call-outs. It was a difficult life, but my children made it joyful. I was able to photograph home décor from a local business in our own house while the children played, and I would post photos and promotions to social media from my phone. I wrote articles for a parenting magazine while my kiddos were sitting the bench during soccer and baseball games. I helped the children with their homework and projects, cooked dinner and tucked them in at bedtime. It was after I put them to bed that I was able to start on my own homework. The schedule was brutal, and my assignments were perpetually turned in timestamped in the wee hours of the morning. Still, this was all temporary. I can do anything for a few years, right? I was building a better future for my children, my husband and myself. Little did I realize when I started my doctoral program in 2020 that I was ensuring a solid financial future for life as a single mother.

The divorce process lasted nearly two full years, and cost tens of thousands of dollars. Typically, a person who felt confident—smug even—in my ability to rely on only myself, I found that I was leaning on others to an extent I never had to before. A brilliant family law attorney in St. Louis was my rock—she came highly recommended, and thankfully, I have a tendency to surround myself with women who are smarter than I am. My doctoral supervisor was as determined as I was that I would finish my research and defend my dissertation. I slimmed down my schedule, let go of the extra money-makers, and continued to reside in the home I built with my husband—with my husband.

Men and women going through divorce tend to believe that if they leave the home, the home will be awarded to the party who stayed. Whether or not any truth to that belief exists, when both people stay in the same home, that forced togetherness becomes a source of much stress and consternation. Months passed in this way. Stress increased. The acrimony ratcheted up to the point that I was treated at the hospital for an ankle injury from being dragged down the driveway, and I slept with my doctoral research-dedicated laptop secured in a bag wrapped around my leg under the blankets each night. I had nowhere to go—I couldn't afford another place. My husband and I owned two large, vacant apartments, but they were attached to his businesses, which meant no privacy for me, as well as another eventual relocation when the divorce was final. When the nurse at the emergency room handed me literature on domestic violence the day my ankle was braced, the words that came out of my mouth so many times came back to haunt me: "Why don't women just pack up and leave?"

Why don't women just pack up and leave? What a simple solution, right? Just pack up and leave! It's so easy! Until it isn't. Here I was, a confident, resilient, educated woman and I was stuck. The relationship was over, but the fear and intimidation continued. Why not just leave?

The question is almost always posed from a place of privilege. Privilege that looks like freedom of finances, movement, expression and autonomy lives behind that question, and although my rhetoric was not ill-intended, it was coming back to roost. Why not just leave? The answer—as anyone who has the lived experience knows—is complex.

Women stay because they have nowhere else to go. Women stay because they lack a network. Women stay because their partner controls the money. Women stay because of language barriers, lack of employment, low self-esteem, fear and shame. Women stay because of the normalization of the paradigm of an unhealthy relationship. My situation was much less dire compared to what others experience. I had tried to leave once—my sleeping daughter was in my arms and my husband stood in the doorway, breath smelling of alcohol. We could not pass. I put her back down in her bed and prayed that the night would pass without further incident as the kids slept. I lay awake with the anger boiling up inside of me that I could not take the children and go. But where would we go? To a hotel? How long could that last? The night passed, and so did many more until one evening, when I returned to the house, kids in tow, after a therapy session for children going through divorce. I unlocked the door to find that most of our furniture and many of our possessions were gone. What looked like a burglary was actually my first night of freedom. I was left with most of what we needed to carry on life as quasi-usual, and it was then that I had my first peaceful sleep. My foot was healing. No bag containing a computer was wrapped around my leg. No footsteps woke me. Just quiet.

A new normal began the next morning. I was on my own—I lived alone with my children. They would eventually start a temporary custody schedule. I would work on my graduate studies on the days the kids were with their dad. I would go to work and pick up the kids from school, cook dinner, spend time with each one, and put them to bed. Even though most of my life looked similar to this even when I was married, I was alone now in a different sense, and it would be OK. And I would be OK. I started therapy with a practitioner who is so intuitive, one of the first things she said to me was, "Congratulations on your upcoming divorce! What a gift to be at a place where you get to rewrite your story and recraft your life." Although it felt (and still feels) unnatural for a mother to only see her children half of their lives, making the best of it is important when circumstances are out of your control.

Throughout that two years of strife, I thought about the women who lacked the privilege I enjoyed. Legal counsel is expensive, but I did have the resources to pay it. Divorce can negatively impact a person's self-esteem, wallet, living situation, relationships and even credit score. Mine did all of those things. I lost friends I never thought I could lose. One friend had been suspended without pay at her job the previous Christmas, and it was me who had the idea to include funds in an amount equivalent to her missed paycheck in a Christmas card to her. It was another friend for whom I took time off of work to testify on her behalf in court for an Order of Protection against a man who hurt her. In the end, even she turned her back on her woman friend who needed her. My credit score took a hit for a brief period of time as assets were bought and sold, and ownership changed. Still, I could not ignore that in a typical life balancing a complexity of influences and events, I still was luckier than most. Sure, I found out too late that my friendships were quid pro quo and transactional, but does that diminish the heart I put into them? Is the fact that I was financially vulnerable for a brief time indicative of my present or future? Does my failed marriage doom me in future relationships? Can I be happy again? Will I want to marry again? Can I ensure the healthy adjustment of my children on my own?

Pivotal moments help us question, adjust and redefine who we are and how we interact with people, events, work and ourselves. Bad friends happen. Relationships can tank. For the parts I played in those things, I accept responsibility and work through ways to improve myself so I do not cause damage to myself or others in the future. For the parts outside my control, I have to at some point shrug and rid myself of the onus of culpability for those. I am thankful to rewrite my story and change its perspective to first-person where I get to narrate authentically, outside the confines of approval-seeking and desperation for acknowledgment and belonging.

Two years have passed since those events transpired. I moved to the St. Louis area, and the children and I are doing well. I fell in love with a man who makes me feel safe and loved, and I married him. My group of friends is small, but true. And thanks to the encouragement of my doctoral supervisor, and the desire for my children to see that their mama does not bend to adversity, I graduated. My lawyer and my therapist maintain their place in my budget. Ever still brilliant in their respective fields, they both help keep me centered. The woman who was once defined as "Mrs." Is now "Dr." I have my own identity. I am blessed.

ABOUT DR. STACEY COLLINS-DIXSON, ED.D

Dr. Stacey Collins-Dixson, Ed.D., is an accomplished educator, psychological examiner and higher education faculty member with more than two decades of experience in K–12 and postsecondary education. Her professional practice is grounded in a commitment to student advocacy, Title IX compliance and diagnostic excellence in special education.

Currently, Stacey serves as a School Psychological Examiner for the Lincoln County R-III School District in Troy, Mo., where she has provided comprehensive psychoeducational assessment services since 2008. Her work ensures full compliance with IDEA and DESE standards, and she plays a vital role in eligibility decisions and individualized educational planning.

In higher education, Stacey is an adjunct professor at both Missouri State University and Missouri Baptist University. At MSU, she teaches in the "Pathways for Paras" certification program. At MBU, she develops and delivers graduate-level instruction in both the Counseling and School Psychological Examiner programs, while also serving as a dissertation reader for doctoral students in the Ed.D. program. Her work as a reader is marked by her exceptional command of APA formatting, grammar, and research methodology.

She holds a Doctor of Education from Missouri Baptist University, where her dissertation—*Analyzing the Influence of Dynamic Title IX Guidance: How University Gender Equity and Title IX Compliance Offices Stay Within the Bounds of the Law*—received recognition for its relevance to higher education compliance and gender equity. She also holds a master's degree in counseling education and certification in School Psychological Examination.

Her early career includes classroom instruction in mathematics and English, as well as speech-language support. She has served as a mentor to graduate students across multiple universities, guiding candidates through the rigorous assessment, interpretation, and communication processes central to the role of psychological examiner.

In addition to her academic contributions, Stacey is a published researcher and writer. Her scholarly work is housed in ProQuest, and she has contributed numerous articles to *Twiniversity*, focusing on family wellness, parenting multiples and mental health. She is also a seasoned speaker, having presented at the Faith and Research Conference and professional development events on topics including gender in education, leadership and institutional wellness. Stacey is currently a contributor for *Clayton City Lifestyle*, *Chesterfield City Lifestyle* and *St. Charles County City Lifestyle* magazines.

With a passion for educational equity, data-informed practice and mentoring the next generation of school-based mental health professionals, Stacey continues to serve as a leader in both her district and the broader educational community.

Stacey is a wife and mother of five children, including twins. She lives in St. Charles County with her family and five fur-babies.

Scan the QR code to watch a full interview with Stacey

Susie Busch-Transou

WHAT FEEDS YOUR SOUL

What feeds your soul? This was the very question that proved to be a turning point in my life and sparked the creation of Hearth and Soul, a gathering place where you can discover unique clothing and accessories for yourself, gifts for your loved ones and furniture, lighting and finishing touches for your home.

I am often asked where the idea of Hearth and Soul began. Smiling and still with a feeling of awe and gratitude I am taken back to a birthday gathering with friends from my college years at Duke University. You see, I innocently drove over to my friends' family home in Georgia for a 50th birthday celebration. At this time my husband, Tripp, and I were happily running our beverage distribution company, raising our daughter (the third of our amazing children, who was still at home finishing her high school years), traveling often to support our boys' collegiate lacrosse pursuits and supporting our local communities through meaningful board service. Little did I know that I would have the opportunity to visit with a life coach, Rev. Catherine. It was during that conversation talking through what feeds my soul and what brings me fulfillment, the idea of Hearth and Soul was born.

We talked about my first 50 years and the common threads of inspiration and joys in my life. Quality time with family and friends, achieving meaningful goals and results in business and in life, travel and discovery of interesting experiences and finds and working to make a difference all fell at the top of the list. It was actually through my board service and community engagement that one of the most rewarding aspects of my life developed. I was fortunate to be able to connect a community need with a resource to fill that need, something that now happens daily at Hearth and Soul.

In keeping with her great intuition about people, Rev. Catherine concluded our visit with the statement: "I see a storefront in your future, a place called 'The Kitchen.'" Inspired and even more curious, I began asking all of the women at the birthday retreat, "What feeds your soul?" And the answers to this question found their way into a home-like setting anchored by a kitchen and hearth room, and featuring women's and men's closets, a library and patio. The concept, brand, business plan and build-out design were developed. The Hearth and Soul family, our team, was engaged, and we opened the doors of our flagship store Hearth and Soul in Tallahassee, Fla. 10 months later.

Today, after 10 years of operating three stores and developing our website, I can honestly say that Hearth and Soul truly feeds my soul. It allows me the opportunity to create, serve, engage, achieve and lead. It is the people that I am honored to work with and to serve that make all of the difference in my life.

Hearth's values are based in friendship and family. Working and living in communities like Tallahassee; Austin, Texas, and St Louis, Mo. has been so rewarding. Through Hearth and Soul, we are able to help meet individual and community needs by bringing together people with like passions through our nonprofit and artist partnerships and book and wellness events. Hearth and Soul creates special gatherings for friends and family to come together filled with all the special details of tabletop flowers, food and samplings of cold beer and wine. It brings beautiful, unique products to market that blend form and function and enhance other people's lives across categories of apparel, design and gifting.

The morale of my story is one of being open to new ideas and opportunities, working hard, putting the highest value on relationships and friendships and pivoting when necessary.

Thank you for living, learning and growing with me.

ABOUT SUSIE BUSCH-TRANSOU

Susie Busch Transou is a business woman, mom, grandmother, volunteer and friend. Growing up in St. Louis, Susie Busch Transou has always taken the Anheuser-Busch philosophy "Making Friends Is Our Business" seriously –both in her personal and professional life. While attending Duke she met Tripp Transou, the man with whom she would move to Tallahassee, raise three children, and through Tri-Eagle Sales (a Florida specialty beverage distribution company) serve north and central Florida's beverage needs.

Susie's love of hospitality blended with the desire to enrich the lives of others has come together to make Hearth and Soul a dream come true.

After years of business and hospitality experience, Susie's entrepreneurial spirit was stoked when she was inspired at a milestone birthday gathering of old and new friends to reflect on unmet needs in her world and what feeds her soul. The answer led Susie to create a unique concept in retail that is reminiscent of the home; a haven within this fast-paced world where friends can connect and an inviting place to shop carefully curated items for oneself, for the home or for that special someone in your life.

A place called Hearth and Soul proudly serves friends in Tallahassee, Fla., St. Louis, Mo., and online at HearthAndSoul.com

Scan the QR code to watch a full interview with Susie

Tessa Greenspan

FAILURE IS NOT AN OPTION:
FROM OUTHOUSE TO PENTHOUSE

Success doesn't fall into your lap — it must be fought for, earned through every heartbreak and setback life throws your way. I know this because I've lived it. I rose from the bottom — from an outhouse — to the top — to a penthouse.

This journey wasn't a straight line. It wasn't a lucky break. It was a battlefield of failures, hard lessons and an unwavering mindset that failure was never an option.

Growing Up With Nothing

I was born into circumstances most people can't imagine. Our house was barely standing. The bathroom was an outhouse in the backyard — a brutal reminder, summer or winter, that comfort and luxury belonged to other people, not us.

We didn't have money. We didn't have connections. What we had was survival, and sometimes even that felt like a miracle.

I remember being a kid, staring up at the stars at night, asking myself: "Is this all life has for me?"

Something deep inside answered: No.

But having a dream and living it are two very different things. Life didn't offer me an easy ladder up. I would have to build it, rung by rung, from scratch.

The First Failures: A Hard Education

School was supposed to be my ticket out. But when you come from nothing, even education is an uphill battle. I worked twice as hard for half the recognition. I wasn't the smartest kid in the room. I wasn't the fastest. I wasn't the most popular.

I was the one who failed the first time I tried something new. I was the one who had to stay after class. I was the one who had to hear the word "no" again and again.

The first job interviews were brutal. I wore hand-me-down clothes and old shoes, trying to look the part. Each rejection letter felt like a door slamming on my dream.

Friends around me gave up. They said, "Maybe this is just our lot in life." I didn't believe that. I couldn't believe that. Failure was not an option.

Every Setback a Lesson

When I finally scraped together enough to start a small business, I thought, "This is it. This is my breakthrough."

It wasn't.

I miscalculated. I trusted the wrong people. I underestimated the challenges. Within a year, I was deeper in debt than when I started.

Bankruptcy loomed over me.

For a moment — just a moment — I thought about quitting. I thought about giving up, blaming the world, blaming my background, blaming bad luck.

But I remembered the outhouse. I remembered where I came from. And I realized — if I could survive that, I could survive this.

I picked myself up. I started again. Wiser this time. Tougher this time. Smarter this time.

Climbing the Ladder: Inch by Inch

Opportunities didn't flood in. They trickled, and only after I proved I deserved them.

Every job I got, I treated like gold. Every connection I made, I nurtured with respect. Every setback, I treated as a classroom.

Slowly — inch by inch — the tide began to turn. Small wins led to bigger wins. Failed deals turned into successful partnerships. Rejected ideas turned into accepted innovations.

I learned one simple truth: Failure isn't real until you stop trying.

Facing the Big Test

Years later, I stood on the edge of a major opportunity — the kind that could change everything. It required everything I had: money, effort, trust, faith.

And just like before, disaster struck.

A key investor pulled out. A contract fell through. Expenses soared.

Everyone around me said, "Walk away. Cut your losses." It was the logical choice.

But success was never about logic. It was about heart.

I doubled down instead. I reinvested. I made the calls. I found new partners. I hustled like my life depended on it — because it did.

And finally, after months of grinding, it happened: The deal closed. The business boomed. The penthouse wasn't a dream anymore — it was my address.

Lessons Learned From Failure

Looking back, failure was never my enemy. It was my teacher.

Failure taught me patience. Failure taught me humility. Failure taught me strength.

Most importantly, failure taught me that there is no shame in falling — only in staying down.

I learned that the world doesn't owe you success. It doesn't hand you your dreams on a silver platter. You have to bleed for them. You have to fight for them. You have to refuse, flat-out refuse, to give up.

Failure is not an option because the alternative is a life of regret — and that is a far worse fate than any setback or stumble.

Today: From Outhouse to Penthouse

When people see me today, they see the success: the home, the life, the rewards. What they don't see are the countless times I fell flat on my face. The sleepless nights. The empty bank accounts. The doubts. The loneliness.

But I see it. I remember it. And I'm grateful for every moment of it. Because every failure sharpened me into the person capable of achieving this life.

From outhouse to penthouse wasn't a miracle. It was a mindset.

It was built on a foundation stronger than brick or steel. It was built on the unbreakable belief that no matter what happened, failure was not an option.

Final Words

If you're standing in your own version of an outhouse today, if you feel trapped by your circumstances, if life keeps knocking you down — hear me now:

You are not finished. You are not beaten. You are just in the middle of your story.

And as long as you refuse to quit, as long as you refuse to accept failure, you are already winning.

The world will tell you to lower your expectations. It will tell you to be realistic. It will tell you to settle.

Don't listen.

Listen instead to that quiet voice deep inside — the one that says: "Keep going. You were made for more."

Because you were. And no matter how many times you fall, remember:

Failure is not an option.

ABOUT TESSA GREENSPAN

Tessa Greenspan, a best-selling author renowned for her inspiring memoir "From Outhouse to Penthouse," which chronicles her extraordinary ascent from poverty to towering success.

She stands as a beacon of hope and guidance, extending her vast business and personal experience as a mentor, entrepreneur and motivational speaker.

With a presidency that spanned over 28 remarkable years, she spearheaded the dramatic turnaround of a health-focused supermarket, akin to the prestigious Whole Foods Market.

Under her leadership, the store rose like a phoenix from the ashes of a $1 million debt, soaring to an impressive $10 million in sales.

Her commitment to excellence in business, combined with a relentless pursuit of creative personal and professional growth, ignites her ongoing mission to empower individuals across the spectrum of business acumen, success strategies and holistic health.

Scan the QR code to watch a full interview with Tessa

Tina Perrmann

THE MIRACLE POWER OF LOVE

"One day you will tell the story of how you overcame what you went through, and it will be someone's else survival guide." ~ Brene Brown

"It's about time for you to experience the Power of Miraculous Love, Tina," my mentor, Natalie's words kept ringing in my ears and heart. Four years post-divorce, defeated, depressed, lonely, unsupported, sad, scared, broke and heartbroken, the truth of my soul still desired to know and be in a Beloved Union. So, my soul's determination and inner work continued. It took emotional courage to work through releasing blocks in my heart-wall of protection. For, I had created a beLIEf system that I was "unlovable", and, at my core, "not good enough", "not worthy" nor deserving of being loved.

The turning point came while attending a funeral for my dear friend's husband. The two of them had been high school sweethearts, married with four children and their last child born just three weeks before his passing of Lou Gehrig's disease. After witnessing their unconditional love story- "Till Death Do Us Part," it invoked the question within me: "I don't know what's more painful - to never know such a love, or to experience that kind of unconditional love and lose it. My heart decided it wanted to know and experience unconditional love.

My mentor continued to work with me and she poured into my soul so I would know God's will for my life is love and complete happiness. Heaven on Earth. She shared a quote from St John of the Cross that became my focus and mantra: "If a person is seeking God, his Beloved is seeking him much more… and the desire for God is the preparation for union with Him."

Natalie instructed me to watch the movie, "Practical Magic" to understand the power of love and know anything is always possible. In the movie, Sally, (Sandra Bullock) and Gillian, (Nicole Kidman) are sisters born into a magical family of witches that have a curse on them around love. It dooms any man they love. After heartbreak, Sally decides to test the powers-at-be by writing a letter, to the universe, to bring her the man she will forever love. And that that man will show up with one blue eye and one green eye so that she will know the curse is broken. In the end, -YES, love wins!!! They learn how to break the generational curse, and the man of Sally's dreams shows up with one blue eye and one green eye. And they love happily ever after. Love wins.

Just like Sally, I, too, felt cursed in the relationship/love arena. So, per Natalie's instructions I decided to write a list to the universe of qualities/ essences that I desired in a GENTLEman – in hopes to attract my Beloved.

MY LIST: (in no specific order)

1. A GENTLEman
2. Supportive and loving
3. Tall, healthy and handsome
4. Emotionally available
5. Creative
6. Lives close by
7. Spiritual/faith in God
8. Loves to cook
9. Sense of humor/playful
10. Open to growing together
11. Respectful
12. Educated and intelligent
13. Financially stable/ entrepreneur energy
14. Has children and is accepting and supportive to my children
15. A man of integrity and character
16. Handyman
17. Open to creating a life beyond our wildest dreams

My mentor constantly impressed upon me that I deserved love, respect and support. But, because of my past experiences of abuse and disrespect, in relationships and a subconscious beLIEf, I didn't believe I was lovable or deserved love, respect and support. She said, "the GEN-TLEman of your dreams (the characteristics on your list to the universe) could show up at a party, pursue you, be everything you desire. But because you don't believe you are worthy, deserve love and is an unfamiliar situation, to your nervous system, you will reject him by making an excuse like you don't like" bald men" or you're not attracted to him, etcetera. In reality, you are unfamiliar with this type of respect, love and support, so you will push it away. I really didn't hear the point she was driving home to my heart at the time. But being so determined, I decided to continue to focus on my love for God, cultivating an attitude of gratitude for everything in my life, daily prayers of invocation and adoration, calling in my angels, doing the homework and using the tools she gave me to attract my Beloved.

Magically, I must have hit a tipping point in my beLIEF system and in my emotional mental and spiritual bodies, because as fate would allow, Steve physically showed up in a serendipitous encounter. Upon our first meeting, I could feel something different stirring within my soul. He wasn't like any other man I had ever met before. He was such a GEN-TLEman. Somehow, intuitively, I knew he was an answer to my prayers, but my fears and heart-wall still put him to the test. It felt safe to talk to him on the phone for hours, but when he asked me out on a date my inner saboteur would cancel.

I wasn't quite sure why I would cancel my scheduled dates with him. Obviously, it was my subconscious, inner saboteur at work. I would make excuses: "I'm not ready for a relationship" or "I'm not attracted to him" or "I don't need a man in my life." Truth, I didn't 'need' a man, but mostly certainly came to believe I deserved a man, who would love, respect and support me and would allow me to do the same back. My soul longed for a Beloved Union.

Then a series of fortuitous Godwinks happened to wake up my heart from a deep, generational pattern of self-sabotaging, because of a beLIEf in a punishing God/Universe and a lack of deserving the power of Miraculous Love. I started to feel God working on my heart-wall.

Standing in the kitchen of my newly purchased home in Kirkwood, preparing food for my daughter, Stephanie's high school graduation party, my mind was filled with stress and anxiety. My body was exhausted and overwhelmed,(with acute adrenal fatigue). Especially because I had just made a big financial and emotional decision to purchase a fitness club. I was thinking about how I was going to manage it all on my own; with one child in college, another soon to follow, and a 10-year-old still at home. On top of that, the immediate party I was throwing for my daughter the next day. Although I acted like I had it all under control, I am sure Steve could intuitively feel my angst and stress. Steve asked me, "Tina, you look overwhelmed to me. What can I do to support you? What do you need? May I cut your grass? Cook? Grill? Run to the grocery store? Clean? Help with your son, Alex?" It was the most attractive, sexiest thing I had heard a man ask me! The tears snuck out of my eyes and rolled down my cheeks. I have never felt so seen or supported on all levels. I didn't remember anyone ever asking me how they could support me before. Being the second oldest of seven siblings, married young and becoming a mother at the ripe age of 19, and a homeowner and business owner at the age of 21, I was the one always supporting others. I aways had to be the strong one. In control. The giver. The supporter. Truthfully, I had longed for support all my life, yet didn't know quite how to receive it. I knew Steve was the one who would teach me strength in feeling the vulnerability allowing help and support.

The next Godwink happened when Steve's S.O.S Rock Band was performing in a Battle of the Bands to open for Ted Nugent. He asked that I attend, gifting me two tickets. It's not my favorite genre of music, but I wanted to go to support him and witness his creative talent and passion for music. Still trepidatious, I invited my lifelong friend, Josie, since she and Steve shared similar musical tastes and, honestly, I needed her opinion. She has always been a great judge of character. When I witnessed Steve on stage with his band, guitar strapped on, fully immersed in his creative talent and passion; I witnessed his Godgift. His Soul. His heart. I had GODbumps!!! Not only was he humbly talented, but incredible sexy and alive! I was mesmerized. He could have played any genre, and I would have loved it, because HE loved it. I loved seeing him fully in his passion. My friend, Josie, confirmed all that I felt about him. Sometimes, you just need your dear friend to push you through your fears and confirm what your heart feels.

The Ultimate Godwink came when Steve enrolled in the last personal growth course I was instructing in St. Louis, since I had just purchased my fitness franchise. I was complete in teaching weekend, personal-development courses. Secretly, I had always longed for a man, who was in a relationship with me, to share this transformative experience. And, to witness my passion and sacred Godgift of intuition in a course room. To see and accept ALL of me. And this would be the last opportunity. We had long, intimate, emotional conversations around personal and spiritual growth and the importance of growth and being responsible for your "stuff" in all relationships. (Matter of fact the night before we physically met - unbeknownst to us - we were both in different personal growth workshops and had declared a goal and desire to be in a relationship and to love again. Serendipitous, we met the next night.)

Something magically happened during the weekend, personal growth workshop. I saw Steve's adorable inner child. I saw his wounded heart. I saw his pain. I saw his Masterful Spirit. I saw his Brilliance. I saw his Soul. I experienced his love language of "being in service to others." I felt his courage to do the inner work with me and take ownership and responsibility for his life. I was elated. I could feel all our prayers in sync and in motion. I felt God had a bigger plan than I imagined for our life and it was at work.

After the weekend, Steve and I had a lunch date, where he handed me a CD of a song, he had written for me entitled, "Angels Touch." He nicknamed me, "Angel," upon our first meeting. Unbeknownst to him, I was obsessed with Angels since my NDE and having experienced an intimate relationship with Angels.

Steve started talking about commitment, marriage and merging and blending our families. When I asked him, "Why do we need to marry again? I have my house. You have your place. We were both 40 years old. Clearly, we weren't going to have more children together and our children weren't accepting our relationship, yet. So why do we need to marry?" He said something so profound, "Without a legal, emotional and spiritual commitment, there would not be a solid foundation to grow our love. And when you become afraid you will want to run or if it got hard, we would want to quit."

I learned Commitment is the glue. When we commit to the power of Miraculous Love providence happens.

Six months later, Steve asked me to marry him. It was surreal. I said, "YES!" We both choose to say YES to the power of Miraculous Love/ God. It was an opportunity for a "Do Over." To love and be loved. And, after all the traumas our children had also experienced from our previous relationships and divorces, it was an opportunity to allow the power of our Beloved Union to heal, forgive, support, model and inspire them with a loving marriage "Til Our Death Do Us Part".

We worked with my mentor, Natalie, for a year to clear our old baggage and allow personal and spiritual growth, for the beauty and grace of our Beloved Union to be nurtured, supported and, more importantly, sustained. She gave us invaluable tools, awareness, insights, hope, support and a vision to create our constructive life together.

The wall of protection I had built around my heart served me well in past relationships but came crumbling down with Steve's safety and persistence. His kind, gentle, loving, support held space for me and my inner child. His determination and tenacity to create a constructive life of love melted my fear. I learned to trust in the power of love again. I learned strength in honesty, transparency, authenticity and vulnerability. I learned the power of putting God first - in ALL relationships. Indeed, I learned anything is always possible with the power of miraculous love. And so, our Love grew bigger than our fears. Our Love for God, our Selves, each other and our children. Love, Faith, Trust, Communication, Respect and Gratitude became our secret weapon to building our successful future together, especially after all the heartache, pain and losses we both had previously experienced.

On May 15, 2004, we had a very intimate ceremony, facilitated by Natalie, merging our sacred, Beloved Union. We walked an outside labyrinth; a microcosm of our walk of faith with God and each other. At Sunset, supported by the Nature Kingdom, we shared our personally-written vows, to each other, before God. We celebrated our love with a wonderful reception at the Country Club with our family and friends. I don't think I ever felt this kind of intimacy and depth of love and commitment. It has sealed the foundation for our love to be nurtured, blossom, grow and sustained so that we are a blessing of inspiration (of Spirit) to each other, our children, grandchildren and all who choose to bare witness.

Just like in the movie Practical Magic, miracles do happen! Generational curses, fears, negative beLIEFS and self-sabotage can be transmuted and transformed. When we surrender and give ourselves to the power of miraculous love, our Beloved shows up in physical form, reflecting the very best parts of our soul.

Twenty-one years later, our Love Story and Beloved Union is fiercely powerful, magical and inspiring, for all who choose to bare witness to the power of Miraculous Love. God.

For alone we can do so little. Together, two hearts committed and beating as one, can accomplish so much more. Miracles.

Love Wins.

ABOUT TINA PERRMANN

Tina Michele Perrmann is the author of BEaUtiFuLL Gracie Angels & Guides. For more than 25 years, as an Intuitive Life Coach and Mentor, she has helped thousands of individuals, couples and business owners heal their traumas, release emotional blocks and provide them tools and spiritual resources to move forward in their goals, heart's desires and dreams.

She created this book and sacred oracle cards to assist others with their spiritual connection, guidance and soul's journey.

Tina is a mother to three children, stepmother to two and grandmother to six beautiful grandchildren. She and her husband, Steve, reside in magical St. Albans, Missouri.

Tina Michele Perrmann
Pure Inspiration International, LLC
St. Albans, MO 63073
PureInspiration22@gmail.com
www.PureInspiration.Solutions

Scan the QR code to watch a full interview with Tina

Tosha Dove-Freund

BEHIND HER

Opening Scene: The Quiet Moment

The soft hum of the diffuser filled the room, blending with the faint rhythm of a clock I hadn't noticed in months. The lights were low, and for the first time in a long time, the silence felt earned. I sat alone at the edge of the treatment bed—still in my nursing scrubs, still in motion somehow—even though the last patient had left an hour ago.

This was my space now. This wasn't the emergency room where I spent countless hours as a dedicated nurse saving lives and families from tragedy. This was my office. My name was on the lease. My brand hung proudly on the exterior of the building, my fingerprints on every detail. And yet, beneath the luxury and polish, I could still feel the bruises of everything it took to get here.

People say I make it look easy. They don't see the nights I cried in my car. They don't know what it cost me to smile when I wanted to disappear. They don't know the sacrifices I endured and the relationships I neglected—my marriage and inevitably the divorce. My son's first 10 years that whisked by as if I had barely blinked, and the next thing I know, he had turned 13. They only see the woman standing, not the one who had to learn how.

This is the story of what's *behind her*—what nearly broke her, what rebuilt her and why she refuses to go back.

The Spark: When It All Began

I wasn't chasing luxury back then. I came from nothing. I know what it feels like to struggle, as my mother did, raising me in a single-parent household. I was chasing *freedom*—freedom and security that no one could take away from me—the kind that doesn't come with a paycheck or someone else's approval, the kind you have to build with bare hands, late nights and blind faith.

Ten years ago, I was standing in the emergency room working under someone else's rules and constant chaos with a dream tucked so deep inside me that I was afraid to say it out loud. But it was there. It always had been. I knew the constant fight-or-flight adrenaline would not be sustainable for the long term.

I remember telling myself, *"One day, you'll have your own,"* not just a business or a brand, but something that felt like truth, like home. One day I would have a place where I could create, heal, grow and pour into others the way no one had poured into me.

I didn't have the blueprint. I didn't have investors. I didn't have a team. All I had was me. What I had was grit and the quiet belief that I was meant for more.

There's a version of me back then who wouldn't recognize the woman I am now. She was the one working double shifts, saving the lives of strangers while losing the lives of my immediate family to sudden trage- dy and loss, running on caffeine and prayer.

She was scared, overworked, underestimated and alone.

Now I walk into my own space with quiet authority and peace stitched into my posture, in front of a team of amazing women that I've assem- bled, who admire me and my stamina.

But she's the reason I'm here. She kept going when no one clapped. She believed in something no one else could see. And every single step I take now—every risk, every win—is a thank-you to her.

The Detours: Everything They Don't See

There's a version of this journey that looks polished from the out- side—the branding, the curated posts, the steady growth. But *that's not the full story.*

They didn't see me breaking down in the bathroom between pa- tients. They didn't hear the silence when I asked for help and no one answered. They didn't feel the fear of watching my account dip below zero—again—and wondering if this was the month it all fell apart. They didn't understand the journey ahead and the education I would need to continue this dream the right way, as I transformed from an ER nurse to a nurse practitioner.

There were times I didn't want to do it anymore, not because I didn't love it, but because loving it hurt too much.

People think the hardest part is getting started. It's not. It's continuing. It's continuing after betrayal, after loss, and after watching people you trusted take pieces of your dream and walk away without looking back.

I've been the girl who worked all day and cried all night. I've smiled through exhaustion, held space for others while carrying my own wounds and stayed quiet about things that should have broken me—because I didn't have the luxury of falling apart.

I had to be strong, not because I wanted to be, but because I *had* to be.

These are the detours no one talks about, the invisible griefs, the unposted failures and the parts of building a dream that don't get shared, because they're too real. But they are the reason I walk differently now. I walk slower, heavier, but more grounded, because everything I carry *carried me.*

The Breaking Point: The Moment That Shook Me

It wasn't loud. It wasn't a dramatic fall or a public failure. It was quiet—almost invisible.

I remember sitting in my car after locking up that night. The parking lot was empty. My signage was well lit. My hands were shaking as I read the email notification, my chest tight from holding in too much for too long. I sat there staring at my signage and the brand I had built as tears streamed down my face, and whispered to no one, *"I can't do this anymore."* And I meant it.

I had poured everything into this dream of pursuing my master's degree in nursing—my money, my body, my peace. And somehow, it still wasn't enough. I was losing myself trying to save something that felt like it was slipping further away because of a malicious attempt to destroy my livelihood and everything I had worked so hard for. Could this really be happening? Why would anyone attempt such hateful endeavors? Why is giving never enough, but instead creates more taking?

The truth is, I didn't want to be strong that night. I didn't want to push through. I wanted to quit, to disappear, to let someone else carry the weight.

But then something happened in that stillness—not a miracle or a breakthrough—a decision. I decided that if I was going to keep going, it would have to be different. There would be no more running on empty, no more pretending, no more shrinking myself just to survive. If this dream was going to live, I had to start choosing me.

I didn't fix everything that night, but *something changed*. It was the first time I saw my breaking as a beginning, not an end.

Sometimes we need to fall apart to realize the pieces we're carrying were never meant to fit that way.

The Climb: Rebuilding Myself

I didn't come back the next day with all the answers. I came back tired but clear. I stopped waiting for someone to save me. I stopped begging for support from people who only clapped when it benefited them. I started moving differently—quieter, more intentional, protective of my peace, obsessed with my healing and fulfilling the truth to protect my integrity. But I didn't do it for anyone else.

I unfollowed the noise. I leaned into stillness. And I listened—to myself, to God, to the whispers that had always been there but were drowned out by the hustle and detours.

I started asking different questions: not "How do I fix this?" but, "How do I learn from this and grow *stronger*?" not "What do they want from me?" but, "What do *I* want for me?" Boundaries became sacred. Rest became non-negotiable. Organization became priority. Silence prevailed over speaking.

I learned to face the added obstacles head on—even when it felt uncomfortable. I focused on moving toward the fears and embracing the anxiety instead of avoiding it. And I let go of the version of me that was addicted to proving her worth through accomplishments.

Little by little, things started shifting. Truth prevailed, and I earned the opportunity to tell my story—the entire story that opened greater opportunities to match my energy. That story earned me the type of respect and credentialing that you can't get from a master's education.

In that moment everything shifted. Peace became more important than praise. My purpose wasn't defined by anyone other than myself. Fear from the actions of others no longer controlled me. Instead, it was replaced with certainty in myself. It was a certainty that only faith and true determination can provide from within.

It wasn't a glow-up. It was a *build-back*—brick-by-brick, boundary-by-boundary with faith over fear and patience over rushing.

It was gratitude without regrets. And for the first time, I felt like I wasn't just surviving my dream. I was redefining and *living* it.

Closing: Behind Her

Now, when they walk into my space, they see calm. They see beauty, luxury, confidence and women building women. They see *her*. They see us—the woman with the business, the vision, the glow, the team.

But behind her? There's a story they don't know. It is a story of the betrayals, setbacks and detours. It is a story of choices I had to make alone with no clear map of the healing I had to do while still showing up for everyone else.

Behind her are broken pieces I learned to hold with grace, lessons I learned the hard way and a strength that was *earned,* not inherited.

I no longer need the world to understand the weight I carry, because now, I carry it with pride.

I built this. I became this. And I'm still becoming.

So, if you ever wonder what's behind her, it's every version of me that refused to give up.

ABOUT TOSHA DOVE-FREUND

Tosha Dove-Freund is the founder and clinical director of Estetica MedSpa, a premier destination for advanced medical aesthetics. With a background in primary care and emergency medicine, Tosha launched Estetica in 2014 out of a deep passion for helping individuals not only heal—but truly thrive in their own skin.

Her journey into aesthetics began with extensive training under internationally recognized experts, where she developed specialized expertise in skincare, laser technologies, and injectables. Tosha obtained her Master of Nursing in 2021 and passed her board certification in 2025; she is currently awaiting Missouri licensure as an Adult Nurse Practitioner.

Tosha's approach combines medical precision with an artistic eye, resulting in personalized, transformative outcomes for her patients. Under her leadership, Estetica MedSpa has grown into a trusted, innovative brand known for excellence in patient care, natural results, and a warm, elevated experience.

In addition to her clinical work, Tosha has built and mentored a dedicated team of medical professionals who share her passion for education, empowerment, and results-driven care. Her work continues to inspire confidence and self-discovery in every client who walks through Estetica's doors.

Scan the QR code to watch a full interview with Tosha

Yolonda Lankford

IT IS NEVER TOO LATE TO BECOME WHO GOD CREATED YOU TO BE

I am blessed that my life's foundation is reinforced by amazing, accomplished and spiritual women who poured into me the values of kindness, empathy and the unwavering expectation of God's promises.

Mother, Dorothy Moore; my aunts Cynthia Boyd and Kate Pride-Davis; and my friends, Joan Gray, Cleo Allen, Beverly Cage and Jackie Baker Green, are a testimony that dreams may be delayed—but not denied. They offered me an open invitation to align my life with divine intention, no matter where I stood on my journey. These ladies taught me that God's purpose for my life was not bound by time, failure or circumstances. Redemption, restoration and hope are my inheritance. I was created for victory.

The process of becoming who you were created to be requires a dose of intentional action, a sprinkle of spiritual growth and a pound of persistent faith.

In this ever-changing world, individuals are often measured by age, achievement or status. Modern society promotes the unrealistic notion that everyone should accomplish their goals by some imaginary timeline. The keyword here is imaginary.

This suppositious timeline suggests that by your mid-twenties you should have completed your formal education. By your thirties, the expectations multiply: a flourishing career, a perfect family, financial security and a crystal-clear purpose. Society would have you believe that once you reach a certain age or stage, the opportunity to live a meaningful, abundant life has expired.

But I am living proof that it is never too late to become who God created you to be.

Now in my late 50s, I consider myself a "seasoned woman." Life, I've realized, is like a well-seasoned recipe—rich, flavorful and perfected with time. Becoming who you are meant to be is a deeply personal endeavor which is rarely predictable and often made up of many twists and turns along the way.

Let me reassure you that whether you are 18 or 90 years old, emotionally exhausted or just beginning, confused or hopeful, it is not too late. Know that your purpose is still valid. Your calling is still alive. It is time to own your now.

When life takes unexpected turns, I pause, take a deep breath, and ask: "What would I tell my 18-year-old self?" The answer always includes the word grace. We give grace to friends and strangers yet struggle to extend it to ourselves.

Remember, you are living this life for the first time. Grace is a gift you deserve. Acknowledge that your life—no matter how broken or delayed—can be repurposed for good. I give myself grace to learn from my mistakes, grace to right my ship and grace to endure my race.

Rooted in scripture and evidenced in my own life, I know this to be true: it is never too late to begin your dream career, fall in love with your soulmate or be a present parent. You just have to be willing to take risks, change direction and explore new paths for growth.

I continually ask God to shine His light on my journey, illuminating each step I take forward. Though the road is not without obstacles, I've learned staying the course brings deep and lasting rewards.

A Late-Blooming Dream

I began my dream career at 53 years old. Throughout my life, people told me I looked and spoke like a news anchor. I would smile and say I'd love to be one—but only if I could report good news. Traditional news didn't align with that vision, so I didn't pursue it.

I already had a fulfilling, successful career and opportunities that were what I call news-anchor adjacent. But during the COVID-19 pandemic, my good friend, Tracie Berry-McGhee, shared an idea. She said, "Let's start a talk show that will uplift our community during this time of uncertainty."

From that spark, the "Own Your Now Show" was born. What began as an online platform to inspire and empower others soon transformed into a television program airing on Nine PBS, and we've since won three Telly Awards. I am proud to be the co-host of the Own Your Now Show.

It is never too late to begin your dream career.

Love, Reimagined

The path to true love can be long and winding. My own journey began more than 30 years ago—with a simple introduction, occasional reconnections and friends who saw our connection long before we did.

It is important to surround yourself with community believers who encourage, challenge and walk with you as you grow into the love you deserve. Like many, I have experienced the heartbreak of a failed marriage and kissed a few frogs along the way. Still, I gave myself permission to love again.

That permission acknowledged my own needs and granted me the freedom to be open to love once more. And I found Ozzie, my No. 1.

It is never too late to fall in love with your soulmate.

The Evolving Role of Motherhood

Whether you have one child or 10, I've learned that the book of perfect parenting does not exist.

I am deeply honored to be the mother of my daughters, Raequel and Danielle. I am also proud to serve as a mother figure to many bonus and community children. As they have grown into adulthood, I've grown into motherhood—evolving from their manager to their trusted consultant.

Every child is unique. Each one develops differently. Being a present parent demands patience, prayer and unwavering support. As much as we plan and dream for our children, we have to leave room for God to implement His plan. Sometimes we can't be present for every big moment—but we can be emotionally present as their lives unfold.

Being a present parent means listening without judgement, holding space without needing to control and releasing the pressure to force our own perspectives.

It is never too late to become a present parent.

Life is a sacred journey of personal growth and transformation.

No matter the road that brought you here, remember; it is never too late to become who God created you to be.

ABOUT YOLONDA LANKFORD

Yolonda Lankford is an energetic, bold and vibrant golden thread in the fabric of St. Louis, Mo. Her formative years were spent in California. Thereafter, she struck out to travel her educational journey where she received a bachelor's degree of Public Administration from Grambling State University. Thirty two years ago she decided to make St. Louis her home. She uses her gifts to uplift girls and women in the St. Louis community through various initiatives. She is an inspirational leader with a powerful presence and an infectious personality.

Yolonda has received numerous awards including an Oprah Winfrey Angel Award, National Counsel Of Negro Women Legacy Award, voted one of St. Louis' Most Magnetic Personalities, Urban League Salute To Women In Leaderrship Award and the Delux Power 100 Award. She has served as Mistress Of Ceremonies for Saint Jude Children's Research Hospital, Salvation Army Doing The Most Good Awards, various events for the St. Louis Cardinals and the Diamond Diva Gala.

Currently, she proudly wears two professional hats. Yolonda is the public relations director of SistaKeeper, a nonprofit organization that is designed to help girls achieve healthy self-esteem, a sense of sisterhood and community awareness. She enjoys the fact that she is making a positive impact on the world one girl at a time. Yolonda is also blessed to be the co-host of the Own Your Now Show, a talk show created to uplift, inspire, and empower! Yolonda's motto – "It is never too late to BECOME who you were created to be!"

Scan the QR code to watch a full interview with Yolonda

KELLEY G. LAMM

AUTHOR • MEDIA PERSONALITY • EMPOWERMENT ADVOCATE

Kelley G. Lamm is a storyteller, speaker and media force whose passion lies in helping others find their voice through hers. As the visionary behind *It's ABOUT TIME*, a powerful anthology of pivotal life moments, Kelley brings together women from all walks of life to celebrate healing, growth and resilience. Her own chapter, *When Love Happened*, reflects the deeply personal journey that led her from silent survival to soulful joy.

A seasoned media entrepreneur, Kelley is the co-host of the *IN YOUR CITY* Radio Show and publisher of multiple City Lifestyle magazines across the St. Louis region. She uses every platform she touches—radio, print, digital and live events—to amplify stories that connect, uplift and inspire.

Her children's book series *OH OLIVE!* champions emotional intelligence through the adventures of an endearing English Bulldog named Olive, teaching life lessons in a voice that both kids and parents adore.

Whether she's writing a children's story, hosting a heartfelt conversation on-air or advocating for the power of second chances, Kelley's message is always the same: you are never too far gone, too late or too broken to begin again. It's never been about perfection—it's always been *about time*.

She lives in Missouri with her husband and business partner Gordon Montgomery, along with their famous Olive the bulldog and her brother Louis, the chocolate poodle. Her greatest joy outside being an entrepreneur is being a mom, nana and wife where love, laughter and storytelling are the heartbeat of everything she does.

Scan the QR code to
visit Kelley's website!